Praise for the international bestseller *The Red Tent*

'Diamant's storytelling is masterful, embellishing the biblical tale with marvellous detail . . . Startling in its originality, *The Red Tent* fairly sings its moral message of love and honor.' —Betsy Kline, *Pittsburgh Post-Gazette*

'*The Red Tent* is occupied by colourful, inspiring characters . . . A read of this evocative story is enough to make you want your own red tent knocked up in the garden.' —Keri James, *The Chronicle*

'Diamant is a wonderful storyteller, not only bringing to life these women about whom the Bible tells us so little but also stirringly evoking a place and time. As with the best writers of historical fiction, Diamant makes readers see there's not much difference between people across the eons, at least when it comes to trial and tragedy, happiness and love.' —Ilene Cooper, *Booklist*

'Here is a book of celebration . . . just keep it close and handy on the nightstand, for any time you need to remind yourself of the simple truths.' —Rebecca Walker, *San Antonio Express-News*

'Diamant succeeds admirably in depicting the lives of women in the age that engendered our civilization and our most enduring values.' —*Publishers Weekly*

'In reinterpreting Dinah—not a woman defiled, but a woman devastated by the murder of her lover—she has created a powerfully imaginative epic . . . She is a fabulous storyteller.' —Zelda Cawthorne, *Herald Sun*

'*The Red Tent* is a fine novel. This earthy, passionate tale, told also with great delicacy, is, quite simply, a great read.' —Jane Redmont, *National Catholic Reporter*

ALSO BY ANITA DIAMANT

The Red Tent

The New Jewish Wedding

How to Be a Jewish Parent: A Practical Handbook for Family Life

Saying Kaddish: How to Comfort the Dying,
Bury the Dead and Mourn as a Jew

Choosing a Jewish Life: A Guidebook for
People Converting to Judaism and for Their Family and Friends

Bible Baby Names: Spiritual Choices from Judeo-Christian Tradition

The New Jewish Baby Book: Names, Ceremonies and Customs—
a Guide for Today's Families

Living a Jewish Life: Jewish Traditions, Customs and
Values for Today's Families

Good Harbor

a novel

ANITA DIAMANT

ALLEN&UNWIN

First published in Australia in 2001
First published in the United States in 2001 by Scribner

Allen & Unwin
83 Alexander Street
Crows Nest NSW 2065
Australia
Phone: (61 2) 8425 0100
Fax: (61 2) 9906 2218
Email: info@allenandunwin.com
Web: www.allenandunwin.com

National Library of Australia
Cataloguing-in-Publication entry:

Diamant, Anita
    Good harbor: a novel.

    ISBN 1 86508 746 7.

    I. Title.

813.54

Printed by Griffin Press, South Australia

10 9 8 7 6 5 4 3 2 1

For Jim

GOOD HARBOR

APRIL

KATHLEEN lay on the massage table and looked up at the casement windows high above her. The sashes were fashioned of rough oak, the glass uneven and bottle-thick. Propped open on green sapling sticks, they were windows from an enchanted castle. Having been a children's librarian for twenty-five years, Kathleen Levine considered herself something of an expert on the subject of enchanted castles.

She smiled and closed her eyes. The massage was a birthday present from her coworkers at Edison Elementary. They'd given her the gift certificate at a surprise party for her fifty-ninth birthday, almost five months ago. When Madge Feeney, the school secretary, had learned that Kathleen still hadn't used it, Madge had harrumphed and made the appointment for her.

Kathleen stretched her neck from side to side. "Comfortable?" asked Marla, who stood at the far end of the table, kneading Kathleen's left instep. Marla Fletcher, who was nearly six feet tall, sounded as though she were far, far away. Like the giant wife in the castle of "Jack and the Beanstalk," Kathleen thought, and smiled again.

She sighed, letting go of the tension of driving from school to this odd, out-of-the-way place. Kathleen had thought she knew every last side street on Cape Ann, but Marla's directions had taken her along unfamiliar roads leading, finally, up a rutted, one-way lane that looped around the steep hills overlooking Mill Pond. She nearly turned back once, convinced she'd lost the way. But then she spotted the landmark: a stone gate, half-hidden by overgrown lilac bushes, weeks away from blooming.

It must have been a stunning estate in its day. Much as she hated being late, Kathleen slowed down for a better look. The great lawn had been designed to show off the pond, which shone platinum in the spring sun. Beyond it, Mill River glittered into the distance, silver on mauve.

She turned the car toward the sprawling hewn-granite mansion. Those windows seemed piteously small to be facing such a magnificent scene, she thought. And the four smaller outbuildings, made of the same majestic stones, with the same slate turrets, seemed oddly grand for servants' quarters.

Kathleen drove past two young couples in tennis whites standing by the net on a pristine clay court. They turned to watch as she pulled up beside the round stone tower, where Marla waited by the door. Rapunzel, thought Kathleen, at the sight of her waist-length golden hair.

Lying on the massage table, Kathleen wondered whether she could translate this amazing place into "once upon a time." She had tried to write children's books, she had even taken classes. But that was not her gift. Kathleen was good at matching children to books. She could find just the right story to catch any child's imagination—even the wildest boys, who were her pet projects, her special successes. It wasn't as grand a gift as writing, but it was a gift. And in her own private way, Kathleen was proud of it.

Yet, here she was, in a castle on a hill in the woods, stroked and kneaded like a happy lump of dough by a kind lady; it seemed like an engraved invitation. Was this the kind of scene that had inspired Charles Dodgson to become Lewis Carroll? Was this the world that Maurice Sendak visited whenever he set out on a new book?

"Time to turn over," Marla said, draping the sheet so Kathleen remained covered. Warm oil trickled over Kathleen's sloping shoulders, velvet drops that soothed and tickled. "Nice," she said, overcome by gratitude to this pleasant stranger who made her feel so well cared for, so . . . cradled. Curious word, Kathleen thought. Curiouser and curiouser. She closed her eyes.

The next thing she knew, two warm hands cupped her face. "Take your time getting dressed," Marla whispered. "I'm going to get you a glass of water."

But Kathleen was no dawdler. She saw from the clock beside her that nearly two hours had passed since she had lain down. She swung her legs over the edge of the table and reached for her bra, fastening the hooks in front, bottom to top, just as her sister had shown her when Kathleen was twelve years old, before she needed a bra at all. She had no idea she was weeping until Marla raced back up the winding stone staircase, an empty glass in her hand.

Kathleen tried to regain control of her breathing. "I have breast cancer," she said, staring down at her chest.

"Oh my God," Marla said softly. She sat down and took Kathleen's hand. "I wish you'd told me. I would have brought up my amethyst crystal. I could have burned myrrh instead of sage."

Kathleen sniffed and stifled a laugh. "That's okay. It was a wonderful massage."

"Do you want to make an appointment for another one? That might be a good thing to do."

Kathleen wiped her nose on her slippery forearm and turned the bra around, filling it with her breasts—first the good one, and then the traitor. "I'll call you after I know when . . . After . . ." Her throat closed. Marla put an arm around her shoulders.

The only sound was the volley on the tennis court below. The juicy pop of ball hitting racket, court, racket, sounded back and forth for a long time before someone finally missed a shot. The players' laughter filtered up through the windows, like an echo from another day, another story.

I AM THE QUEEN of compromise, Joyce thought as she walked into the empty house. "Lowered Expectations 'R' Us," she muttered.

The sound of her heels—somehow it had seemed necessary to wear good shoes to the closing—echoed against the bare surfaces. She wandered from room to room, reminding herself that the roof and furnace were new, and that there wasn't a shred of shag carpeting anywhere. The house was on a corner lot, and most of the yard faced south, which meant Frank could have the garden of his dreams.

She told people it was a sweet little house, but in the light of day, it was six pinched rooms, aluminum siding, and small windows that cranked open and shut. The kitchen had been mercilessly updated with avocado-green appliances in the 1960s by the Loquasto family, who had bought the house new in 1957 and raised five kids in it.

There was no ocean view, no fireplace, not even a porch. Her Gloucester dream house was a boxy Cape on a residential street three blocks up from the oily moorings of Smith's Cove, on the way to Rocky Neck.

"Aren't you sweet?" Joyce said to the green refrigerator.

Maybe someday she would write a best-seller, and she and Frank could afford a white refrigerator with an icemaker in the door. They would knock down walls and hire an architect to design a loft and porches and a widow's walk, so she could see the water.

Nah. If she had that kind of money, they could just buy the million-dollar condo on Marten Road she had looked at "just for fun." Two fireplaces and water views from floor-to-ceiling windows in every room.

"Get a grip!" said Joyce, who caught sight of her scowling face in the bathroom mirror. She tucked her curly, dark hair behind her ears and sighed. She looked okay for a forty-two-year-old woman with five extra pounds on her backside and a slight overbite. "What have you got to bitch about?" she scolded, widening her striking gray eyes. "You just bought a vacation house for God's sake. Nine-tenths of the world's population would kill to live in your garage!"

So what if it wasn't a big, fancy dream house? It was on Cape Ann, and she could smell the ocean. At night she would hear foghorns and halyards, and it was only a short bike ride to Good Harbor beach.

Maybe she and Frank would start cycling again. They had taken bike trips all over New England when they'd first met, making love in cheap little motels, eating peanut butter sandwiches every day for lunch. People sometimes took them for brother and sister, because they both had dark hair and gray eyes. Maybe they could take a little trip while Nina was at camp this summer.

Or maybe she would take a watercolor class, and Nina could come along with her.

No matter what, Joyce promised herself, this house would be her own private writers' colony. She would get up early every morning and write five pages. And not a sequel to *Magnolia's Heart*, either. This book would have her real name on the cover.

Joyce Tabachnik didn't sound like the name of a romance novelist. So she had had no objection when her agent suggested a pseudonym; after all, this book was just a means to an end. She and her journalist friends had complained for years about their finances and vowed that *someday* they'd write a mystery or a thriller that would pay their kids' college tuition *and* buy them early retirement in the south of France. Joyce's dream was a house on Cape Ann—her favorite place on earth, less than an hour's drive north of Boston but still somehow off the tourist track.

On her fortieth birthday, Joyce had gotten depressed. "I am such a cliché," she had moaned into her pillow. She wanted a dramatic change in her life, but what? She couldn't bear the idea of revisiting the high-tech hell of infertility medicine for a second child. And, as she told her book group, years of freelance freedom had ruined her for the office politics that go with a "real" job. She decided that a house by the sea would cure what ailed her, so between assignments for *Parent Life* ("How to Tell If Your Baby Is a Brat") and *AnnaLise* ("Who Fakes Orgasm and Why"), she devoted Tuesdays and Thursdays to writing a romance novel.

Romances were a secret pleasure she had acquired during the last trimester of her pregnancy with Nina, when a near-hemorrhage had landed her in the hospital on bed rest. One sleepless night, a nurse had loaned her a few old Silhouette paperbacks, and she was immediately hooked on the fast-lane plots, the dependable triumph of good over evil, and the sex, which was a little rough but always satisfying.

For years, she made a Memorial Day ritual out of shopping for a bathing suit for her daughter, a new tube of sunscreen, and a pile of well-thumbed paperbacks from a malodorous thrift store in downtown Waltham. She read them all, fitfully, while Nina played on the beach. But once Nina turned nine and started going to day camp, Joyce set aside the bodice rippers and joined a book group dedicated to reading serious literature.

Even so, she never stopped searching for the right premise for *her* romance novel. Nina's fourth-grade Black History Month report on women and slavery provided the setting. Joyce read all the women's slave narratives she could find, engineered a family vacation to Charleston, South Carolina, and studied the cuisine of the Old South, as well as the layered striptease of nineteenth-century lingerie: wrappers, corsets, crinolines, bloomers, petticoats, shifts.

Her heroine was Magnolia Dukes. The blue-black daughter of an African prince, Magnolia survived her master's various cruelties, learned to read, and triumphed in love with Jordan LeMieux, the second son of a down-and-out white landowner. Magnolia was wild and brave in ways that Joyce hadn't planned. Frank confessed to being shocked by the violence (especially the beheading), the vertiginous foreplay, the operatic orgasms.

Joyce took Frank's discomfort as a good sign, which was confirmed by an enthusiastic phone call from the first literary agent she tried. Mario Romano III, a local man, new to the business, actually brought a copy of his birth certificate to their introductory lunch, just to prove that his name was no figment of a genre-fevered imagination. For Joyce, he suggested a *nom de romance* at that first meeting. "Any ideas?" he asked over salad in Harvard Square. She shrugged.

Mario, short, dark, and very handsome, offered a method reputedly used by drag queens to concoct stage names: combine the name of your first pet with the street you lived on as a kid.

"That would make me Cleo Lehigh," said Joyce.

"Very nice," Mario said. "Was Cleo a dog or a cat?"

"Parakeet."

Mario nodded. "Nice to meet you, Cleo." He raised his glass.

Within a few months, they had a modest but respectable offer, with an option for three more Magnolia titles. And when Lifetime

TV bought the rights to produce a miniseries, Joyce's Cape Ann fantasy shifted from pipe dream to Plan A.

Frank, always cautious about their finances, wanted to put the entire windfall into IRAs and bond funds. After months of arguing, he finally conceded that seaside real estate would be a solid investment, too. There was no disagreement about where to focus their search on Cape Ann; both preferred Gloucester to Rockport, which seemed too Waspy for a family of Tabachniks. A remnant of Gloucester still fished for a living, and the city smelled of it.

Which is how Joyce came to be standing in a ten-by-twelve-foot living room covered in blue cornflower wallpaper, staring out at the neatly raked yard.

"Oh, shit," she said, feeling her mood suddenly plummet.

What on earth had she done? Joyce and Frank hadn't gone cycling for ten years. Nina would never agree to a painting class with her mother; her daughter was a jock, not an artist. And spending time alone here would only prove that Joyce couldn't write "serious" fiction.

She *was* a cliché, a bored and boring suburban baby boomer. With a statue of the Virgin Mary in her front yard.

The five-foot-tall cement statue had nearly kept Joyce from looking at the house. Frank said don't be silly, but she wasn't being silly. Just put off.

Joyce was not religious. When asked about her affiliation, she quoted her grandmother's line: "We're lox-and-bagel Jews." She and Frank lit a menorah for Hanukkah and ate too much at their friends' Passover seder, and that was pretty much the extent of her family's Judaism. Even so, that statue gave her the creeps. From the window, Joyce had a great view of its modestly draped back-side. "The Holy Mother's tushy," Joyce whispered to herself.

A warm breeze wafted in through the windows, which gleamed

spotless in the bright sunlight. Joyce inhaled the ocean air. There was a sudden blast from a big ship in the harbor.

Reminded of her great good fortune, Joyce looked up at the ceiling and said, "Okay, God, I get it."

BACK IN HER OLD green Taurus, Kathleen looked down at the seat belt between her breasts. Why on earth had she kept this appointment?

All that Catholic-school training dies hard, she thought. But crying and blurting out her troubles to a stranger like that? She could imagine her grandmother's reaction: "Family business stays in the family." The loud echo of Gran's disapproval surprised Kathleen. But then, she wasn't herself.

She hadn't been herself for a week, since the radiologist had used the word *cancer*. Five years ago, after the first needle biopsy, she'd been ready for that pronouncement. In fact, she'd been so sure of a cancer diagnosis, she had reread her will before the appointment. She had searched through the filing cabinet for the deeds to their funeral plots—hers and Buddy's.

But after that lump had turned out to be benign, she'd gone for her regular mammograms without dread. That was stupid, she now realized. What had made her think she was going to get away with it? Breast cancer had killed her sister; it was bound to get her sooner or later.

When he'd delivered the bad news, Dr. Barlow had tried to be reassuring. "All we see so far is DCIS," he'd said. "Hopefully, the surgeon won't find anything else."

Back from the doctor's office that afternoon, she called her sons in New York and California. She left a message for her friend Jeanette, in Florida. But she waited to tell Buddy until he got home. They sat at the kitchen table, and Kathleen watched the lines on her husband's face grow deeper.

Lying in bed that first night, Kathleen realized that she had already left the world of small talk and gardening and current events. She was in the airless, out-of-time place she knew from the long, murderous months of Pat's breast cancer. She'd been to that place with Danny, too, though it had been much quicker with her little boy. It was only that one horrible week in the hospital. Not even a week.

In the morning, Buddy sat beside her as she called the surgeon, Dr. Cooperman. And when she got home from school that afternoon, Jack was in the kitchen, a pot of soup and a pan of frying onions on the stove. "Mom," he said, and swept her into a hug.

"I didn't add the dill," Jack said. "Even though chicken soup is way better with dill, I know you don't like it."

Kathleen ran a finger through his thick black hair, just like hers when she was young. "Nice beard," she said, passing her knuckles across the soft growth. "It makes you look a little like my grand-dad, in that photo when he was just off the boat."

Jack was her youngest, twenty-three years old, sous-chef at a three-star restaurant in Manhattan. His framed diploma from Johnson & Wales hung over the kitchen table.

"How's Lois?" Kathleen asked, trying not to show how curious she was. She had never met his live-in girlfriend; only spoken to her on the phone.

Jack stirred the onions. "She's great. She sends her best. Her show opens next week, though I don't suppose you'll be coming down to see it—now." The word hung in the air, and he looked stricken.

Jack would need her reassurance as much as Buddy did. She was going to have to keep her guys propped up, all the way through her surgery and "follow-up treatment," whatever that meant. Dr. Barlow said the surgeon would explain.

The kitchen clock presided over the silence until the phone rang. "Mom? Did you get my messages?" asked Hal without preliminaries, as usual.

"No, honey, I just got back to the house. Jack's here."

"Tell him hi. I surfed the Net for a while last night," Hal said. "I've got six Web sites for you to visit and I've E-mailed a list of books and magazine articles you should read. Whatever happens, you should get second opinions." Hal had taken premed courses for three years, and even though he'd switched his major to English and worked as a technical writer for software companies, he still entertained thoughts of himself as a doctor. So did his mother.

"I'm planning to," said Kathleen. "I'd really like to get into Boston to see Jane Truman, the one who wrote that book, you know?"

"Yeah?" he said, impressed. "That would be great! Her name's all over the bulletin boards and chat rooms."

Kathleen promised to log on and read Hal's messages later that night. "Dr. Barlow thinks it's the ductal carcinoma in situ."

"Yeah, I read about it. Some people consider DCIS not really cancer at all, but a kind of precancer."

Kathleen frowned. Was that supposed to cheer her up?

"Sorry I'm so far away," he said.

"This is still a guilt-free zone," Kathleen said, reading from the cross-stitched sampler she had put above the kitchen sink twenty years ago. She noticed that the frame needed dusting.

Buddy's voice broke into her momentary trance. "Where's my son, the dishwasher?" he called from the door.

Kathleen said good-bye to Hal as Buddy Levine tramped into

the kitchen and reached out to hug Jack. Buddy was six feet, a few inches taller than his son, and apart from a slight paunch, in very good trim. He still had a full head of hair, and the toothy smile that remained the working capital of Levine Electric: A Cape Ann Tradition Since 1930.

"You knew he was coming, and you didn't tell me?" Kathleen said, poking her husband gently. "You sneak."

"Why ruin his surprise?" Buddy said, and hugged her. She looked up into his face. Years of fishing had baked Buddy's face to leather, but he was still a handsome man. They were both lucky in their looks, Kathleen knew. Her eyes were even bluer now that her hair—the chin-length bob unchanged through years of family photos—had gone white.

They sat at the dinner table for a long time that evening. Kathleen and Buddy praised Jack's meal of elegantly presented comfort food—chicken soup, meat loaf and mashed potatoes, apple pie. Bite by bite they oohed and aahed, and laughed, as they always did, about the way he'd overcome the unlucky marriage of Irish cooking and Jewish cooking.

Kathleen was reminded of how easy it was with just the three of them. When both her sons were at the table, one could get sulky while the other took center stage. She stared into her wineglass, wondering if they'd ever outgrow that. She caught Buddy's and Jack's anxious eyes on her and stood up to clear the table. "I wasn't even thinking about it," she said, surprising herself with the sharpness in her voice.

"I'm sorry," she said, sinking back in her chair. "I guess I'm kind of tired."

Jack moved his chair closer to hers and took her hand. "It's okay, Mom." They all sighed in unison, then laughed at themselves for being such peas in a pod.

*   *   *

Jack left for New York early the next morning, and Buddy decided not to go into the store, even though Saturday was a busy day. He and Kathleen took their coffee cups out to the deck and read the papers, bundled up in wool sweaters. All day they reached for each other—a hand on the shoulder on the way to the bathroom, a kiss on the cheek over the kitchen sink.

On Sunday, Buddy suggested a walk at Good Harbor. As they crossed the wooden footbridge at the southern edge of the beach, Kathleen reminded herself to look. This place was so familiar to her that she sometimes walked halfway across before lifting her eyes to see the day's singular display of cloud and surf.

Not even a mile from end to end at low tide, the graceful sweep of Good Harbor was her elixir, her secret potion. When she dreamed about Good Harbor, she woke up refreshed. Today the water was flat as a pond out to the horizon, but Kathleen had seen plenty of angry seas with six-foot swells here, too.

She and Pat had walked the length of Good Harbor thousands of times, back and forth, sometimes six lengths at a go, talking nonstop. Buddy called it "chewing the fat." "You two get all the flavor out?" he'd ask when they would finally sit down for a picnic with him and the boys.

The sisters had remained close, even after Pat had entered the convent and Kathleen had started her marriage and family. A Jewish family at that. They called each other every week, and when Pat came to visit, they never stopped talking.

Buddy took her hand as they started down toward the water's edge. Kathleen hadn't talked to anyone like that since Pat died. She'd gotten pretty close to Jeanette before she'd moved to Boca Raton—finally convinced by a bad winter, a broken hip, and an insistent daughter. But while she and Jeanette had had some good chats at Good Harbor, they were nothing like Kathleen's talks with Pat.

Kathleen missed Pat so much.

Buddy gave her hand a squeeze. He's good company, Kathleen thought, squeezing back. A wonderful listener, but somehow, her husband didn't know how to keep a conversation flowing or how to direct it forward, or whatever it was that had worked with Pat. Whatever it was that seemed to work so effortlessly between all the women around them, walking and talking on the beach. As usual, pairs of women outnumbered the man-woman couples.

It just isn't the same with men. Why is that? she wondered.

"You okay?" Buddy asked.

"Fine."

A black Lab raced past them and leapt three feet into the air to catch a Frisbee. "Next dog, I want a German shepherd," she said firmly.

"And I bet you already have a name picked out."

"Maurice."

"Really?" Buddy said. "After Kirchel, I figured it would be Wolfie. Or Amadeus."

"Maurice Sendak introduced me to Mozart in the first place. I think it's only fitting."

"Couldn't we call him Max?" Buddy asked. "I sure am going to feel silly hollering 'Moe-ree-eece.'"

"You'll get used to it."

On Monday morning, Buddy didn't go fishing, even though the weather was fine. He read the paper until Kathleen left for work. He walked her to the car, opened the door, and waved as she pulled away.

Kathleen watched him in her rearview mirror.

"Thank you," she whispered, and then shook her head, realizing that she meant it as a prayer. "No atheists in foxholes," she muttered, turning on *Morning Edition,* hoping that they might run one of Dr. Truman's commentaries that day. As qualified as Dr. Cooperman might be, Jane Truman had the reputation as the best breast surgeon in Boston—maybe in the whole country. She was also a local celebrity, thanks to her occasional two-minute radio essays about her patients, her colleagues, and her little girl.

When she got to school, Kathleen sat down in the little office beside the teachers' lounge and called Dr. Truman's office. She was told, very politely, even kindly, that Dr. Truman was booked solid until September. She locked the door to the teachers' bathroom and wept, trying not to make any noise.

The gym teacher, Fiona Kent, was waiting for her when she finally emerged, and within a few hours, the whole school knew the whole story, right down to the details of her phone call to Dr. Truman. After the third-period bell, Madge Feeney marched into the library, where Kathleen was staring out a window.

"Don't you worry, dee-ah," said Madge, who had grown up in South Boston and still drove all the way down there for mass every Sunday. "My niece, Ellen, works in that Dr. Truman's office." Madge shook her head sadly, sighed, and said, "You know, my ma had it, too."

As the day wore on, Kathleen heard that refrain again and again. Like a parade of cats with dead mice in their teeth, five teachers, two aides, and a lunch lady came to the library and laid the tale of their mother's, sister's, cousin's, best friend's breast cancer at her feet. As though she didn't have Pat's story, her own sister. Good thing I don't have a daughter, she thought.

At noon, Madge's niece left a message: Kathleen should bring her mammogram and test results to Dr. Truman's office the following Monday morning.

"Oh, Kath, that's so great," Buddy said when she called to relay the news. He cleared his throat, and the noise on the other end of the phone was muffled. Kathleen never knew what to say when Buddy got choked up.

After school, Kathleen stopped at the town library. But when she got to the 600s, half the titles on breast cancer were already gone. I guess someone else got bad news this week, she thought, and wondered about all the other women who had stood in the same spot, hearts racing, hands shaking.

Even so, there were plenty of books left to choose from. She took three, worrying, as she checked them out, about where to hide them. She didn't want Buddy stumbling across *What to Do If the Doctor Says It's Cancer, The Breast Cancer Guidebook,* and *Survivors: Ten First-Person Accounts by Women Who Beat Breast Cancer.* But Kathleen found she couldn't look at the books without starting to sweat and returned them a few days later, unopened.

She and Buddy decided to keep the appointment with Dr. Cooperman, who seemed as competent and reassuring as a thirty-year-old surgeon could be. But every night that week, Kathleen dreamed she could feel the cancer pushing from the inside of her breast, threatening to break out of her skin. She took to adding a jigger of brandy to her bedtime herbal tea. In the morning when Buddy asked how she had slept, Kathleen would say, "Like a baby." What she thought but didn't say was "Like the dead."

JOYCE'S ROUTINE HAD turned into a secret rut. She dropped Nina off at school, cruised through the Dunkin' Donuts drive-through for coffee, and mentally scanned her to-do list: the kitchen cabinets needed washing and fresh liners, she had to measure the windows for blinds, and all the walls needed paint. Every morning she vowed that as soon as she reached Gloucester, she would get to work.

But most days, once she'd made the hour-long drive to the house, she collapsed in an orange beanbag chair she had rescued from a neighbor's trash heap and read magazines until it was time to pick Nina up from school. One Monday she stripped the paper off the shelves, imagining Mary Loquasto picking the green teacup pattern to match the appliances. Another day, she vacuumed the crawl space in the attic. But those were exceptions.

She promised herself, over and over, to get off her butt. She should be finishing the articles that were still due. She ought to make more of an effort to talk to Frank, who was preoccupied and consumed by the goings-on at Meekon, the most recent start-up software company on his long, high-tech résumé. Rumors of a Japanese takeover were flying again, and it was all he could talk about. Which made it hard for her to pay attention.

Every day, she got out of bed resolved to make serious headway on the house, spend a little time at her desk, fix a good dinner, keep her cool with her increasingly surly twelve-year-old daughter, and have a real heart-to-heart with Frank. But every day turned out pretty much the same as the day before. By the time Joyce crossed the bridge and saw the fisherman sign welcoming her to Gloucester, her good intentions had evaporated. She ended up in the beanbag, staring at the wallpaper until it was time to drive home in a guilty funk that lasted until bedtime.

Joyce finally got herself to Ferguson's Decorating Center to buy scrapers, brushes, and paint. On the way to the cash register, two gallons of Linen White cutting narrow grooves into her palms, she caught sight of the color charts. "No more white," she muttered.

This was, she knew, an extremely unoriginal urge. Everyone in Belmont already had a red dining room or a green den. She walked over to the Benjamin Moore display, which looked like an altar to the Greek goddess of the rainbow; Joyce tried to remember her name. Maybe she could tell me which one of these ten thousand shades of green would make my avocado refrigerator look retro and chic. Joyce grabbed a handful of color strips and walked out, leaving the cans of white paint like offerings to Iris (that was her name!), messenger of Olympus.

Driving back to Belmont, Joyce spread the samples on the passenger seat and nearly swerved off the road while reaching for Calvin Klein's Forested. Maybe that would help. Or not. Joyce frowned at herself in the rearview mirror.

"I'll call Francesca!" she crowed a moment later, smacking the steering wheel triumphantly. Francesca Albano was a soccer mom who had hosted a parents' team meeting the previous fall. Touring Francesca's enormous house, Joyce felt as if she'd been trapped inside the interior decorator's infomercial. But her jaw had dropped in pure admiration of the kitchen. Who would have thought that bright blue and gold were a good combination for anything but cheerleader uniforms?

At the dinner table, her announcement of the decision to call Francesca was met with stares.

"Mom, are you okay?" said Nina.

"Yeah, Joyce," Frank chimed in. "Maybe you ought to lie down or something."

"Why?" asked Joyce. "I think it's a great idea."

"You wouldn't even let me paint my room light yellow, remember?" Nina said, twirling a strand from her long, dark ponytail.

"Isn't there a clause about Linen White in our prenup?" Frank teased.

Joyce was getting annoyed. "I'm simply admitting my inadequacy here."

"I still think we ought to take your temperature," Frank said lightly.

"Don't tease Mom," said Nina, suddenly rushing to her mother's defense.

"It's okay, honey," said Joyce.

"No, it's not," Nina said, a hysterical catch in her voice and tears in her eyes. "He's so mean to you."

"Nina," Frank warned, "knock it off."

"Really, Nina, he's just kidding around," said Joyce.

"Now you're ganging up on me."

"That is not true," Frank said, emphasizing each word. "And your behavior is not acceptable, young lady."

"You hate me," Nina screamed. She ran for her room.

"Let it go," said Joyce. "There is no point in arguing when she gets like this. She can't help it."

"She has to learn to control herself, and you shouldn't undermine me like that in front of her." Frank got up and headed for the computer. Joyce cleared the table and brooded. Life with Nina was a minute-by-minute drama, and Frank's anger only made it worse. There was no predicting her daughter's behavior, and no consoling her confused, abandoned husband.

Nina had been such a daddy's girl as a toddler, and all the way through grade school they had spent part of every weekend in the park, just the two of them. First swings and slides, then balls and bats, then soccer. They had private jokes. They quoted lines from *The Simpsons* at each other. Or they used to.

Not anymore. As hard as Nina was on Joyce, she was ten times pricklier around Frank. Everything he said or did seemed to drive her crazy.

Frank is grieving, Joyce thought, and he doesn't even know it. She started the dishes, remembering when this had been a sweet spot in her day. Nina would perch on the countertop and squeeze dishwashing liquid on the sponge while Frank read a chapter from one of the *Narnia* books. Could that really have been last fall?

There was no more reading aloud. No more spontaneous hugs, not even any TV couch time. Nina's life revolved around her friends and soccer, a game that made Joyce go limp with boredom.

I guess I'm grieving, too.

As she rinsed the last pot, she heard Frank yell to Nina through her closed door, "Are you doing your homework in there?"

Frank still thought there was a strategy for avoiding the thunderstorms of Hurricane Nina, but Joyce was beginning to suspect that there was no way through the next few years without getting drenched every few hours. Maybe that's why I'm up in Gloucester so much, she thought, as she looked up Francesca's phone number and muttered, "Duh, as my daughter would say."

Francesca was all that Joyce remembered, breezing into the Gloucester house later that week. Joyce followed her hot-pink linen pantsuit from one room to the next and felt her modest vacation home morph into a tacky double-wide trailer.

In the kitchen, Francesca stopped and in a near whisper said, "Well, at least they didn't leave you with orange linoleum and yellow countertops. I've seen much worse."

Joyce felt both murderously defensive about Mrs. Loquasto's taste and mortified at her association with it. "Coffee?" she offered.

"No thanks," Francesca said, and opened an enormous book of color samples on the counter. She flipped straight past the greens to a page of dark purples and explained that in "situations like this" it was better to go for contrast.

Joyce's face betrayed her. "Purple is neutral," Francesca reassured her. "Besides, someone as interesting and artistic as yourself should have an interesting and artistic home," she said, snipping out swatches named Pretty Putty, Golden Light, Bluish, and Lemon Crème and laying them beside Summer Aubergine, which Joyce continued to eye with suspicion.

"Buy a quart and just paint a swatch. Live with it for a while," Francesca said. "If it still doesn't work for you, call me."

Joyce waved as Francesca backed her sleek black Saab out of the driveway. She walked over to the Madonna, whose gray concrete arms reached down toward last year's withered mums. "I like being told that I'm interesting and artistic," she said to the statue, and pinched its solid cheek. "Don't you?"

At Ferguson's, the clerk advised against the cheap brushes she brought to the counter. "A good brush gives you a nice finish, even if you use lousy paint," said the young man, who smelled faintly of beer. "Since you're springing for the good paint, you may as well get the good brushes. That's what my uncle tells me. And he's a professional."

He was a good-looking kid, twenty years old, if that, with deep brown eyes and sandy hair that hung over his shoulders. He told Joyce how to wash and hang the brushes so they would stay in good shape. There was a tattoo on his forearm, a little blue star or maybe a starfish.

Joyce thought about leaning down to kiss it.

Later that day, waiting in the car for Nina to get out of school, she remembered the tattoo and wondered what the hell was going on with her. Nina slammed the door hard.

"Hi, sweetie."

"I'm in a bad mood, Mom," Nina warned.

"What's wrong?"

She shrugged violently and said, "Lucy and Ruth were talking about me behind my back. They say I'm stuck-up and fat."

"Fat?" Nina's ribs were practically visible through her T-shirt.

Nina flashed Joyce a look that warned against disagreement.

Joyce took a breath. No matter what she said, it would be wrong, though saying nothing wouldn't work either.

"Mom," Nina demanded, "do you not even care that my back is killing me and my throat hurts?"

"Of course I care," Joyce said as sympathetically as possible.

"Yeah. Right." Nina pounded the button for her radio station and crossed her arms. Through her daughter's silence Joyce counted six commercials—acne remedy, a television show, running shoes, a contest for concert tickets, a candy bar, another TV show—before they arrived at the field.

"Jenny's mom will pick you up," Joyce shouted as Nina slammed the door and ran toward the other girls, her aches and pains forgotten.

Joyce drove around the corner and pulled over. She tried to put things in perspective. She thought about how much she really loved her daughter. She thought about how supportive Frank was of her decision to freelance from home. She thought about how much she loved the beach at Good Harbor.

But it didn't work. She turned off the ignition, leaned back into the headrest, and let herself cry.

KATHLEEN BARELY SLEPT the night before her appointment with Dr. Truman. Startling awake every hour, she counted Buddy's sleeping breaths to calm herself and finally took the first birdsong as permission to get out of bed. She walked to the end of the block, threading her way between the neighbors' houses to watch the tidal river turn gray, then blue in the growing light. By the time she returned, Buddy had the kettle boiling.

They left home an extra hour early, planning for traffic in Boston, but the roads were oddly empty and they arrived at the medical complex before Dr. Truman's office opened. Buddy and Kathleen shared the elevator with a young woman who had a gold stud in her nostril and who turned out to be Madge's niece, Ellen. When Kathleen started to thank her, Ellen raised her hand like a traffic cop stopping a car. "Having a little bit of pull is the best part of this job. And don't you worry. Our patients get the best care in the world."

Kathleen noticed Ellen didn't say "Our patients get well," but that was okay with her. Honesty in a doctor's office is a good thing, she thought.

They sat in the mauve-and-cream waiting room as the office staff arrived and started swapping stories about the weekend. A receptionist, who looked to be about forty, had been out on a blind date. The nurse with cornrowed hair had a colicky baby at home.

The phone rang and the smell of fresh coffee saturated the room. Kathleen felt as though she'd fallen down another rabbit hole. But I'm in better shape than Alice, she figured: I feel like I know everything and everyone here.

When Ellen warned them that the doctor was running a little late, Buddy let out a loud "Huh." Kathleen had forgotten the way he held his breath when he was nervous. He squirmed in the flow-ered armchair that was far too small and feminine for him and reached for a copy of *Good Housekeeping*.

Ten minutes later, Dr. Truman barreled through the door, white coat flapping over khaki pants, a stack of folders in her arm. She lifted her finger at the desk staff, signaling that she needed a moment, and hurried down the hall.

Kathleen watched her go. The doctor was shorter than she had pictured her: maybe an inch over five feet, and no string bean. Not fat, but substantial. Her hair was longer and darker than Kathleen remembered from the newspaper photographs.

When she realized that Buddy was holding his breath again, Kathleen touched the tip of his nose and he snorted, embarrassed.

"Mrs. Levine?"

Kathleen looked up.

Dr. Truman had her hand out. "Mr. Levine?" Buddy stood. "Come on down." She gestured for them both to follow her.

Kathleen was glad for the window in the doctor's office and for the chestnut tree it framed. "Sit down, Mr. Levine, Mrs. Levine. Or would you rather I called you Kathleen? Or is it Kathy?" Dr. Truman closed the door.

"Kathleen," she said. The wall behind the desk was decorated with diplomas and photos: Dr. Truman shaking hands with Bar-bara Bush, with an arm around Barbra Streisand, behind a lectern with Barbara Walters.

"You've got a theme going there," Buddy said.

"Yeah," the doctor said. "I'd like to get Barbara Kingsolver. Too bad Barbara Stanwyck is no longer with us."

Dr. Truman pulled up a chair next to Kathleen and asked about her children: Two sons? Where did they live? What did they do?

She asked about how long it took to drive in from Cape Ann, and about Kathleen's job. When the doctor heard the words "children's librarian," she grabbed a notepad and asked about books for her daughter, who was just on the verge of reading.

Kathleen mentioned four titles and thought of a few others while Dr. Truman led her into the adjoining examination room. She took off her blouse and bra and lay down on the table while the doctor washed her hands. They were big, Kathleen noticed, the nails cut flat across the top, like Buddy's. The doctor palpated her left breast and then the right without any change in expression.

After Kathleen dressed, Dr. Truman clipped the mammograms to the light board and, using a pencil, pointed to a scattering of what looked like white grains of sand contrasted against the shadowy mass of her breast. "These are the calcifications," the doctor said, and described how a wire would be inserted into that area to guide the incision. "But let's go back into the office and talk all this through with your husband, so you both get the whole picture."

From the doorway, Kathleen was startled at how pale Buddy looked in the light from the window.

"Okay now," said Dr. Truman, looking from one anxious face to the other, "I'm not telling you to pretend that this isn't serious or to act all stiff-upper-lip around each other. But we caught this early, and there's every reason to be optimistic."

Buddy let out a breath.

"Mr. Levine," Dr. Truman said.

"It's Buddy," he corrected her.

"Well, Buddy, I believe Kathleen is going to be around for a long time. And I'm not feeding you a line."

Buddy and Kathleen nodded.

Quickly, but not too quickly, Dr. Truman reviewed the options. Since the biopsy had confirmed DCIS, they had to decide between wide excision with radiation or mastectomy—with or without reconstructive surgery.

"Dr. Cooperman didn't say anything about a mastectomy," Kathleen said, alarmed.

"Yes, she did," Buddy corrected quietly.

"That is a more radical choice," said Dr. Truman, "but some women choose it to avoid the radiation, or just for peace of mind."

Kathleen reacted instantly, instinctively: no mastectomy.

"That's fine," Dr. Truman said, and explained that if the margins around the excision were cancer-free, there would be no need for further surgery.

"And if the margins aren't cancer-free?" Kathleen asked.

More surgery, Dr. Truman said gently, but cautioned against getting too far ahead of the facts. "At this point, I want you to be perfectly clear that you do not have the kind of disease that killed your sister. Your sister had inflammatory breast cancer, which is rare. Back in the 1970s, it was almost always fatal. But that is not your diagnosis."

"I understand," Kathleen said. "But I want you to do the surgery, the excision. Will you? Will you do it?"

"Sue Cooperman is a very good surgeon, Mrs. Levine."

"Please," said Kathleen, leaning forward in her chair. "I know you're busy, but it would mean the world to me if you could do it."

The doctor started to explain that her schedule was very busy when she noticed the yellow Post-it note on Kathleen's chart. "You have an inside track here, but the fact is, I don't control my own OR schedule. Dr. Cooperman could probably operate much sooner. You'll have to make that decision yourselves."

At the desk, Ellen looked at the computerized calendar, pinching her mouth over to one side. "Gee, the best I can do for you is the very end of June. But I'll call if there's a cancellation. It happens. Not often, but once in a while, and you're right at the top of that list. So you be ready and keep a good thought."

Kathleen tried to smile and said, "I'll do that."

But in the elevator, she started to panic. How could she get through two more months with this thing inside her? Maybe she should let Dr. Cooperman do the surgery. But Dr. Truman had made her feel so much more taken care of. So . . . cradled.

She wanted to talk about it on the way home, but the traffic was bad and Buddy was too tense to pay the kind of attention she needed.

When Jack heard her dilemma, he said, "I'll try to get an extra day off and come home next week." Hal spent an hour on the phone with her, going over the pros and cons. Finally, he declared that medically there was probably no harm in waiting for Dr. Truman, but if it would drive her crazy, she should schedule the surgery with Dr. Cooperman.

Kathleen felt as if she were wearing a lead cape. She couldn't bear waiting nine weeks. Still, she needed Jane Truman to take care of her. And yet, she was also convinced that it made no difference which doctor did the surgery. Kathleen was certain they would find more cancer. She knew it in her bones. No question.

She tried calling Jeanette again, but hung up as soon as the answering machine switched on.

After another sleepless night, she made an appointment to have Dr. Cooperman do the surgery on May 9. But the following day Ellen called to say there had been a last-minute cancellation. Next Monday. Six days away. In the meantime, she would have to come down to Boston for a pre-op visit with the anesthesiologist, and to meet with one of their nurses. She'd also need to get a clean bill of health from her own internist.

"See you soon, Mrs. Levine," said Ellen, sounding as if Kathleen had just booked a haircut.

She wrote down her assignments and then put the receiver down a little harder than necessary. "This must be my lucky day."

Driving to school, she was suddenly furious. She counted all the ways she was angry. About having cancer, about being too scared to sleep, about having to disrupt everything in her life. And it was going to ruin the whole summer.

It *would* have to happen *now*, she fumed. Summers in Gloucester could make you forget the miseries of winter, just like those drugs. What were they called? Amnestics.

Summers on Cape Ann erased the cumulative assault of January darkness, the relentless February chill, the raw misery of March, and the final heartbreak of April, when the light returns but the wind still stabs you in the back.

In May, there are birds everywhere, and by the end of June the beach roses bloom and the supermarket fills with sun-stunned vacationers loading their carts with chips and lemonade.

In June, every wave and rock and gull is lit up from inside, the sky is a daily miracle. But I won't be able to enjoy it, Kathleen thought bitterly. The margins won't be clean. They'll find invasive cancer cells on the margins. There will be more surgery, and radiation and chemotherapy, and God knows what. I'll be too weak and nauseated to sit up, much less have energy to pull weeds or plant bulbs.

Kathleen loved the steep, rocky hill behind the house. It had been a "nature preserve"—her own euphemism for scrubby and neglected—while her sons were growing up. But once they left home, she fortified the worn-out soil with coffee grounds and manure, and now there were flowers everywhere, daylilies mostly, in and around the ten granite boulders on the hillside. A few years ago, Buddy had hired a cherry picker so she could get up to the top, and she had planted a big stand of yellow Stella d'Oros up there. They bloomed the whole summer.

She wouldn't be planting anything this summer. No new lilies. No tomatoes. Nothing.

By the time she pulled into the parking lot, she was in a rage. "Damn it!" she shouted. "Damn it all to hell."

She leaned back in the seat and calmed down enough to walk into the building, retrieve her date book, and tell the principal that she would be out the rest of the week. He put his arm around her shoulder and said, "You take all the time you need." Then he got that look on his face and Kathleen knew what his next words would be. "My sister had breast cancer."

Back home, she called Buddy to tell him the news. She called Hal and Jack. She talked to receptionists at medical offices. "We can fit you in Friday, but it may be a long wait," said the woman at the internist's office. "Bring a book."

Kathleen sat in one waiting room after another, unable to read. She picked at her cuticles and wondered what had happened to the woman who had canceled her surgery with Dr. Truman. Had she come down with the flu? Found a better surgeon? Did she decide she'd just rather die?

The last stop was at a lab for a final blood test to rule out anemia. A child's outraged wail filled the silence in the waiting room outside the lab. The grown-ups in the chairs around her smiled at each other and shook their heads in sympathy. "Poor thing," said the woman sitting next to Kathleen.

Danny hadn't cried. He was knocked unconscious by the car. And then they had put the tube down his throat. Pat had promised Kathleen that her little boy wouldn't remember the pain or the disgusting procedures they did on him—because of the drugs. Amnestics.

*　　*　　*

Buddy and Kathleen spent the Sunday night before surgery at a motel near the hospital in Boston. The bed was as hard and flat as a frozen pond, but somehow they managed to fall asleep, waking at dawn to get to the operating room on time.

Within minutes of entering the building, Kathleen lay gowned and shivering on a gurney. She was so frightened—trembling and almost blue at the lips—the anesthesiologist asked if she'd like a mild sedative once they hooked up the IV. Kathleen was mortified at her cowardice, but said yes. Was it Fiona or Madge who had told her about some woman, diagnosed with DCIS and dead of metastatic breast cancer a year later.

Buddy sat beside her in pre-op, alternately silent and gasping. She thought about reminding him to breathe, but she couldn't spare the energy to form the words.

Lying between the green curtains, she remembered Pat's last days in the hospital: the foul, metallic smell of her sister's breath, her face, bilious and yellow, distorted into a bloated circle. And then Pat in her casket. "Isn't she the picture of peace?" the old nuns had said. But Kathleen had been horrified. Who had picked that lime green polyester suit? Who had turned Patty into a frump for a roomful of strangers to peer at and pronounce "at peace"?

She closed her eyes tighter against the memories and the bright light and the cold of the pre-op room. Why did they keep it so cold?

Dr. Truman walked into the room, transformed by the green operating scrubs into an outsize elf. The doctor's fingers felt dry and warm on Kathleen's arm as she crouched down close enough for Kathleen to feel her breath against her cheek. Kathleen smiled at the sound but didn't pay attention to the words. The voice was calm. "Okay, Doc," Kathleen said. At least she thought she said it.

The doctor vanished, Buddy kissed her, and Kathleen was

wheeled into an even brighter, even colder room. She shuddered under the sheet. A voice told her to take three breaths, and she fell back.

She woke up vomiting into a blue plastic basin in another curtained cubicle. A West Indian nurse held her by the shoulders. "There you go, darling, you'll be feeling better now." She wiped the inside of Kathleen's mouth with a minty swab and asked, "Ready to see your husband?"

Buddy walked in with a broad smile across his face. "Dr. Truman says you were great. She says we can go home whenever you feel up to it."

She nodded and closed her eyes, just for a moment, just to rest from the strain of retching. But she woke up much later, in a hospital bed. The room was illuminated only by the fading daylight slipping through narrow blinds. She stirred, aware of the bandage on her breast, a dull ache beneath it.

"Buddy?" He was asleep in the chair beside her.

"What!" he said, jumping up.

"I'm ready to go home."

An aide helped Kathleen out of bed and wheeled her out to the curb. They drove home without speaking, and both fell into bed, exhausted, with their clothes on.

Dr. Truman called in the morning to ask how Kathleen was feeling. They would meet the following Monday to review the pathology report. "Don't worry," Dr. Truman said. It was a stupid thing to say, and Kathleen tried to forgive her for it.

Kathleen did nothing but worry. It was a school vacation week, and it rained. The phone rang and she told her sons she was doing fine. That's what she said to Madge and Fiona, and to Louisa, her next-door neighbor, who brought over a pie.

"Waiting is hard," she admitted when they asked how she was feeling, but she said nothing about the ugly bruises from the intravenous lines, or about how the steady beat of fear kept time with the dull throbbing of the incision. She certainly didn't talk about how she woke up sweating, the sheets twisted around her arms and legs, or about how she was trying to get used to the idea of never seeing her sons married, never meeting her grandchildren.

Buddy rented movies he thought Kathleen might like. Eating popcorn and fruit for dinner, they watched a succession of recent comedies, which neither of them found especially funny. Finally, after a damp weekend that included—on Buddy's insistence—a long walk through a crowded mall, and a nearly silent dinner at the White Horse Inn, they were ushered into Dr. Truman's office for the verdict.

The doctor was smiling. "Good news, Kathleen. The best news I could give you today. The margins were clean, and there was no evidence of invasive cancer cells anywhere." She looked down at Kathleen's chart. "Of course, given your family history, we want to be extra careful. After the radiation, you'll need to be checked every six months. But it looks good. And you understand that the surgery confirmed that your diagnosis and prognosis are completely different from your sister's."

The doctor closed the chart and talked about radiation treatment, but Kathleen had stopped listening. Her ears pounded. For a moment she thought she might faint. She wasn't going to die. At least not this summer. She wasn't going to die.

"Is it okay to get the radiation closer to home, instead of down here?" she heard Buddy ask. Thank goodness he was paying attention, taking notes on the little pocket pad he used for orders at the store. Kathleen tried to look interested in the conversation. But she was busy reclaiming the summer. The light, the garden, the beach.

Thank You, God, thank You.

Dr. Truman recommended a radiation oncologist in a new clinic near Beverly. Buddy wrote as she described the probable treatment: every day for six and a half weeks.

I'm not going to lose my hair or throw up or turn yellow and die like Pat. Forgive me, Pat, Kathleen prayed silently, lying on the table while the doctor examined her incision and pronounced her a "good healer."

Walking to the car, Buddy said they could schedule her treatments to start after school let out for the summer. Kathleen would likely be fully recovered from the surgery by then. He would map out the quickest route to the clinic. She'd be done early in August, so the summer wouldn't be a total loss. Come September, she'd be rested and ready to go back to school.

Kathleen said almost nothing all the way home. How did I get away with this? she wondered. Why Pat and not me? I'm sorry, Pat. You didn't deserve to die. God forgive me, but I'm glad to be alive. You'll forgive me, too, won't you, Pat?

They approached the end of the "mainland," passing the last of the malls and condo developments. Then there was nothing but trees to look at, all on the verge of green.

Kathleen rolled down the window and took a deep breath, letting herself feel how much she wanted to be in school next fall. The kindergarten class included several "grand-students"—children born to parents she had taught. At the open house last month, she'd met SueEllen Puello's daughter, Jasmine, a delicious girl with big black eyes. And she had a feeling that Alex Maceo would be a lot like his dad, an active boy she'd turn into a reader.

Then they were at the A. Piatt Andrew Bridge, which meant almost home. Hal and Jack used to compete to see which one of them could say it the most times as they drove over.

"A. Piatt Andrew?" Buddy asked, grinning. "A. Piatt Andrew.

A. Piatt Andrew. A. Piatt Andrew. A. Piatt Andrew. A. Piatt Andrew. A. Piatt Andrew.

"How many was that, Mom?" he asked, the way the boys would ask, every time.

The tide was high and bright in the midday sun.

She might yet see grandchildren. Please, God. She squeezed her eyes shut for a moment. Please. And thank You.

MAY

JOYCE groaned when she found out that her book group had chosen *Anna Karenina*. She groaned again when she opened it and faced the barrage of -evitches, -ovitches, and -ovnas. She couldn't keep any of the names straight and, after one hundred pages, put the book down.

"I give up," she said.

Frank, beside her in bed watching the news, said, "Does it matter? You always say Marie dominates the whole conversation, anyway."

It was true. "The whole group feels more and more like homework, anyway," Joyce said. "Other women's book groups seem to have more fun."

Frank, apparently mesmerized by the weather report, said nothing.

"Hello? Frank?"

He turned to her. "So quit and find another one that's more fun."

"What a rotten thing to say."

"What? If you don't like this group, why not make a change?"

Joyce turned her back on Frank, switched off the bedside lamp, and fumed. She'd missed a few meetings, but she couldn't afford to quit her book group entirely.

She was lonely. After four years of working at home, she had started to feel like a hermit. Her coworkers at the magazine had stopped inviting her to lunch a while ago; she'd just said no too many times.

But that wasn't the main source of her isolation; she hadn't been all that close to the people at work, anyway. Her two best friends had moved: Lauren and her husband were in Atlanta, and Pia's assignment in Paris had been extended twice.

Joyce was down to her second string, which was unraveling. Missing book group yet again would only add to her funk.

When she walked into Heidi's living room for the meeting a few nights later, Marie was, indeed, holding forth. Four women were gathered around the blond Danish coffee table, where cups and plates were artfully arranged around an uncut cake. But Marie wasn't talking about *Anna Karenina*. For a moment, Joyce wondered if she'd been in an accident; the circles under her eyes were so dark they looked like bruises. But no, it was just the exhaustion, as Marie was explaining, of taking care of a nearly three-year-old with absolutely no interest in using the toilet, while at the same time contending with her teenage twins. "Forty-seven is just too old to be doing this," she said.

Heidi, a fifty-two-year-old pediatrician married to a shrink, was the oldest member of the group. Joyce, at forty-two, was the youngest member. The rest of them had started when all their kids were in elementary school. Now, Heidi's oldest was in college, and their occasional non-book-related conversations revealed the changes. A few months back, before Heidi—the group's schoolmistress-cum-den-mother—could rein them in, there had been a hilarious debate about whether there was a causal relationship between hormone replacement therapy and the exponential increase of VW Beetles in Boston's western suburbs.

But no one was laughing tonight. In the long pause that followed Marie's confession, Alice blurted, "I moved out of the house."

Marie's mouth dropped open. They could hear a door close upstairs.

"What happened?" asked Heidi, her long, blue caftan swishing around her legs as she sat down next to Alice.

"Nothing happened," Alice said slowly. "There was nothing left with Tim. It was just . . . empty."

"What will that do to Petra?" Marie said a little too quickly. Alice winced at Marie's typical rush to judgment.

"Joint custody."

The room went silent again.

"I had no idea you were unhappy," said Joyce, who had always liked Tim, who seemed like such an easygoing guy; Frank liked him, too.

"Did you guys try counseling?" Heidi asked gently.

"No. It's me. I'm in therapy," Alice said. "Actually, I'm, um, taking Zoloft."

Joyce giggled. Four pairs of eyes turned to her, and she felt her face redden. "I'm sorry. It's just so much, isn't it? All at once, I mean. Isn't anyone here having a torrid affair? Then we'd have a complete set of midlife crises."

Marie tried to lighten it up and, with a mock leer, pointed at Joyce. "Hey, I figured that's what's been keeping you away."

"Not me," Joyce said, "maybe that's why Susan's not here," trying to deflect attention away from herself.

"Actually, Susan is in Cleveland to help move her father to a nursing home," said Marie. "The Alzheimer's got to be too much for her mom to handle."

"Oh, God," Joyce said, "I haven't talked to her in ages." She and Susan used to walk around the high school track twice a week, but that had stopped when Susan went back to school last fall.

Heidi headed for the kitchen and returned with two bottles of wine. "I don't think decaf is going to cut it tonight," she announced.

Alice didn't want to say more about her problems, so Marie took up where she'd left off. They all knew the story of her last pregnancy; her husband hadn't wanted another child, and her fifteen-year-old boys weren't the least bit interested in baby-sitting for their little brother. "I think I had a baby so I wouldn't have to deal with the rest of my life," Marie said, as close to tears as any of the women had ever seen her. "But now I'm bored out of my skull at home all day with Ryan. Al is working eighty hours a week, and the boys are going to spend the whole summer at my sister's house on Nantucket. I think I made a terrible mistake."

Diana, the therapist, put an arm around Marie. Diana had a "challenging" son, too, a thirteen-year-old who was perpetually failing in school. "Hang on, Joyce," Diana said by way of warning. "I, too, have a tale of woe.

"I didn't tell you before, but Dylan was arrested for shoplifting a couple of months ago. The judge ordered tests, and they came back with a diagnosis of ADD and depression. Herb insisted we try Ritalin and his grades are up. He's hanging out with other kids more." Diana paused. "He's happier. He even said so." She raised her glass for a refill. "All those years I wouldn't let him be evaluated because I thought the teachers and counselors just wanted to drug my creative, free-spirited boy. God forgive me."

The phone rang and Heidi hoisted herself off the couch to answer it. Joyce used to think Heidi carried her extra weight stylishly in her long skirts and Navajo jewelry, but tonight she just looked dated and tired.

There was a pause as they waited for Heidi to return. Then, Alice turned to Joyce and asked, "So, what's really up with you, Tabachnik?"

"I, um, wrote a novel." Joyce's timid announcement was met by an outburst of congratulations and questions. Did she have an agent? A publisher? Who? When?

Joyce smiled weakly. "It's signed, sealed, and available in a supermarket near you."

The faces around her went blank. Taking a deep breath, she said, "It's a romance novel."

That shut them up. Joyce figured that these women might read the occasional British mystery, but they were more likely to subscribe to *Soldier of Fortune* than pick up a romance.

She felt herself begin to sweat. "You guys know that none of my nonfiction projects panned out. Three different agents tried on the last one, but no one wanted to buy a book about the Children's AIDS program. Too depressing. Too many AIDS books."

Joyce was ashamed for parading her "serious" credentials, but she continued anyway. "I decided to go commercial."

She entertained them with a description of the how-to-write-a-romance workshop she'd attended, quoting sample phrases from handout sheets: "Her body vibrated in response to his presence." "He felt a numb certainty that the moment was wrong."

She told them about her lunch with Mario Romano, but stopped short of revealing her pen name.

Joyce emptied her glass and excused herself. The buzz from the wine was starting to turn into a headache. Serves me right, she thought, as she walked out of the bathroom. I'm such a hypocrite.

They agreed to postpone the discussion of Tolstoy until after the summer. Marie offered her house for the September meeting, and the women said good-night to each other.

Joyce and Alice walked out together. "That's great news about your book," Alice said. "But you seem a little tense. Are you okay?"

"I'm fine. What about you? And how's Petra taking this?"

"Petra will be okay," Alice said as she unlocked her car. "Kids are resilient. I stayed with Tim for a lot longer than I should have, for Petra's sake. But I just can't anymore. My marriage is empty, and I know it sounds stupid, but all I really want is to fall in love again. I want to feel alive like that again. Besides, it can't be good for her if I'm miserable."

"Alice, I wish you all the best," Joyce said. "It takes a lot of courage to do what you're doing."

"Yeah. Or mental illness."

Joyce's scalp prickled. Hadn't Alice said she was taking antidepressants?

"Call me?" asked Joyce.

In the car, Joyce switched off the radio. She felt like a rat about the way she'd made fun of her own book. It's not a bad book, she thought. It's pretty good, actually. "Magnolia would spit on me," Joyce muttered, glancing at herself in the rearview mirror. "And she'd be right."

Alice was a wonderful woman, a sweet person, but no great beauty. Her skin was leathery from all the years of working in her father's landscaping business. What were the odds of her finding a new love?

Joyce recognized the fantasy, though. After eighteen years, who didn't? Her marriage was stuck in its own mud. All the conversations she and Frank had these days turned into skirmishes about Nina. They hadn't been to a movie for ages. She could count on one hand the number of times they'd had sex in the last year.

Sex with someone new. Conversation with a man whose eyes locked on hers. Shopping for new sheets hand in hand. She'd seen women her age in love, glowing like lanterns. Was it endorphins or gratitude? God, it would be great to feel like that again.

But it would kill Nina. All that "resilient kid" stuff aside, Joyce could imagine the scene at the kitchen table: "Your father and I have decided . . ." Her daughter would crumble.

Frank didn't deserve that, either. He was a good husband. Not hostile, like Marie's. Or arrogant, like Heidi's. As for Alice's Tim, Joyce had to admit, he was dull, bordering on dumb.

The big problem with Frank was the way he withdrew into things—his work, his gardening, whatever book he was reading, or even a TV show. When they'd first met, Joyce had fallen in love with his self-sufficiency—especially after two high-maintenance boyfriends. But now his independence felt like distance. Most of the time, he seemed a million miles away. The only thing they seemed to share anymore was Nina. And the mortgage. And a billion memories.

Back in her own driveway, Joyce sat in the car looking at the dark windows. To be fair, she wasn't exactly knocking on Frank's door these days, either. He'd probably respond if she said something, but she couldn't muster the energy.

They'd had these long dry spells before, and each time Joyce had been the one to insist they find their way to water. One time, she'd shanghaied Frank—left Nina with a sitter, picked him up at work, drove them to New York City for dinner, a play, and a night in a hotel. Once, she insisted they talk to a therapist.

But this dry spell was starting to feel like the Sahara. Joyce was tapped out and pissed off that it was up to her to make the effort, start the conversation, take the initiative. Wasn't it Frank's turn yet?

Oh, well. At least she wasn't as bad off as the women in her book group. Nina was a pain in the ass, but soccer was going to get her daughter through the "Ophelia" years. Frank was not stupid or hostile. Hell, she'd bought a house in Gloucester.

It's all relative, right? Joyce thought. And things are relatively good.

Then she remembered the blank, almost frightened expressions on her friends' faces when she'd said "romance novel." Not one of them had asked the name of her book. Not even Alice.

Joyce brushed her teeth, swallowed two aspirin, and picked up *Anna Karenina* again. "Happy families are all alike; every unhappy family is unhappy in its own way." Joyce couldn't remember if that sentence had seemed wise when she'd read it in college.

She left the book on the couch and crawled into bed, careful not to wake Frank. She tucked herself into the far side of the comforter and thought about her book group. Compared to them, her family seemed rock solid. But Joyce wasn't so sure she would go as far as "happy."

KATHLEEN COULDN'T remember the last time she had used the Sabbath candlesticks. Buddy's parents had worked in the store seven days a week, so her husband had no childhood attachment to the Friday-night rituals of wine and bread and candles. But Kathleen loved the weekly celebration she'd studied in her conversion class, especially the candles. As a little girl she'd looked after her grandmother's votives, which burned in every room, sending up prayers to the Blessed Mother, to Saint Jude, to Saint Teresa, the Little Flower. At Christmas, there were red and green candles everywhere—even the bathroom.

She welcomed the Jewish routine and made it her own. Every week when Hal and Jack were growing up, she'd polished the candlesticks, warmed a challah bread in the oven, and polished the sideboard with lemon oil. Her sons told her they still associated those smells with Fridays.

Holding a match to the bottoms so they would stay in place, Kathleen wondered if her candle lighting was for Jewish purposes or out of Catholic nostalgia, but decided it made no difference. "Light is a symbol of the Divine," she said, quoting a line from a long-ago sisterhood Sabbath service.

Kathleen had cooked Buddy's favorite dinner, the fat grams be damned: orange-glazed chicken, pan-fried potatoes, green beans, and chocolate mousse. When he saw the container of cream on the counter, he said, "Trying to get rid of me, eh?"

"Well, now that I'm going to live to be ninety, I thought I'd find myself a younger fella," she said from inside Buddy's lingering hug. "I do have a favor to ask, though."

"That mink coat you've been hinting at?"

"I won't need that until November," she said, teasing back. "But I would like to go to temple tonight."

Kathleen had converted to Judaism the week before they married, thirty-three years earlier. It didn't bother Buddy that Kathleen Mary Elizabeth McCormack wasn't Jewish. He had been one of a handful of Jewish kids growing up in Gloucester. The working-class Italian and Portuguese boys in school never bothered him about being different, maybe because he was a head taller than most of them. For Buddy, Judaism was a matter of holiday foods and honoring his parents' traditions. But Mae and Irv Levine both wept for joy when Kathleen told them she was going to convert.

It hadn't felt like a momentous decision to Kathleen at the time. Catholicism had stopped making sense to her at the age of fourteen, and no one in her own family had objected to her becoming Jewish. The grandmother who would certainly have objected, and loudly, on the grounds of Kathleen's immortal soul, was dead by the time she got married. Kathleen had no memory of her father, who had walked out when she was three. She didn't recall her mother saying anything, but then, her poor mother seemed congenitally unable to object to any awful thing life laid in her lap. As a teenager, Kathleen had secretly prayed, "Please, God, make me be different from my mother."

Pat heard her calling to religious life in college and was Sister Pat by the time Kathleen met Buddy. Pat wrote a long letter wishing her sister "shalom in her new spiritual home" and, on the day of Kathleen's conversion, sent a dozen long-stemmed roses, a huge extravagance back then.

Rabbi Flacks, the perpetually tired man who tried to teach her
the Hebrew alphabet, took her for a perfunctory ritual dunk in a
tiny pool in the basement of a run-down Boston synagogue. Afterward, in the parking lot, with her hair still wet, Buddy gave her a
simple, gold Star of David on a chain. She'd worn it at their wedding, at the boys' circumcisions and bar mitzvahs, during the Jewish holidays, and whenever she went to temple—even if only for
a committee meeting. She had worn it to her one and only job
interview, too.

They had joined Temple Beth Israel in Gloucester when the
boys started kindergarten. Kathleen drove them to religious school
faithfully and even worked on a few fund-raisers, but Buddy didn't
like going to services. He said he found the seashore more spiritual, and he wasn't interested in the social life of the congregation.
He would have let their membership lapse long ago, but Kathleen
kept paying the dues.

She was attached to the place. Buddy's folks had been there for
the bar mitzvahs, basking in the reflected glory of their grandsons'
performances. The organ played the same melody when each of
her boys carried the Torah scroll up and down the center aisle in
the sanctuary. Leading that joyful pageant, they clutched the blue
velvet covers with white knuckles. They were very different, her
boys: Hal serious, Jack sunny. But for their bar mitzvahs, they'd
been identically proud and nervous in their brand-new suits, identically self-conscious and fearless of their changing voices.

Patty had been there both times, too. She and Mae and Irv had
blown their noses after Hal's speech, and the sound of their com-
bined honk had brought down the house. Whenever Kathleen
walked into Beth Israel's long, spare sanctuary, she remembered
the three of them sitting in the front pew, laughing and crying
together.

Mae and Irv had been buried out of that sanctuary, too. And

Danny. Had she worn the star for Danny's funeral? She couldn't remember.

Buddy didn't say anything about the reappearance of challah and candles. He stood close to her, his arm pressed against hers, as she bowed her head. She closed her eyes and remembered how Hal and Jack used to fight over who got to blow out the match. "Knock it off, monsters," she had said every Friday. "Time to kiss and make up."

She turned to her husband. "Time to kiss and make up, eh, Bud?" He held on to her until the kitchen timer went off.

On their way to the temple, Kathleen played with her necklace, running the star up and down the chain absently. They hadn't been to services there for well over a year; they'd been visiting Hal in California last High Holidays, which was pretty much the only time they went anymore, and they still hadn't met the new rabbi.

According to the article in the local paper, she was just a few years out of rabbinical school. Kathleen had meant to attend one of the get-acquainted coffees when she was first hired, but somehow the dates had slipped her mind, as had the new rabbi's name.

"Rabbi Michelle Hertz." It was posted on the sign outside the building. "Let's see if she's better than Avis," Buddy said as they walked in. Kathleen didn't even bother to roll her eyes.

At least forty people were in the sanctuary. "Pretty good crowd," Buddy whispered. The congregation swelled in July and August, when the summer people showed up, but in May it was still just the locals.

Kathleen and Buddy settled into what had always been Irv's High Holiday pew, fourth from the front on the left, and waited for the service to start. Kathleen folded her hands, lowered her head, closed her eyes, and prayed, "Thank You."

Buddy took her hand and kept his eyes on their interlaced fingers, so neither of them noticed the rabbi walk to the lectern. They looked up when she started to sing. Her unaccompanied voice, reedy but pleasant, delivered a tune familiar from the boys' years in Sunday school. "Shalom Aleichem," she sang.

After one stanza, the rabbi waved for the congregation to join in. After a second solo verse, she stopped and shook her finger at them. "I'm warning you, I don't start the service until everyone is singing, and I don't mind singing all night. There's a transliteration on page seventy-nine, and we can even do it without words." She was smiling, but it was clear she meant business.

Rabbi Michelle Hertz was in her late twenties, Kathleen decided; nice looking, with a heart-shaped face, big brown eyes. No discernible makeup. Her yarmulke was a boxy, multicolored third-world cap pinned onto dark curls pulled back into a low ponytail. Her prayer shawl, though, was the kind worn by old men in Orthodox synagogues, black-and-white and very big. How traditional, Kathleen thought, especially compared to the last rabbi's bare head, black robe, and skinny, little prayer shawl that had always reminded her of a priest's stole.

After four more stanzas that included a lot of "Yi-dee-di," everyone was singing. Even Ida Rubelsky, who wore a hat and gloves to services, though much of the crowd was in sweaters and jeans.

Smiling approval, Rabbi Hertz slowed the tempo, ended the song, and asked the congregation to turn to the prayer book and read with her.

The old *Union Prayer Book* was gone, replaced by a softcover book in which God had changed from *He* to *You.* As though God were sitting across the table, close enough to ask to please pass the salt. There seemed to be more Hebrew in this book, a language that would always remain an inaccessible mystery to Kathleen.

Her only D in school had been in Spanish, an everlasting shame. But the English translations were graceful, and the singing more than made up for her distance from the Hebrew.

Kathleen smiled at the rabbi's performance. Or maybe that wasn't the right word for it. It occurred to her that Michelle Hertz might be a good match for Hal, if Hal were interested in women. She suspected that might be why he lived out in California. Thinking about her son, Kathleen sighed. Buddy cast a concerned eye in her direction; she reassured him with a pat on the arm and turned her attention to the readings.

The service was so unusual that even Buddy was still paying attention when they got to the sermon, if you could call it that.

Rabbi Hertz hiked the prayer shawl over her shoulders and came down from the altar. "This is one of everybody's favorite Torah portions," she said, walking up and down the aisles, handing out copies of the weekly Bible reading, smiling as she made eye contact.

"This is the part where God gives Miriam leprosy for yelling at her little brother, who just happens to be Moses, who is—like it or not—God's all-time favorite human being."

The rabbi made her way back to the pulpit and said, "This section has always bothered me. I mean, Aaron does exactly the same thing as his sister, but he gets off without so much as a mosquito bite! So who wants to read the first verse?"

Ida Rubelsky stood, adjusted her hat, and in a pungent North Shore accent rhymed *Hazeroth* with *Reheboth* and intoned the name of the "Laud." She read on and on, ignoring the rabbi's frequent "Thank yous."

Buddy whispered, "I haven't had this much fun at temple since I was seven and my grandmother nodded off and fell out of her seat."

The rabbi finally got Ida to stop and returned to the top of the page, soliciting comments about Moses' relationship to God, Miriam's "raw deal," and the reason why it took seven days for her to heal. After extracting a few tentative remarks, Rabbi Hertz eased into her own interpretation of the story.

"Let's assume for a moment that Aaron isn't a bad guy," she said. "He doesn't run off congratulating himself on his good luck while Miriam's skin turns white and she goes to solitary confinement for a week. Let's imagine that Aaron is horrified by what happened to his sister, and that he suffers for her.

"What does Aaron think, at that particular moment, about the God they've been chasing around in the desert? A God who would do such a terrible thing to his kid sister, the only one in the family who can sing, who composes beautiful songs in praise of Adonai?

"'What kind of deity am I serving,' he thinks. 'What kind of God punishes Miriam and not me?'

"Maybe Aaron wonders if he could have protected his sister. Maybe he's thinking, 'Why didn't I challenge God and ask why she got punished and I didn't?' Maybe Aaron suffers over what he perceives is his own cowardice." Rabbi Hertz took a long breath and scanned the room before going on.

"Now, as biblical characters go, Aaron doesn't have a lot of charisma. We don't know a whole lot about him, and besides, we tend not to trust high priests. But I imagine Aaron sitting beside his sister's hospital bed with his head in his hands. I see him as just a regular Jew, like the rest of us. Guilty. Afraid. Wondering about the meaning of pain. Struggling with his faith and searching for comfort. But also connected by blood and history and love to his brother, Moses, to his sister, Miriam, and to the Jewish people's unending project of discerning and creating meaning in a seemingly random, sometimes cruel universe."

Kathleen's cheeks burned. She felt as if the rabbi were speaking directly to her and almost looked around to make sure no one was staring at her. But everyone seemed intent on the rabbi's story. Even Ida, notorious for fixing her lipstick during sermons, was listening.

Kathleen struggled with the rabbi's words. *Why didn't I argue with God about my cancer?* She had been frightened and worried, but she'd borne her cross (hah!) without complaint, like a martyr.

But she knew why she didn't argue. She believed her cancer was a punishment. The doctor had cut a hole into her breast as retribution. She had survived Danny's death. What kind of mother reads stories to other people's children after throwing dirt on her own son's coffin?

It should have made a louder sound, but the box had been so little. She had wanted to climb down into the too small hole, cut into the warm soil. The world had smelled so good that day. The damp earth, the cut grass. She had wanted to die.

She had gotten cancer because it was her turn to suffer, as Pat had. Though Patty hadn't deserved it.

Kathleen realized that everyone else was standing and scrambled to her feet. Rabbi Hertz asked that anyone who had come to honor the anniversary of a loved one's death now speak that person's name. Voices came from different corners of the sanctuary, some barely audible.

"My father, Moshe, who died twenty-five years ago this week."

"Lena Swartz, my sister."

A woman in the back said, "My father, Charlie, the atheist, who would have been mystified to see me here."

The rabbi didn't have to do nearly as much coaxing to get the congregation to sing a final song, and the melody caromed off the thirty-foot-high dome, doubling the sound. "Now that was some really joyful noise," Rabbi Hertz said, beaming. "Please do stay for our Oneg Shabbat coffee hour, which is provided by our wonderful sisterhood. The only requirement is that you say hello to at least two people you've never met before—and that includes me."

Kathleen was the first to greet the rabbi. "I enjoyed your service so much," Kathleen said, watching the rabbi fold the prayer shawl and tuck it into a red velvet bag. "It was exactly what I needed tonight."

"And what was it you needed?" the rabbi asked, taking Kathleen's hand and not letting go.

"A place to be grateful, I guess. I had good news this week."

The rabbi, still holding on, raised her eyebrows quizzically.

"It seems that I'm not going to die from breast cancer."

"I'm so glad. My mother had breast cancer, too."

Kathleen started to laugh and, mortified, clapped her hand over her mouth. "Oh, no. Sorry, I, oh . . . it's just that it seems every time I tell anyone, they tell me about their mother or friend. I'm sorry. I must be at the end of my rope." Kathleen lowered her voice. "How long ago did she die?"

The rabbi laughed at that. "My mom is alive and well. In fact, she's off in India on an elder hostel."

Kathleen didn't know how to respond.

"You must be going through a lot," the rabbi said. "Is it okay if I say a Mi Sheberach for you tomorrow morning?"

Kathleen, embarrassed, admitted she didn't know what that was.

"It's a traditional prayer for spiritual and physical healing for members of the congregation and their families."

"That sounds awfully, um, Catholic," Kathleen said. "I mean, when I was a child, we prayed to all kinds of saints for healing."

"Did it work?"

Kathleen didn't know how to respond. How could the rabbi be so cavalier about a question of faith? "I don't think it works that way," she finally said.

"Neither do I," said Rabbi Hertz, putting a hand on Kathleen's shoulder. "But I know that public prayer can work like an embrace for people in pain, and there's no such thing as too many hugs when you're hurting."

Kathleen, almost stammering, said she wouldn't be there the next day.

"That's okay. You'll be in our thoughts. Thanks for coming up and saying hi, Kathleen. Let's get together, soon," the rabbi added, and turned to greet the young couple waiting behind her.

Kathleen walked toward the coffeepot at the far end of the sanctuary. "Genevas are my favorites, too," she told a dark-haired woman who had just picked up the last one. Joyce smiled, snapped the oval neatly in half, held out one piece to Kathleen and said, "It tastes better if you share it. Or at least, that's what I used to tell my daughter when she was little."

Kathleen accepted the half-Geneva. "Are you a regular?" she asked. "I haven't been here for ages. The last time I was at services, the rabbi was an older gentleman who looked like Ichabod Crane."

"This is my first time here, ever." As Joyce spoke, Kathleen realized she was talking to the woman who had described her father as an atheist. "My dad died fifteen years ago tomorrow. I never go to services for kaddish, but I couldn't find any of those memorial candles in the supermarket. And I wanted to do something real, something physical, to remember him."

"The candles are by the shoe polish at the Star Market," Kathleen said, smiling.

"I'm glad I came, anyway." Joyce smiled back. "I always wondered about the Gloucester synagogue. It's kind of a conceptual oxymoron—a Yankee temple. But the service was pretty interesting, much better than the last one I went to, which was just deadly. That must be five or six years ago for a bar mitzvah."

"Are you here for the weekend?" Kathleen asked, admiring Joyce's outfit, a casual but sophisticated cream-colored chenille sweater over black silk pants. Her silver earrings caught the light as she talked.

"Actually, my husband and I just bought a little house up here—near East Gloucester square, you know? Over by the theater? We'll be summer people, I guess, though we'll probably have to rent the place most of the summer to help cover the mortgage.

"We hope to come up on weekends during the school year. My daughter's at a sleepover tonight. She's twelve, so she's almost always at a sleepover."

"My sons are long gone," said Kathleen. "It's just me and my husband, who's here somewhere."

"Frank's here, too." Joyce looked around the room. "Actually, I'm kind of mystified that we're here at all. Normally at this hour, I'd be in bed with a book."

"Oh? And what are you reading?"

"I'm about to start the new Amy Tan. And you?" Joyce asked, approving of Kathleen's elegant posture, her thick, white hair and the darkest blue eyes she'd ever seen.

"I'm just finishing the latest of the Harry Potter books—belatedly for me. It's work as well as pleasure; I'm a children's librarian."

"Ah, a librarian." Joyce put her hand over her heart and bowed her head. "May I kiss the hem of your garment?" She grinned. "I can't tell you the number of times librarians have saved my deadline."

"You're a writer?"

"For women's magazines, mostly."

The trays were being cleared as the two of them started for the door, where Buddy waited with a dark-haired man, who held out a jacket to Kathleen's new acquaintance.

The women turned to each other and laughed. "This is my husband, Buddy Levine. I'm Kathleen."

"Joyce Tabachnik. This is Frank."

"You mean you don't even know each other's names?" Buddy asked. "You've been over there gabbing like you were long-lost cousins."

The four of them walked out of the synagogue and paused on the steep stairs to the street. The building had served the town's Jews for a century, but it would always look like the foursquare New England church it was built to be. Below them, the lights of the docks and the big fishing boats were mirrored in black water.

Joyce took a deep breath and said, "God, it smells good up here." Kathleen shivered and Buddy rushed over to help her into her sweater. They said their good-byes.

"Nice people," Buddy said as he and Kathleen got into their car.

"Nice people," said Frank as he and Joyce pulled out of the parking lot.

A FEW DAYS LATER, Kathleen thought she saw Joyce ahead of her in the produce aisle at the Star Market, but she then caught sight of the Naked Coed Golf T-shirt. The woman she had talked to at temple wouldn't wear such a thing in her own bathroom, much less in public.

Kathleen wondered if Joyce would trade an insider's tour of Gloucester in exchange for a trip to the mall. The corduroy jumper she had worn to services that night must be fifteen years old.

Joyce had walked past the same bananas earlier the same day, keeping an eye out for Kathleen. "That's what I want to look like when I grow up," she had told Frank on their way home from services. Joyce thought about calling Kathleen but worried that she might not want to have coffee with the author of a romance novel—though of course she hadn't mentioned *Magnolia's Heart* when they'd talked.

The following week, Joyce heard her name as she walked into Tomaso's. "I was hoping to run into you. I see you already know about one of Gloucester's crown jewels," Kathleen said, opening her arms in adoration of the crowded Main Street storefront. Mismatched metal shelves held tomatoes, pasta, oil, and tuna with unfamiliar Italian labels crowding out the American brands. Dean Martin crooned from unseen speakers.

While the women behind the counter took orders, Kathleen

explained the merits of the special sandwiches, named for neighborhoods and saints. "The calzone always sells out early in the summer."

Joyce nodded and inhaled the store's heady mixture of yeast, sawdust, and salami.

A grim-faced woman wearing orange lipstick and a green T-shirt asked for their order.

"Hi, Ginny," Kathleen said. "How are the grandkids?"

Ginny's frown dissolved as she pointed to a photograph taped to the counter. "The best."

Kathleen introduced Joyce and mentioned the house on Forest Street.

"Mary Loquasto's house," Ginny said, nodding. "You the writer?"

Joyce blushed and nodded.

"It's a nice house," Ginny added, almost daring Joyce to disagree.

"We're very lucky," Joyce said.

"There are no secrets in a small town, you know," Kathleen whispered. She bought a loaf of scali bread; Joyce ordered three dozen cookies for Nina's soccer team. Dean Martin followed them out into the street. "Sometimes they play opera," Kathleen said, pointing up at the speakers under the awning. They stood for a moment and listened to the end of "Return to Me."

"Are you in a rush?" Kathleen asked. "The pastry shop over there has wonderful cappuccino."

As they walked into the café across the street, the woman behind the counter said, "Hi, Mrs. Levine."

"Hi, Philomena," said Kathleen. "Is Serena over her cold?"

"She'll be back in school next week," said Philomena, who lowered her voice and added, "And I hear you're going to be okay, right?"

Kathleen brushed off Philomena's question and the quizzical look on Joyce's face. "I'm fine. Can we have two of the world's best cappuccinos?"

As she steamed the milk, Philomena got started on other people's business. "So, is that Mrs. Fry who teaches second grade pregnant, or not?" She set down a couple of biscotti with the coffees. "On the house."

Philomena was about to pull over a chair to join them when the phone rang. Kathleen and Joyce exchanged relieved glances. They stirred their coffees with exaggerated care, each wondering where to begin.

Maybe I'm too old, thought Kathleen. She tried to remember how she and Jeanette had started to be friends. It had taken them two years to talk about anything more important than the weather. And now Jeanette was out of her life. Kathleen knew why she hadn't called: too many friends and family members had been diagnosed with cancer in the past few years, and Jeanette was terrified. Still, Kathleen would never be able to forgive her. For a moment, she considered sticking to the weather. But then Joyce smiled, revealing two perfectly matched dimples Kathleen hadn't noticed the other night at temple.

"What brought you to Gloucester in the first place?" Kathleen asked.

"Actually, Nina found it," Joyce said. "She was a colicky baby . . . what a horrible three months that was. She would only sleep in the car, and even then we had to be doing at least fifty. Frank and I drove up and down 128, taking turns napping. So one night, late, maybe three in the morning, Frank pulled over alongside Good Harbor beach. There was no moon, and the stars were just staggering. I could see the Milky Way like it was an address, you know? Like a real pathway through the sky. Eventually, all of us fell asleep, and when we woke up, the sunrise closed the sale.

"After that, we came up for vacations. We rented cottages all over the place: Annisquam, Lanesville, Rocky Neck. We were in an apartment near Bass Rocks for three years until the place went condo. By then, I swore if we ever had the money, we'd buy a place up here."

Kathleen nodded, her eyes fixed on Joyce's expressive face. She must be forty, Kathleen thought. I can see the little lines around her eyes. Gray eyes, very striking with the black hair.

"Of course we couldn't afford what we wanted," Joyce went on, "which is a water view. Our place is about three blocks up from Smith's Cove, near the theater. Oh, right," she said, remembering Ginny's comment. "I guess everyone knows that."

"It's not bad, to be known by your neighbors."

"I'll have to get used to it. Belmont is totally anonymous by comparison."

Kathleen nodded, encouraging Joyce to go on with her story.

"I love it up here. But when I try to explain what made me pick Gloucester, I end up sounding like a Hallmark card. How can you describe the sky and the light up here without getting all gooey?"

"It's hard to describe love of a place," Kathleen said. "I can't do it, and I've been here nearly thirty-five years. I remember reading a poem that said the harbor here is big enough to hold the sky. Something like that. It was Charles Olsen. He used to live in Gloucester, you know. And there was also a line about how Gloucester was still a place to go fishing from. I should find that again."

"I'd like to read it," said Joyce. "Did you know Olsen?"

"Oh, no. I heard him speak at a town meeting once. Strange guy. A shame he died so young."

There was a pause, and then it was Joyce's turn to ask a question. "Do your sons live nearby?"

Kathleen told her about Hal, her oldest, twenty-nine and living in San Francisco, a computer programmer; and Jack, twenty-three, a chef in New York, with a Broadway actress for a girlfriend.

Kathleen asked about Nina. "She is totally into soccer," Joyce said. "And most of the time she wishes I would vanish from the face of the earth."

"Oh, dear. That sounds painful."

"It is," Joyce said, shocked to find herself instantly close to tears. "Her room is right off the kitchen at home, and from the time Nina was a baby she made us keep that door open. She liked to listen to us moving around. She liked to know we could hear her. She told me that once.

"But in January—God, it was just a few months ago really— she closed the door. I remember it was a Sunday. And that was it. One day we were friends, tickling, and going to movies together. The next day I was a terrible embarrassment, clueless, terminally annoying.

"I wonder if the whole adolescence thing is going to be harder for me because Nina is an only child, or because she was a miracle baby. I had three miscarriages and two surgeries before we had her. I used to give myself hormone shots in restaurant bathrooms, like some kind of junkie." Joyce paused. "I haven't thought about that part of my life in ages. We worked so hard to get her. Now that she's such a royal pain in the ass, I should probably remember how much I wanted a baby. But that's not my first response when she screams at me for asking if she needs lunch money."

"I think boys are easier," Kathleen said. "But there is an undeniable loss when they get to this age. And it's never as sweet as when they're little and sitting on your lap."

They sat quietly for a moment, each savoring memories of little shoes, effortless kisses, bath time.

They smiled at each other. This is good, thought Joyce.

The conversation turned to work, and Kathleen talked about

the never-ending budget battle over funding for the library. Joyce told Kathleen how her first national magazine article was completely "edited" to say the opposite of what she had intended.

They agreed to a second cappuccino and traded favorite authors.

"Jane Austen, Margaret Atwood, Toni Morrison," Joyce said.

"Beverly Cleary, E. B. White, Maurice Sendak," said Kathleen.

"Oh, Sendak is a genius."

Kathleen beamed. "Absolutely."

"Did you ever try writing a children's book yourself?"

"Once upon a time. It was pretty awful. I'm good at helping children find books to love."

The door opened and two men walked in, shouting greetings to Philomena in Italian. A moment later, four Japanese tourists crowded in. Kathleen looked at their cameras and whispered, "They're early this year."

Out on the sidewalk, Joyce suggested that Kathleen and Buddy come for dinner the following week; the deadline would help her get some painting done.

Kathleen hesitated and the invitation hung in the air for a moment too long.

"Don't feel you have to," Joyce said.

But Kathleen heard the catch in Joyce's voice. "It's not that I don't want to. It's just that . . . I, umm, I'm facing radiation treatments, and I don't feel like very good company."

"Oh my God. I'm so sorry. What is it? I mean, why are you having radiation?"

"Breast cancer."

"Oh, shit." Joyce flinched, afraid Kathleen would think she was crude.

"It's not that I don't want to get together again. I'm just . . . I don't want to talk about it anymore and I don't want to be treated like a patient," Kathleen said, a little louder than she'd intended. "They're all as sweet as can be—my family, neighbors, people at school—but ever since the diagnosis, it's all anyone can talk about. Any room I'm in just fills up with cancer. My cancer. Their best friend's cancer. Their dog's cancer! Honest to goodness! One woman cornered me and told me about her twelve-year-old dog's liver-cancer treatment, like I was an expert on the subject.

"Oh, dear. I sound furious, don't I?"

"Well, why the hell shouldn't you be furious?" Joyce said softly.

They smiled at each other. They were going to be okay.

The next day, Joyce called to say that she had found the Olsen poem about Gloucester, and they chatted about the weather for a minute. Then Kathleen said, "I'm getting measured for the radiation in a couple of days. They're going to make some kind of a plastic form for me to lie in so the ray goes to the right place. And then they are going to"—she took a deep breath and tried to sound casual—"put tattoos on me. So they zap me in the right spot, I guess. Or maybe so they don't shoot the wrong one by mistake."

"That sounds hideous!"

"I think so, too," Kathleen agreed. "They say it's not going to hurt, and I'm usually pretty good at putting things like this into perspective, but I'm dreading this tattooing thing so much, I can hardly stand it. Is that silly?"

"Nothing about how rotten you feel is silly. You're not going to a day spa, for God's sake. The whole thing sucks."

Kathleen giggled.

"Excuse my language," Joyce said. "But even the littlest part of this sucks. And don't let anyone try to tell you different."

Kathleen felt better after she hung up. She hadn't told anyone else how upset she was about the tattoos. Thank goodness Joyce hadn't tried to cheer her up.

Joyce knew she'd said the right thing—or at least that she hadn't said the wrong thing. After her first miscarriage, people had said nothing but the wrong thing to her. One ex-friend patted her hand and said she should be glad "Mother Nature was taking care of her mistake."

The doctor who did the D&C said, "Don't worry, hon. We'll get you past this and within a year you'll have a healthy baby and forget this ever happened." After he left, the nurse snorted in disgust. "What a crock of horse manure," she'd said, crossing her large arms. "Losing a baby is a heartbreak that you never forget." Nurse Phyllis Burkey was a woman Joyce remembered with fierce affection. "It sucks," Phyllis Burkey said, "and don't let anyone try to tell you different."

JUNE

THIS IS ridiculous," Kathleen said when Buddy insisted they leave two hours before her first appointment. "I don't want to sit there any longer than I have to." But when he crossed his arms and lowered his head, she knew he wasn't going to back down.

She slammed the car door too hard, and they drove through the morning fog and over the bridge without speaking. Just past the Ipswich exit they ran into traffic, and the radio announced a four-car accident a mile ahead. Buddy glanced over, but Kathleen refused to meet his eyes and admit he was right.

She looked out her window and tried not to think of the crash as an omen. Buddy wiped his palms on his pants.

Once they passed the backup, the silent breach between them closed. "The trees are beautiful," she said softly, staring at the woods, filled in and fully green for the summer.

"It was all that rain we had," he said, squinting into the rearview mirror.

Dr. Truman had recommended this doctor, but the building did not inspire confidence in Kathleen or Buddy, who remembered its earlier incarnation as St. Jude's Hospital for Incurables. Metro-North Medical Center was a brutally ugly, low-slung, yellow-brick building. "It still looks like a tire factory," Buddy muttered.

Inside, the crucifixes were gone and the lobby alcove where

Saint Jude had once held court had been turned into a spiky garden of flowering bromeliads. The blue plastic pond was carpeted with pennies. They followed the signs to the elevators and down to the basement, where the gray carpeting exuded the faintly toxic smell of renovation. The magazines were up-to-date, and there wasn't a speck of dust on the silk flower arrangements. Someone had tried to soften the light in the waiting room by unscrewing a few of the fluorescent bulbs and adding some table lamps, but they only cast weird shadows on the acoustic-tile ceiling.

Kathleen thought she had never seen a bleaker place. Like the waiting room for the best-behaved residents in hell, she thought, and decided Joyce would get a kick out of the image. Maybe Joyce would write a novel and dedicate it to her, as a posthumous memorial.

Kathleen was surprised by that morbid turn in her train of thought. After all, the prognosis was, officially, "excellent."

Five pairs of eyes looked up as they walked into the waiting room. Two women in their sixties—one wearing a head scarf against a naked skull—interrupted their whispered conversation and looked first at Kathleen and then at Buddy, trying to work out which one was the patient. An elderly man in a pressed shirt and clip-on tie leaned forward on his cane and smiled a weary welcome. A young black man—a teenager—stared blankly. Beside him, his mother glared protectively. Buddy put his arm around Kathleen and steered her to the desk, where the receptionist greeted them as though Kathleen were a long-lost girlfriend.

"Oh, hi, Mrs. Levine. Marcy will be right out for you."

"Marcy?" asked Buddy.

"She's your nurse. She'll set you up before you meet with Dr. Singh. I'm Carla." Carla handed them a clipboard. "You can get started on these in the meantime, okay?"

Sitting next to Buddy, Kathleen saw that the forms asked for the same information she had supplied a dozen times in the past weeks: her insurance policy number, her weight, her height, her family history, her social security number, her primary care physician's name. She couldn't concentrate and handed Buddy the pen.

Kathleen kept her eyes on the floor. The young man wore an enormous pair of gleaming white Nikes; his mother, a pair of cracked black patent leather flats. The two other women wore identical pairs of sneakers with short white socks. The older man's tasseled loafers looked expensive.

Buddy's tan work boots were the same ones he'd been buying at Sears ever since she'd met him. Each pair lasted between three and four years. Kathleen calculated that this would be his eighth or ninth pair since they were married.

Her own blue, beaded moccasins, bought years ago at an outlet store in Maine, suddenly seemed ridiculous. Hal had teased her about them when they were new.

Kathleen wished Hal didn't live so far away. Her hands were icy, and she could feel her heart pounding. She didn't know how to manage this fear. She was supposed to feel fortunate. Noninvasive tumor and clean margins. DCIS is barely cancer at all. It was the right breast, so the heart is clear of the ray. And she was left-handed. All good news.

Then she recalled Joyce's "This sucks" and smiled grimly.

"Mrs. Levine?"

The voice caught her by surprise, and she sprang to her feet. A pretty Asian woman wearing a red dress introduced herself as Marcy Myers and extended her hand, holding on to Kathleen's until the meaning of her grasp was abundantly clear. Oh, for heaven's sake, Kathleen silently scolded herself. She's just being nice.

In the office, Kathleen forced herself to listen while Marcy explained what would happen next. After Dr. Singh met with them, they would take a tour of the center and see the radiation machine and the simulator, which was used for taking measurements. Measuring would take up most of the morning. Marcy recited the radiation litany, which Kathleen already knew by heart: no deodorant before treatments, cornstarch instead of powder, no perfume, and no lotion apart from the ones they would give her.

Why was Buddy writing this down again?

Then Marcy started talking about the "application of permanent landmarks."

"You mean the tattoos, right?" Kathleen asked, unable to keep the edge out of her voice.

"Do you have a religious objection to tattooing?" Marcy asked.

"I don't understand."

"Are you Jewish?"

"Yes," Kathleen said, instantly defensive. Kathleen Levine was never an easy name to explain.

"Some of our Jewish patients refuse the permanent markings on religious grounds."

"I never heard of that."

"Well, according to Orthodox law, tattooing is forbidden."

"We're not Orthodox," said Kathleen.

"All right, then," Marcy said gently. "Our patients say the tattoos don't hurt. You can barely even see them, and oncologists prefer the permanence."

Kathleen said, "I know. They do it so that if they have to treat the other breast, they'll know which is which. I thought I already signed a paper agreeing to this."

Buddy winced when she said "the other breast."

Marcy looked at the bottom of her checklist, put down her pencil, and lowered her voice meaningfully. "Mrs. Levine," she said, and then urgently, "Kathleen. I would like to emphasize the importance of support for women undergoing breast cancer treatment." It was the first time Marcy had used the words *breast cancer*. She cited statistics about the benefits of mentors and support groups.

Kathleen had seen the pamphlets about support groups, but she couldn't imagine complaining about her paltry symptoms to women who were throwing up and losing their hair. Besides, she didn't want to devote any more time to this thing than she had to. She wanted to preserve the summer. She wanted to plant lilies, visit Jack in New York, spend more time with Joyce.

Or maybe she would die, and what good would a support group do then?

Kathleen could sense Buddy's concern, but she wasn't even looking at Marcy anymore. Her eyes wandered around the wall behind the desk, at a vaguely cubist rendering of Rockport's famous red fishing shack, the college diploma issued to Marcy Yamaguchi, a nursing degree for Marcy Y. Myers, and a framed photograph.

The picture had been taken at a rocky seaside overlook. Marcy and a burly, bearded man wearing a blue T-shirt and a yarmulke smiled into the camera, their arms around two little girls. The older one looked to be about ten; the younger one had Down's syndrome.

Kathleen focused on Marcy with new interest, but just then Dr. Singh arrived and everything stopped.

He was the most breathtakingly handsome man Kathleen had ever seen. He shook Buddy's hand and resumed a conversation the two of them had begun in the hospital.

He had seen them after her surgery, he said, and Kathleen realized she must have been out cold. There was no way she would have forgotten these black eyes, the full arch of these red lips. He was so good-looking that Kathleen blushed.

"Would it be all right if we stay in here, Mrs. Myers?" he asked Marcy with a wave of his long fingers. His accent was British and formal.

"Have you found a house yet?" Buddy asked, picking up the thread of a conversation that was new to Kathleen.

"In Marblehead," said the doctor. "We moved in last week. My wife and I feel fortunate to be living in such a beautiful place. But if we don't find the television remote control very soon, we may end up in divorce court."

Kathleen felt her cheeks color again, in anger now. This wasn't a cocktail party. This was her funeral, thank you very much, and the corpse would like to remain the center of attention. She coughed into her fist.

The doctor seemed to take the hint and began describing the treatment for what seemed like the sixth time. He described the possible side effects: fatigue, aches and pains, swelling or shrinking of the breast, a kind of "sunburn" caused by the rays. Buddy scribbled furiously as Kathleen looked deeply into the doctor's eyes and wondered if his wife was from India.

Good heavens, he was a masterpiece.

The doctor stood up and took Kathleen's right hand between his. "Setting the machines properly will take a week or so," he told her, "and then we will meet again for the first treatment. I shall see you every week, and Mrs. Myers will watch out for you as well. You may call upon us anytime, with questions.

"Mrs. Levine," he said, drawing an inch closer and lowering his voice, "try to rest easy. We will take very good care of you here, and your husband will take excellent care of you at home, I'm certain. For your part, you must eat well, rest, and keep up your spirits.

"I also prescribe long walks by the ocean," he said, letting go of her hand and holding up both index fingers, like an orchestra conductor. "I am quite serious about this. The exercise alone is beneficial, of course. But the gifts of the sea are precious. Surely you know what I mean."

"Oh, yes," she said, transfixed by the attention and his touch. "I love to walk on the beach," she said, almost stammering.

"Of course you do."

As Dr. Singh left, Kathleen and Marcy caught one another's eye. Marcy put a hand over her heart and fluttered her fingers. Kathleen laughed out loud. Buddy looked at them, clueless.

"I'm going to show you the treatment room first," Marcy said, leading them down a hallway. She opened the door to a room as big as Kathleen's library at school. The radiation machine loomed in the center, like an oversize prop from a 1950s science-fiction movie.

Marcy introduced Terry and Rachel, who would be her regular radiation techs. Terry showed them how the treatment table moved up to meet the movable "head," which delivered the ray. Rachel pointed to the mobile hanging from the ceiling: four angels made out of clothespins and glitter. "A patient's daughter made it," she said.

When Terry turned the lights down for a moment and a red beam bisected the room, Kathleen gasped. "The laser is used only for alignment," Terry explained quickly. "I think they should change it to blue or green, don't you? The red is so, I don't know—red."

"Alarming," said Kathleen.

"Scary, yeah," said Terry, a pretty blonde with high cheekbones and four gold hoops in each ear.

In the simulator room down another hall, Kathleen put on a hospital johnny. The room was dim and cold, and she was mortified as her nipples hardened and stayed erect during the endless measurements by John Marino, a young man who used to work construction and knew Buddy from the store. John was muscular and quick, running in and out to control-booth monitors and computers. "Sorry this is taking so long, Mrs. Levine," he said. "But we've got to get it perfect." Kathleen admired the professional way he arranged her arm and measured the contour of her breast without even seeming to touch her.

Then she caught sight of her reflection in a mirrored panel on the door. "Oh, God," she whispered. Staring at the frightened, haggard, old woman, she thought, how else would he touch me? Her breast looked mutilated, the scar still red and angry-looking.

The disease of old age. Where had she read that? I'm an old lady with cancer. She squeezed her eyes tight. Marcy walked in just then and said, "Hang on, Kathleen. We're nearly done."

But they weren't. Rachel, a short, round brunette who wore her hair in braids, brought in a tray with a small bottle of india ink and a box of individually wrapped needles. She noticed Kathleen's eyes widen and pointed to two small blue freckles on her thumb. "This is what it looks like. I did it to myself so I'd know what it felt like, too. It only pinches for a sec. Not even as much as a bee sting."

Rachel and John took great care in locating the exact spots for the tattoo marks, but Kathleen felt herself getting more and more agitated.

"Here we go," said Rachel, swabbing the cold antiseptic on Kathleen's breast. The needle felt hot.

"Only three more," Rachel said.

"Okay," said Kathleen, her voice tight and high. Marcy held her left hand. They were right. It didn't hurt much at all, but the tears came anyway, down her cheeks, into her ears. She held very still.

On the way home, Buddy tried to ask how she was feeling. Kathleen shook her head and closed her eyes.

"Tired, huh?"

She nodded and leaned back into the headrest. An old word floated into her head: *Stigmata.*

As they approached their driveway, Kathleen told Buddy to drop her off and go back to the store, but he got out of the car, made her a cup of tea, and tucked her in for a nap.

Kathleen got in bed to humor him, but as soon as he left, she dressed and went out into the yard. Pulling a few weeds, she inhaled deeply and savored the smell of warm soil layered on ocean air. Joyce had said something about how Tomaso's smelled like heaven, but this was pretty darned divine.

She went inside and picked up the phone. "None of us Tabach-niks can answer you at the moment," said the machine. "Please wait for the beep and leave a message."

"Hi, Joyce. It's Kathleen. Let's go for a walk at Good Harbor. Call me."

JOYCE LISTENED TO Kathleen's message a few days later as Frank carried the cooler into the kitchen and Nina stood in front of the open refrigerator. "There's nothing to eat in this house," she said. "Who's Kathleen?"

"Shut that door will you?" said Frank. "I'm going shopping in a minute. Mom and I met her at the temple."

"Where was I?"

"Sleeping over at Sylvie's house," he said.

Joyce picked up the receiver.

"You're going to use the phone now?" Nina said, sounding incredulous. "I have to make a call."

"It'll have to wait," Joyce said, carrying the receiver into the living room. Nina poked her head through the door and wordlessly registered her impatience, but Joyce pretended not to understand.

"Sorry I couldn't call sooner," Joyce said. "When do you want to walk?"

"I could be there in fifteen minutes."

Joyce grabbed the car keys and announced, "I'm meeting Kathleen for a little while."

"You can't go now," Frank sputtered.

"Drop me off on your way to the store," Joyce snapped. "Kathleen will drive me home and Nina will be fine on her own for half an hour."

In the car Frank asked, "Is Kathleen okay?"

"What kind of question is that? She's got breast cancer, for God's sake."

"Well, yes, I know," he said, embarrassed into a silence that lasted until they pulled over beside the footbridge that led from the shore road, over the tidal river, and onto Good Harbor beach. Joyce had the door open before the car came to a stop.

There was no sign of Kathleen yet, so Joyce leaned over the weathered wooden railing. The river below was barely a trickle, making it hard to tell if the tide was coming in or going out. I should have said good-bye to Frank, she thought. I should be nicer to Frank. And Frank should be nicer to me. She hoped the long hours he was putting into this company paid off in a big way.

Joyce reached her arms over her head to stretch, glad that Nina wasn't nearby to tell her to stop acting like a weirdo in public. Not that there was much of a crowd this late in the afternoon. Most people were leaving, lugging chairs and coolers, going home.

Four lifeguards went by, looking like a commercial for *Baywatch*, despite their ugly regulation-orange bathing suits. A handsome black kid with a washboard stomach was wearing a pair of silver hoop earrings exactly like Joyce's. I can see them, she thought, but to them I might as well be one of those gulls. The birds were busy cleaning up a mess of corn chips, screaming and flapping at each other. "Oh, dry up," Joyce said softly.

She raised her eyes to the horizon and took a breath. She loved this slice of the coast, from Salt Island to the granite fortress of the Bass Rocks. Something about the way the beach held the sky unlocked her. It inspired her to ponder the direction of her life and set her to wondering whether she believed in God—or Something. She often thought about her father at Good Harbor—he had loved the ocean, especially when there was a strong wind and a loud surf.

A late sun worshiper wearing a bikini and two-inch platform

sandals clopped past on the bridge's weathered wooden boards. Joyce glanced over her shoulder. She smiled at herself and how easily she could be distracted from cosmic ruminations. That lady was sixty-five if she was a day, but at least she looked okay in a skimpy bathing suit. The same could not be said of the truly elephantine women Joyce had seen out here, parading around in next to nothing. Were they oblivious or intentionally outrageous? She didn't know whether to avert her eyes or applaud.

People-watching at the beach was one of Joyce's great pleasures. Endless questions and stories occurred to her. How did sixty-something couples, holding hands and bumping shoulders, manage to keep the spark alive? Or were they newlyweds who had found each other after burying longtime spouses they had come to loathe? Were the lesbian couples in matching khaki shorts local girls or tourists from the Midwest? Was the man in black socks and sandals a recent immigrant from a landlocked country, or a clumsy spy?

Joyce also considered herself a connoisseur of T-shirts. Like a bird-watcher, she kept a list of oddball favorites: "When the going gets tough, the tough get duct tape." "What are you looking at?" "She Who Must Be Obeyed."

And tattoos. Once the sole property of veterans, they'd been taken up by macho boys and nubile girls, and an unpredictable assortment of middle-aged men and women. But from now on, they would all make her think of Kathleen's tattoos. The brand of One-in-Eight.

Joyce hugged her own shoulders until she felt her joints grumble pleasantly. She was free. Yesterday she had shipped the last of her magazine assignments. Mario had left a message asking about the Magnolia sequel, but she hadn't returned his call. She wanted to try a serious novel. She wanted to give it the summer, at least.

Frank would be at the supermarket by now, buying food for the weekend and staples for the rest of the summer. It was their first time in the house, all three of them, the first spring weekend without a soccer tournament. On the way up, Frank had cleared his throat and announced in a brave voice that he was going to be an assistant coach for Nina's team next season.

"Don't worry, sweetie," he had said over his shoulder to Nina, trying to head off her inevitable snit, "I won't be telling you what to do. I think my main job is going to be putting together the schedule. Tom says that it's so complicated, they need a spreadsheet. That's where I come in."

Nina scowled, put on her Walkman, and started singing along to the unheard lament of a woman in love. The summer before, she had sung their silly family car song. "We all went to the barber, to look sharp for Good Harbor. We don't turn to the starboard till we get to Good Harbor." She went on and on until Joyce, worn-out, had snapped, "That's enough!"

This year they had had to bribe Nina with a promise of new CDs to get her to come at all.

"What are you thinking about?" asked Kathleen, suddenly at Joyce's side.

"I was thinking about Nina. I'm so glad you called."

"And I'm glad you could get away today. Want to walk? It's doctor's orders."

"Smart doctor."

"I don't want to talk about my treatment," Kathleen said, trying to sound casual rather than brittle. "It hasn't started yet anyway. I just went to get measured and marked."

"The tattoos, right? Did it suck?"

"Yes. But I don't want to talk about that either. Tell me what's going on with you."

They left their shoes next to the green trash barrels at the end of the bridge and headed over the tidal plain to the water's edge.

The last tide had sculpted the beach into a wavy pattern made of tiny crenellated dunes; each one held a scrap of blue sky reflected in warm water.

A pair of gulls swooped overhead and skimmed the shoreline until they found a spot to their liking and started strutting, on the lookout, as always, for food.

"Is the tide coming in or going out?" asked Joyce.

"Going out," Kathleen said.

"It's such an undramatic difference at this point. You have to be really tuned in to know it."

Kathleen laughed and said the only reason she knew was because Buddy had told her. She turned the talk to Joyce. What was new? How was the house? Was she writing? What was for supper?

"I have no idea what we're eating," Joyce said. "I'm going to paint the kitchen a very strange color. I'm not writing at all. But I do have tidings of strange goings-on with my Virgin Mary."

"Your what?"

"I didn't tell you about her yet?"

Joyce described the statue: her surprising height, the detailed pleats in the veil, the way her hands stretched out as if she were inviting the flowers to grow. Frank had been too busy to come up and get rid of it. This was his first time in Gloucester since the weekend they'd met at temple.

In the meantime, her Virgin had spawned a mystery. "A few weeks ago, she sprouted a crown of plastic flowers on her head. Then someone left a pot of marigolds at her feet. So I figured I'd better try to move her myself. I rooted around a little, but the cement goes way down, much further than I could dig with a trowel. We're going to have to hire someone to take her out.

"Today, I found a bunch of lilacs lying next to her. Now I'm wondering if we've got a local shrine on our hands."

Joyce felt shy about asking her neighbors what to do with the statue. She couldn't even get up the nerve to ask the two guys who lived next door, even though they always smiled and said hi when they walked their golden retriever.

"So how do I deep-six the Mother of God without pissing off the whole block or starting a pogrom?"

Kathleen laughed. The sound pleased Joyce immensely.

"I think you might want to call in a priest," said Kathleen.

"I don't need an exorcism, do I?" Joyce said in mock horror. "Her head isn't spinning around or anything like that."

"Oh, no. I just think you might need help in getting the BVM out of there respectfully."

"The BMW?"

"Blessed Virgin Mary," Kathleen said. "Try the priest over at St. Rita's."

"I've always wondered about Saint Rita. Is she the patron saint of waitresses or meter maids or what?"

Kathleen laughed again. "There's a million saints I've never heard of, but I'm pretty sure Saint Rita is the patron of matrimonial trouble."

"You're kidding."

"No, I really think so. Whoever she was, St. Rita's is near your house, so that's the parish priest to contact."

"Okay then. I'll call him."

Kathleen stopped and faced out to sea. Her right hand shaded her eyes and then she pointed to the horizon. "He's out late."

"He?"

"The sailboat."

Joyce hunted for the boat. The thumbnail-sized sail seemed stuck against the sky, like a scrap of white paper on a pale blue bulletin board.

"What a day," said Kathleen, studying the distance.

In the silence, Joyce wondered if Kathleen was thinking about her cancer. She wanted so much to be a worthy friend, a confidante.

"Father Sherry!" Kathleen said suddenly.

"What?"

"That's the name of the priest at St. Rita's. I met him last year at some school event. I remember thinking what a funny name he had. Father Sherry. It reminded me of that old priest in *Going My Way* who was always taking a medicinal nip. Not that this man is anything like Barry Fitzgerald.

"Father Sherry is in his late forties, a big man. And he belongs to a diving club. I saw him once over at Folly Cove wearing a wet suit. I thought it was so funny—a diving priest."

"With or without the clerical collar?" asked Joyce.

"You call Father Sherry. He'll know what to do."

They had reached the far end of the beach, where the sandbar out to Salt Island was fully exposed.

"You know, in all the years of coming here, I've never been up there," said Joyce, pointing to the top of the island.

"There's nothing there but the view. And a sense of accomplishment," said Kathleen. "I used to take the boys. They hated that I made them bring shoes and socks and long pants. But they never once got poison ivy when I was with them. I'll take you sometime."

"That would be great."

"Do you want to walk out now?"

"I should get home," Joyce sighed. "Frank is cooking."

They turned to start back. "It's always amazing to me how big this beach is," Joyce said. "The walk from the bridge never feels that far, but when I get all the way down here, it looks twice the distance. It's like two totally different places."

"Rachel Carson has a wonderful line about how the shore has a dual nature," said Kathleen.

"*Silent Spring?*"

"No. It was in a book about the ocean. She said the seashore was, let me see if I can remember it, a place of unrest, of dual natures. It's wet and dry. Old as the earth, but never exactly the same from one tide to the next."

"Like people," said Joyce.

"You don't think people are the same from one day to the next?"

"Well, biologically they're not. We're not. I mean, we're made of water, and that's always in flux. Don't you think that's what she meant?"

"I suppose so," Kathleen said. "Do you think people have a dual nature?"

"Do you mean good and evil? I'm not that much of a philosopher," Joyce said, pausing. "But we're all living and dying at the same time. Cells dividing, making more cells, shedding the old ones." She stopped, worried that she'd said something wrong.

They lapsed into silence and picked up the pace a little. A jogger approached and breezed past with a wave.

"I think we're eating fish tonight," Kathleen said. "Buddy finally caught something big enough to eat."

"Who cleans them?"

"He does. And he cooks them."

"Frank likes to cook, too."

"Tell me about Frank," said Kathleen. "And what kind of name is Frank for a nice Jewish boy?"

"His birth certificate says Franklin, after FDR. The Democratic Party was his family's real religion."

"And how did you two meet?"

"At a party. I liked the way he danced. And then I liked the way we danced together."

"Sounds very romantic," Kathleen said. "I met Buddy at a

dance, too. But he didn't dance, and neither did I. We found each other in the wallflower seats."

"That's pretty romantic, too. And since you brought it up, what about your name, *Kathleen Levine?*"

"That's Kathleen Mary Elizabeth McCormack Levine. I converted before I married Buddy."

"Was your family okay with that?"

"Yes," said Kathleen, remembering Pat's roses. "It was okay, even for my sister the Sister. Did I tell you that my sister was a nun?"

"No. Are you close?"

"Pat died of breast cancer."

"Oh, my God."

"I have a different kind, as all my doctors like to remind me." Kathleen briefly described her diagnosis and treatment.

"It sounds like you're going to be okay."

"It's not a death sentence. I won't even lose my hair."

"You have beautiful hair," Joyce said.

"Thanks. I'm still pretty vain about it. And I wanted to thank you for what you said the other day."

"What did I say?"

"About not letting anyone tell me this wasn't an ordeal."

"Oh. You mean, that it sucks."

"You have such a way with words. I guess that's why you're the professional writer," said Kathleen. "The radiology doctor told me to go for walks by the ocean during these treatments. It was the only decent part of that whole awful day."

"I can't imagine what you're going through," said Joyce.

"Count your blessings that you can't."

On the bridge, they stopped to lean over the railing, elbows almost touching, looking down to the riverbed, the wet sand waiting for the return of the tide. "Sometimes I think I can hear the difference," said Joyce. "When the tide's going out, the pebbles get dragged. So the sound is a little lighter coming in."

Kathleen cocked her head to listen and nodded.

Joyce asked Kathleen for a ride home, and as she slid into the car, Kathleen said, "Next time, you have to tell me about how you did the research for *Magnolia's Heart.*"

"Oh, my God. How did you find out?"

"Never underestimate the powers of a librarian in the age of the Internet."

"You looked me up?"

"I bought a copy yesterday."

Joyce covered her face with her hands. "Please, just rip the cover off, okay?"

"That is quite a pair of pants he's wearing."

"You noticed?"

"They took out a piece of breast. My eyes are fine. For your next cover, they could take a picture of my radiology doctor."

"Do tell."

Kathleen tried to do justice to the surpassing beauty of Dr. Singh during the short drive to the Tabachniks' house. As they pulled up, Joyce pointed to the statue and said, "Let me introduce you."

They stood on either side of Mary in silence for a moment. Kathleen bent down to pick up the crown of plastic flowers, which had fallen to the ground.

"My sister disliked this sort of thing: the crowns, the May processionals, all that. She said it made Mary into a kind of beauty queen. Pat thought of her as one tough cookie, a fierce soul. But I think Pat was the fierce one. She projected herself onto the Blessed Mother."

Joyce didn't know what to say. "Jews know so little about Mary. Or Jesus for that matter. How do we get away with that, living in this culture?"

"I don't know," said Kathleen. "Fear? Defensiveness?"

Joyce tried to look at the statue defenselessly. The half smile on the Virgin's face was pensive. Back erect, head inclined to the right, she seemed to be listening. She held her hands at an intentional angle, like a dancer, her fingers reaching, inviting you to approach. It was a gesture of welcome that seemed both formal and genuine. Nice body language. Gentle and still. Attentive. The mother we all wish for.

"She's always young, isn't she?" said Joyce.

"What?" Kathleen had been thinking about the way Pat had prayed over Danny's body after the doctor had removed the ventilator.

"Mary is always young in these statues, isn't she? Firm chin, no wrinkles, no regrets."

"No regrets," repeated Kathleen. "I never thought of that. Maybe that's why I'm not a Catholic anymore." Joyce had no idea what Kathleen meant, but she didn't ask her to explain. It seemed too personal a question—like asking to see the tattoos on her breast.

They parted with promises to walk again.

From the rearview mirror, Kathleen watched Joyce wave goodbye. She looks sad, Kathleen thought. I'll call her tomorrow.

KATHLEEN SAT ON the deck and counted seven pots of sweet william. I guess that's one good thing about getting older, she thought. Everyone knows your favorite flowering annual.

Buddy had brought home two big plants from the supermarket, Hal had shipped one, Madge Feeney had collected money and sent one from the staff, the principal had sent over another on his own. Louisa from next door left hers on the porch with an envelope containing three marijuana cigarettes and a note that read, "Proven appetite booster." Jeanette wired her flowers from Florida with a printed card that said only, "Get Well Soon."

Kathleen decided she'd plant the whole bunch in one big clump near the lone granite boulder in the front yard. They would make a great shout of magenta in one of the few spots she hadn't filled with daylilies. But not just this minute.

She leaned back in the chaise, put her feet up, and squeezed her eyes shut, feeling the warmth on her forehead, her nose, her forearms. Kathleen had never been much of a sunbather, but she knew that once she started radiation, she'd avoid the sun, even though no one at the clinic had said she had to take extraordinary precautions.

"I'm thinking about gardening by the light of the moon and grocery shopping at midnight," she said to Hal and Jack, both of whom had taken to calling every night.

She lingered for a few minutes on this golden morning and savored the smell of new mulch.

The book slipped off her lap and landed with a thud. Kathleen was nervous about starting *Magnolia's Heart* and regretted having told Joyce she knew the identity of Cleo Lehigh. What if it was really bad? Could she lie convincingly if she had to? Could she be a friend to the writer of a bad book? And if not, what kind of person did that make her?

As she reached for the paperback, the phone rang. Saved, she thought, jumping up.

A familiar voice introduced herself as Michelle Hertz and Kathleen tried to summon a face. "I found out that we live in practically the same neighborhood and I wondered if you'd like some company."

Kathleen suddenly remembered the young rabbi.

"Or if this isn't a convenient time . . . ," the rabbi said.

"No, of course. Please," Kathleen insisted. "Come join me for iced tea."

Rabbi Hertz said she'd be there in a few minutes. "And don't make a fuss. I won't stay long, and I promise not to pray or anything."

Kathleen washed the breakfast dishes. She wiped down the counters, pulled out a couple of tall tumblers, sliced an orange, and picked two sprigs of mint from a pot on the windowsill. Was this a pastoral visit? The only other time a rabbi had been in her home was after Danny died.

Glancing out to check the tidiness of the deck, she noticed *Magnolia's Heart* on the chair. Forgive me, Joyce, she thought as she hid it under a stack of magazines. I suppose I'm hopelessly conventional, but I really don't want the rabbi to think of me as a randy old lady.

The doorbell rang a moment later.

"See? I really am right in the neighborhood," Michelle said, taking both of Kathleen's hands in hers. She wore a long khaki shift and stylish black sandals that showed off crimson toenails. "I didn't realize that you were the one with the incredible rock garden."

Kathleen led her through the house—a thirty-year-old split-level, furnished with big, comfortable chairs and local antiques. The rabbi slowed down to look at the family photographs that covered the hallway walls, but Kathleen moved ahead, eager to show off the beautiful part of her home. The kitchen sliders led onto a relatively new redwood deck that overlooked the steep yard. Flowers bloomed around the granite boulders, jutting up at odd angles on the hill.

"This is spectacular," Michelle said. "And the rocks are like sculptures, aren't they? What's that deep blue flower over there?"

"Lobelia."

"And the yellow?"

"Alyssum. But you have to come see it once the rest of the lilies are blooming. The whole place comes to life."

"No vegetables?"

"A few tomato plants, a little basil and parsley." Kathleen led the rabbi back toward the table, set with iced tea and cookies.

"I didn't mean for you to go to any trouble."

"No trouble." Kathleen felt her cancer take one of the empty chairs. She hated the way her mind worked these days.

"Ah," said the rabbi after taking a long drink. "That's perfect. What did you put in here? Mint?"

Kathleen nodded. "I grow my own. Though actually, mint grows itself."

"Nice." After another sip, Michelle put down her glass, took a breath, and leaned forward. "But I have to confess to an ulterior motive in visiting."

"What is that, Rabbi?" said Kathleen, smiling at how lightly the title sat upon this young-enough-to-be-her-daughter woman.

"It's the library in the temple."

Kathleen frowned. "But there is no library in the temple."

"Exactly. It's a shame, don't you think?"

"Well, yes. We tried to get one going but, oh, that was a long time ago."

"I know. I was reading through old board minutes; you were on that subcommittee."

"You're reading minutes from the early seventies? That must be pretty dull."

"You'd be amazed how much history you can pick up from them, and from the old temple bulletins. I'm the new kid in town. I have lots to learn."

Kathleen wondered if this was the rabbi's way of telling her that she knew about Danny. It was so strange to meet people, to know them for years even, without their having a clue about the death of her second child. She never spoke of him. Not even to Buddy—especially not to Buddy, who couldn't bear to hear Danny's name.

She thought about Danny every day. In the garden. On the beach. At school, when one of the kindergartners giggled in the same key. Did Buddy think of him like that, or was it just a mother thing?

Michelle Hertz let the silence last for a moment, gazing at the potted flowers on the deck. "By the way, I did say that prayer for you.

"I only used your Hebrew name; that's also in the records. Rabbi Flacks saved everything. With your permission, I'll keep saying it through the summer."

Kathleen looked at her glass.

"I know I'm young," said Michelle gently, "but I am no stranger to illness. Let me know if I can help or if there's something the congregation can do. And I mean anything from dropping off food to driving you to appointments, to just coming over to say hi. Okay?"

"It's nice of you. But from what I hear, the radiation isn't too debilitating. That's all I have to endure right now."

"Well, whatever you need, we're here for you." Michelle took a cookie, broke it in half, put it down again. "And if you feel up to it, I want to ask you to help me make a library for the temple."

Kathleen was startled. She shook her head, starting to make her excuses, but the rabbi spoke first. "I just received a donation of five thousand dollars specifically for the library. That's a lot of money for a collection that, as of today, includes about one hundred mostly outdated books with broken spines and torn pages. I'd like to make a big announcement about it, call the newspaper, the whole schmear. But I don't want to do that until I have a committee in place. Since you're the only professional librarian in the congregation, you're the natural choice."

Kathleen pressed her lips together and tried not to look annoyed.

"You would be the official chair, but there would be no meetings, I promise, and no heavy lifting, of course. I have a bunch of young moms who volunteered to do shelving and carding and stuff like that. There are a couple of contractors in the temple who've agreed to build new bookcases. I need help on the children's section. I can suggest plenty of titles for the adult collection, but I know almost nothing about children's books. Someday I hope to"—Michelle shrugged—"but not yet.

"I know there are loads of new Jewish books for kids, and I'd like to make sure we'd be getting the best. The donor actually stipulated one-quarter of the gift for the children's section. So what do you say?"

Kathleen was put out. Here she thought she was getting a nice pastoral visit from the rabbi, when she was actually being recruited for a fairly big job. She knew nothing about Jewish books for children, though, of course, she could learn, and she did know quality.

Kathleen realized she was also flattered. "It's kind of you to think of me. I'm just not sure I'm going to be up to it."

The rabbi put her hand on Kathleen's arm and said softly, "I went through this with my mother. And while I don't presume to know what it's going to be like for you, my bet is that you'll be able to do some reading. All I'm really asking is for you to go through what we've got and help with a list of titles. I'll find you some catalogs, and you could check out the Web, maybe visit a bookstore, or one of the big temple libraries. I can even ask someone to drive, if you like.

"I really need this to happen. I'm trying to revive the religious school, and there's talk of starting a preschool. But we don't have a single children's book published after 1975."

"That's terrible," Kathleen said, professionally offended. "No one's bought anything since then?"

"If they did, the books are long gone." Michelle glanced at the kitchen clock. "But I've got to get going. I don't want to be late for my first Cape Ann Interfaith Clergy meeting. Jim Sherry told me there'd be a good turnout. Seems everyone wants to meet the first lady rabbi on the North Shore. Cool, huh?"

Kathleen walked her to the door and thanked her for coming.

"I'm not letting you off the hook," the rabbi said. "I really do need your help. More to the point, the temple needs your help. Please say you'll think about it."

"I'll think about it," said Kathleen, smiling at the hard sell.

"Good-bye," said the rabbi.

"See you," said Kathleen.

"God willing."

"God willing?" Kathleen repeated softly, closing the door. What an awful thing to say. It makes me feel doomed, she thought, heading back to the kitchen. The meadow of Sweet Williams on the deck flashed into sight. Doomed or blessed. Either way, the rabbi was right. It was out of her hands.

JOYCE FELT AS IF she'd wasted the first half of June in the car driving to and from soccer practices, and soccer games, and soccer dinners.

Nina's team had led their division all year and was now in the play-offs, and Nina was a big part of their success. She was a great ball handler, a generous teammate, and an apparently fearless player who inspired the other girls. Joyce was in awe of her daughter's athletic ability; Frank had to be the source of those genes, just as he was the source of her long toes and shell-like, little ears.

Joyce went to the games because Nina wanted her there, especially now that each match mattered so much. And Joyce was glad to be there, especially for the time-outs and pauses in the action, when Nina sought her eye. Those moments recalled the days when her daughter would shout, "Look at me, Mommy," in the pool or on her bicycle or swinging upside down on the monkey bars. "Mommy, look at me."

By now, Joyce understood the language and basic strategy of the game; even so, soccer bored her silly. She tried to distract herself by watching the crowds, but the other parents were too predictable: white of skin, khaki of pant, never an amusing T-shirt in the bunch. And unlike her, they seemed genuinely interested in what was happening on the field.

"From the outside, I may look like a soccer mom," she confessed to Kathleen on the phone one night after a game. "But on the inside, all I want is for my kid to pick up a book and read of her own free will. Don't get me wrong, I'm really proud of Nina. But I do envy the parents of kids who are into chess or dance or theater. I'd rather watch sixteen performances of *Annie* than sixteen soccer games. Although I'm sure that gets old."

Kathleen looked forward to Joyce's calls and stories. Her own days dragged, hour to hour. "All this waiting is doing me in," she said. "First, there was the waiting for the lab report, then waiting for the incision to heal, and for school to end, and for treatment to start. I can hardly sit still long enough to read the newspaper. My garden is keeping me sane, though. If I didn't have to weed and water, I'd jump off the A. Piatt Andrew Bridge."

"Oh, you can't do that," Joyce scolded. "You promised to take me out to Salt Island." She loved hearing how Kathleen's voice grew lighter during their conversations.

When Kathleen began the radiation treatments, Joyce mailed her a rusted toy metal ray gun she found at a thrift store. Kathleen sent back a note on a postcard from Three Mile Island. Whenever they spoke, Joyce found a new use for the word *zap*, and Kathleen laughed every time.

Nina's last day of school was followed by the make-or-break soccer match of the year. Belmont was playing Newton, which had won the past three state championships. Joyce and Frank stood, shoulder to shoulder, cheering as Nina took the field. They high-fived each other and hooted when she assisted on the first goal.

That turned out to be Belmont's solitary score. "Let's go, Nina," Frank shouted between cupped hands. "Go, Belmont," he yelled until he was hoarse, but Newton racked up one goal after another.

Joyce felt her neck and shoulders get tighter and tighter. Finally, mercifully, it was over.

On the way home, Nina asked Joyce to sit in the backseat and sobbed on her shoulder. Joyce stroked Nina's hair silently, remembering the days when she really could "make it all better" for her daughter. But what could she say now that wasn't totally stupid? You had a good season? You'll win next year?

At home, Nina shook her mother off, shut her door, and cried to her teammates on the phone. Joyce and Frank sat at the kitchen table, wrung out by the loss, wrecked by Nina's disappointment. "It was so much easier when she was little," Frank said, taking Joyce's hand.

It occurred to Joyce, once again, that their entire relationship revolved around being parents. Less than a year after they'd got married, they'd started trying for a baby. After another year, they'd begun infertility workups and treatments, miscarriages, surgery, and finally her high-risk pregnancy.

The nurses oohed and aahed over the way Frank cared for Joyce through the months of hospital bed rest. And he'd been a champion in the labor room, huffing and puffing, weeping and beaming. "Hold on to this one, honey," the anesthesiologist had advised.

She looked at Frank's fingers, now interlaced with hers. They were good parents. Nina could be a royal pain in the ass at home, but her teachers loved her and she had loyal friends. That's the way it's supposed to be, Joyce knew. Nina was honest and bright. She would grow up to be a good person.

But there was no denying that she had crossed the threshold leading out of their lives. The end is near, Joyce thought, and laughed softly at the melodrama of the phrase.

"What?" asked Frank, smiling, waiting to be let in on the joke.

"We're almost done."

"With what?"

"Nina's on her way out the door."

"She's only twelve."

"Twelve going on twenty. It's happening so fast." Joyce thought about what the women in her book group had said about the speed of their kids' high school years. "What are we going to do? She's the center of our lives," Joyce said, then more tentatively, "of us."

Frank frowned. "Joyce, for crying out loud, we've got five more years until she goes to college."

"But don't you see the end of it from here? She's changing so fast."

"You're rushing her." He withdrew his hand. "She's still a child, and I think that you're letting her get away with murder on the grounds that she's *going* to be a teenager."

"Frank, she's always been precocious. She talked early. She walked early. C'mon. It's not just her attitude, it's her body. She's developing breasts, or haven't you noticed?"

Frank stood up. "I think I'll order pizza for dinner."

"Are you kidding?" Joyce yelped.

"Would you rather have Chinese?"

Joyce stared after him as he went to ask Nina what she wanted to eat. Frank was worse off than she'd realized, but she lacked the energy—or maybe it was the inclination—to do anything about it.

The next morning, Sylvie's family picked Nina up for a week on Cape Cod. Nina took the bag of brownies from Joyce's hands, gave her a quick, sideways hug, got into the van, and didn't look back.

Joyce felt her mood plummet. Now she had no reason to get up at seven, keep the refrigerator stocked with milk and juice, or even cook dinner. With Nina gone, Frank would probably work straight through until nine or ten every night.

She had to do something. Immediately. Joyce unplugged her

computer and loaded it into the car. As she packed some extra underwear and T-shirts, she dialed Frank. "I'm going up to Gloucester."

"Nina gone?" Frank asked sympathetically.

"Yes. I'm taking my computer."

"Isn't the laptop already there?"

"I hate that keyboard."

"You never mentioned anything," Frank said.

"Yeah, well, I do."

"Call me later?"

"Okay." Joyce slammed down the phone and got in the car.

Joyce was furious at Frank for the way he had walked out on their conversation the previous night. His problem with Nina's sexual development was probably a textbook case, but if they couldn't talk about Nina anymore, what the hell could they talk about? They used to talk about music. When they'd first met, they used to go to jazz clubs. They hadn't done that in a dog's age.

She reached the house in thirty-five minutes. That's a stupid record, she thought, a little frightened by what she'd just done.

The house was stuffy and sad-looking, the living room still empty but for the beanbag. Joyce cranked open the windows as she dialed Kathleen, who picked up on the first ring.

"Hello?"

"Kathleen, it's Joyce. I'm here for the week. Want to take a walk?"

"How soon can you get there?"

It was high tide, which meant Good Harbor was reduced to a dark, wet skirt of sand up near the dunes. From her perch in the center of the footbridge, Joyce watched the morning fog evaporate in wisps over the flooded plain. A parade of women passed by, bearing umbrellas, chairs, coolers, towels, plastic buckets, canvas bags, plastic bags, paper bags. Children ran ahead, heedless of their mothers' voices, rising like birdcalls: "Be careful!" "Wait for me!"

A girl who looked to be no more than sixteen yelled, "Joey, come back here," as a skinny four-year-old with a pierced ear raced by. She put down her beach bags and chair to light a cigarette. She rolled her eyes at Joyce and hollered, "Joey, I'm gonna kill you."

Kathleen arrived, wearing a wide-brim straw hat and a long-sleeved man's white shirt over white, drawstring cotton pants.

"You look very elegant," said Joyce.

"Thank you." Kathleen patted Joyce's hand on the railing.

"Can I ask about the treatment?" Joyce said tentatively as they set out.

"You can ask." Kathleen shrugged. "There's not much to tell. It's not terrible, it's, oh, I don't know." She paused. "Strange. Pain-less. And it's very fast. I get there, they zap me"—she used the word pointedly—"and then I go home.

"There are no side effects from the radiation itself. Nothing. Sometimes I wonder if the machine is even switched on. Of course, they say you don't really notice anything until it's almost over, and I've just started. Then my skin could get red, like having a sunburn, and maybe peel. And who knows what else."

"Yikes."

"My biggest problem is that I'm not sleeping well. But they say that's nothing to do with the treatment. It's the worry. And that's all there is to it." Then Kathleen abruptly changed the subject. "So Nina's off with her friend for the week, right? Talk to me about life among the living."

Joyce tried not to flinch.

"Sorry," said Kathleen. "I shouldn't have said that."

"No. Say what you want."

"No, really, I'm sorry."

They walked for a while without talking. Kathleen kept her

face turned to the water. Finally Joyce said, "Nina's team lost the big game last night. She was heartbroken. I was heartbroken. Frank was heartbroken. But the dirty little secret is that I'm relieved that soccer is over for the year, which makes me feel like a total shit. Here my daughter is shattered, and I'm thrilled that I don't have to watch another game until next fall.

"I wish I felt differently, but this is just something I can't get enthused about."

"It's a hard age."

"I suppose. But I keep telling myself that she's doing well in school, and she has friends and all."

"I meant it's a hard age for parents," Kathleen said. "I remember when Hal was fourteen or fifteen, and one summer all he wanted to do was watch television. I said, 'Why can't you go for a bike ride or read a book, like you used to.' And he said, 'Mom, it's never going to be the way it was before.'

"It was as if he'd thrown a bucket of cold water on me. All of a sudden I saw the hair on his legs, and not that invisible baby down, either. A man's hair. It took me months to get over that."

"But I feel like I'm screwing up our whole relationship," Joyce said. "I blow up at her for no reason, and I'm such a nag. Clean up your dishes, get your shoes off the floor, do your homework, brush your teeth, put on deodorant, get off the phone, take a shower, pick up your room. Bitch, bitch, bitch, bitch, bitch. She starts crying, and I know I ought to be quiet, but I don't stop.

"And Frank seems totally unwilling to admit that she's growing up. He gets on her case about schoolwork or talking back to him, and then I get furious at him for picking on her, and we fight about that."

"Don't worry, Joyce," Kathleen said gently. "It's just a stage. You'll grow out of it. And then she'll go to college."

"And then what do I do?" Joyce asked, her voice suddenly pinched.

Kathleen faced out at the ocean and chose her words carefully. "There's work. Reading. New interests. Hobbies. You start talking to your husband about things besides the kids. It's good. It's never the same, but it's good. And it fills you up, pretty much. In time, it really does fill in. A lot of people seem to take music lessons. And then someday, maybe you get grandchildren."

"Nina is twelve! I don't want to see grandchildren for a long time, thank you very much."

"I've been ready for grandchildren for ages, but my sons don't seem to be anywhere near it. In the meantime, I took up daylilies. Sounds prissy, but they are the love of my life." Kathleen smiled. "Don't tell Buddy I said that, okay?"

Joyce held up a hand in the "Scout's honor" position.

"I knew nothing about plants until the year Jack left for college," Kathleen said. "I took one of those garden tours and met a woman, a bit of a kook really, who had three hundred varieties of daylilies in a wonderful rock garden. Now I have, oh, probably thirty kinds myself. Seeing which ones are blooming is one of the great joys of summer for me."

They were already in front of the red motel, which marked the end of the beach when the tide was this high.

"I suppose I could take a drawing class," Joyce said.

"If that's something you're interested in."

"Not really. It's a generic kind of fantasy. I don't have any talent for it. Besides, it doesn't solve my work problem. I'm not sure I can fake a shred of interest in school bus safety, which is my next big assignment."

"But, Joyce, you have to go back to Magnolia and tell what happened next."

"Oh, my God, you read it! And you're still willing to be seen in public with me?"

"Come on. It's good. How did they let you get away with it?"

"With what?"

"The politics, I guess you'd call it. The race politics. A black woman and a white landowner is hardly the usual romance formula, is it? Isn't the man supposed to be older and more experienced? Isn't the girl supposed to tame the man? Jordan was so restrained, and she's such a, well, *hussy* sounds so politically incorrect, but, heavens." Kathleen put her hand to her heart in mock shock.

"There are so many issues: literacy, race, secrets. The sex is only one part of it. Though the racy parts are plenty racy. All that black and white skin. It makes one wonder," Kathleen said, arching an eyebrow.

"The imagination is a wonderful muscle," said Joyce. "At first, I thought all I was doing was writing something commercial that would allow me to buy a house up here. The means to an end. But I really got into her, into Magnolia, and the story. And the historical period. I'm glad you saw the politics."

"You must have done a lot of research. Where did you find out the little details like how they starched the petticoats, and where they got ice?"

A high-pitched voice interrupted Joyce's answer.

"Mrs. Levine." The girl on top of the lifeguard stand was on her feet, with a megaphone to her mouth. "Mrs. Levine, up here. It's me, Krista!"

Kathleen waved and walked toward her. Joyce followed.

"Krista! How are you?" Kathleen asked, holding on to her hat as she looked up at the big, blond girl above them.

"I'm good. And you?"

"On a beautiful day like this, how could I be anything but fine," Kathleen said brightly. "This is my friend, Joyce Tabachnik."

"Hello, Mrs. Tabachnik."

"What are your plans for the fall?" Kathleen asked.

"Salem State."

"Oh, good for you. I'm so proud of you."

"Yeah, me, too," Krista said shyly.

"Let me know how it goes, will you? I'll even help you with your homework."

Krista laughed. "You were always so nice to me."

"That's only what you deserve, dear. Good luck. Come see us, okay?"

Krista picked up her megaphone and answered, "Bye, Mrs. Levine."

"Beautiful girl," said Joyce.

"Lucky she's alive."

"Was she sick?"

"Her stepfather used to beat her up. She was the most defeated little thing as a kid. Totally convinced she was stupid. And then in high school, she got involved with an abusive boy. I was really afraid for her."

"She stayed in touch with you?"

"She used to come back every few months to see Helen Holden, her third-grade teacher. I tutored her a few times, but it was Helen who really stayed in touch."

"I envy the way people know you around here."

"Mostly it's a good thing," Kathleen said. "Though I do wish I could just walk into a store without someone asking me how my treatment is going."

Instead of going directly back to the bridge, Joyce and Kathleen walked toward the receding sea through shallow water, already lukewarm from the sun. "It's going to be a perfect day," Kathleen said. "I wish I didn't have to sleep through most of it. I didn't fall asleep until three last night, and then I had to wake up before seven." Joyce took her arm as they walked back to the bridge.

"So what's happening with the Holy Mother at your house?"

Joyce hadn't even looked at Mary when she'd arrived, but she promised, again, to call Father Sherry about "getting rid of Her Holiness."

Kathleen laughed at the phrase. "Do you have time to walk tomorrow?"

"I have nothing but time this week. I'm staying up here until Nina comes back from Hyannis."

When Kathleen got home, she found a breathless message on the answering machine. "Oh my God, Kathleen, someone painted Mary! She's all white and shiny. High gloss! Jesus, I mean, oh, shit. And there are more flowers. Kathleen, I think I've got Lourdes going on in my front yard."

KATHLEEN SAT UP in bed, her thin cotton nightgown soaked, the pillow damp, her heart pounding. The digital clock glowed in the dark: 3:10. Buddy let out a soft groan and turned over as she slipped out of the room.

Gripping the edge of the kitchen sink, she stared out into the dark yard, trying to calm down. It had been a long time since she'd had a nightmare about Pat, and this was a new one. In the old dream, her sister was lying in a metal casket, weeping softly. But tonight, it was Kathleen in the coffin, pounding a slatted wooden lid above her. Danny was with her. He was dead, but not a baby anymore, a boy with long legs and arms tight around her neck. She heard Pat's soothing voice repeating the phrase "It's all been taken care of." Kathleen had woken up on the verge of a scream.

Pat had been so certain of life after death. She used to talk about Danny in heaven as if he were just in a room upstairs. Even when she was dying, she had that kind of faith. Rabbi Flacks had sat with Kathleen and Buddy and cried with them. But he had never said anything about seeing her son again.

She splashed cold water on her face and walked out to the deck. The wood felt cool and alive under her bare feet. If Buddy knew, he'd be after her about splinters. He had become such a mother hen since the boys left. Sometimes she liked being fussed over so tenderly, but sometimes it got on her nerves.

A clotted river of stars filled the moonless sky. "My goodness,"

Kathleen whispered, lowering the back of the chaise. After a moment, she realized she had assumed the position she took every day under the machine—only it was the left arm bent above her head and there was no headrest or armrest to keep her from moving. She stretched her arm and twisted her torso, just because she could.

The techs were nice. That Rachel was pregnant didn't seem to concern anyone but Kathleen. "I'm not even in the room when it's on, Mrs. Levine," she explained sweetly, but Kathleen worried about the baby.

Funny how quickly I've gotten caught up in their lives. They probably have to check my chart to remember my name, but I'll always remember them. Terry's hands are cool. Rachel's are warm, probably due to the pregnancy, or maybe she just has that kind of metabolism. Terry's boyfriend is a nurse. Rachel's husband works for Wildlife and Fisheries. Terry loves chocolate. Rachel drinks Diet Coke, which can't be good for the baby.

Kathleen let her hand seek out the scar, feeling the seam in her flesh through the nightgown. Terry said she was better off being small-breasted. Bigger women flopped around, which made it harder to line up the machine accurately.

Better and worse, lucky and unlucky. New definitions.

After the first day, the radiation machine itself didn't bother her. Some patient's child once said it looked like a dragon, and ever since, the techs had taken to calling it Puff. They joked about painting a face on the movable head, putting arms on the trunk, and a tail at the base. Kathleen whistled the tune to "Puff the Magic Dragon" while she got on the table and waited. Terry and Rachel sang along and kept it up from the control room. They talked to her over the intercom, filling every moment she was alone in the treatment room, stopping only when Puff turned his head to zap her from another angle. Rachel asked, "You all set, Mrs. Levine?" before they let the next dose fly.

"Mrs. Levine is all set," she answered meekly or brightly,

depending on how little sleep she'd had the night before or on the amount of roadkill she'd seen on the way in. Kathleen didn't understand where her moods came from anymore.

The wind shifted and the scent of beach roses reached her. It was such a sweet aroma, though it always made her feel wistful. She closed her eyes to concentrate on the smell, which faded in and out on the breeze. Starlight and roses. Lucky me.

She woke up with Buddy sitting beside her, frowning. A cotton blanket was tucked around her toes and neatly folded below her chin.

"What time is it?" she asked, confused by the dim light.

"Five-thirty. You should have woken me up."

"Oh, Buddy. What's the point? Why should you be exhausted all day?"

"I just want to do something for you, Kath."

"Well then, get me a cup of coffee," she said, yawning.

The clouds were low, and it smelled like rain. No walk today, she thought. Buddy brought out two cups. "How about if I drive you to your appointment today? Miguel can open. We could get some breakfast after?"

Kathleen looked at him. He was asking her for something. "What is it, Buddy? What's the matter?"

He shrugged. "I don't know. I want to help you. Something. But there's nothing to do. You're so quiet. I miss you."

"I have been kind of preoccupied."

"Of course," Buddy said, quickly apologetic. "I don't know what I mean."

"Sure, why don't you drive me in today. And then we can go over to the Spar for breakfast. It's been a long time since I had those blueberry waffles."

Buddy took her hand and kissed it. She held on, swung her legs around, and pulled herself to standing.

"I don't want to die, Buddy." She put her head on his chest. "I know this cancer probably won't kill me. But I think about dying all the time. I dream about it. What do you think? Do I get to see Pat on the other side, or do I just lie there in the dirt forever?"

Buddy took the cup out of her hand and put it down gently. It was so much a gesture out of a movie, Kathleen almost laughed. Buddy wrapped his arms around her and drew her close. "I think dead is dead," he said softly, near her ear. "But that's not so bad. I think of it as following. Following the rest of them."

"The rest of them?" She leaned back and looked up into his eyes.

"Yeah. My mother and father. Your sister, your mom. But not just them. All of them. All of us. People." He dropped his voice and she wasn't quite sure if he said, "Danny."

"I don't know," he continued. "Maybe it's just a way to feel less lonesome about the whole thing, but I think of dying as a path we all go down separately at first, but eventually, together."

Kathleen looked up at her husband. "That's so beautiful. Where did that come from?"

He smiled. "You're not the only deep one around here."

Kathleen shook her head. "Buddy, you're a fucking well."

"Kathleen Mary Elizabeth! Such language."

"We cancer patients can say whatever the hell we want," she said, defiant.

"Says who?"

"Says Joyce."

"Oh, well, if the wise and wonderful Dr. Joyce says so."

Kathleen sneezed.

"Time to go inside," Buddy said.

"No," she protested, holding him. But the moment had passed.

"Time to go," he insisted, and picking up the cups, led her into the house and the rest of the day.

IT RAINED HARD THE rest of the week. Joyce spent the mornings stripping wallpaper. Afternoons she sat at the computer and made a dutiful stab at her novel, a story about three sisters, serially married to the same man. *Stab* seemed like the right word, since all she did was slice at the opening paragraphs over and over.

She met Kathleen for cappuccino at the café on Main Street one gray afternoon and told her about how walking through Charleston, morning, noon, and night, had helped conjure up the world of *Magnolia's Heart:* the fine ironwork fences made by slave labor, the paving stones laid by slave labor, the mahogany faces of impassive black women, sitting on blankets in the touristy marketplace, selling baskets woven in ancestral patterns.

"I don't think I ever enjoyed writing as much as when I was working on Magnolia," she said. "I actually couldn't wait to get to the computer to find out what she would do next."

"You sound happy when you talk about it," Kathleen said.

"Yeah, but I'm not having much luck on my current project."

"Why don't you bring Magnolia and Jordan up here? Doesn't Jordan have an abolitionist aunt in Boston? They could settle in Gloucester. Think of all the research you could do on Yankee underwear!"

That made Joyce laugh, but she remained unconvinced. "I want to do something one hundred and eighty degrees different. And the truth is, I want my own name on the cover. I want to be invited to talk at the local bookstores and at the Belmont library. Magnolia would call me a dog-faced coward. And she would be right."

"I understand, but Magnolia is very alive to me. I want to know what happens to her next."

"Thanks," said Joyce, who wanted to know, too.

Apart from the checkout girls at the supermarket, Kathleen was virtually the only person Joyce saw all week. Frank called every morning, promising he'd try to come up that night, but by the afternoon there would be a crisis he didn't want to leave with "the kids," which is how he referred to Tran and Harlan, the twenty-two-year-old MIT entrepreneurs who had started the company. Their new search engine was to be launched at the end of the summer, and Frank, who had already been down several of these yellow-brick start-up roads, was their key adviser on several fronts. Frank thought their product had great potential, and he was betting on it taking them all, finally, to the Emerald City. Besides, he liked the kids a lot.

Frank would have enjoyed sons, Joyce thought.

"I'll be there tomorrow night for sure," Frank said.

"You said that last night."

"I promise."

"Sure," she said, annoyed. "G'night."

"Good night, Joyce. Love you."

She drove in and out of Belmont one morning after rush hour, just to check the mail and pick up a sweatshirt and an extra pair of jeans. Mario had left two more messages asking for news of Magnolia. Joyce called him back late at night, when he was sure to be out of the office, telling his machine, "Magnolia is on vacation. She will return when she's totally rested."

She left Frank a note on his pillow: "Come up and see me some-time."

But she wasn't entirely sure she did want him in Gloucester. Lonely as the evenings could be, she liked knowing the sink wouldn't generate dirty dishes whenever she turned her back. She liked the peace of going to bed alone.

They almost never had sex. Either Frank was tired, or she was. Or she was angry with him, or he was preoccupied. Or she went to bed hours after he did, or his back hurt. On the rare occasion they lay down together, there was always a moment's tension. Would one of them make a move? Would one of them turn away?

Maybe this was what happened to people after so many years of sharing a bed, Joyce thought. Maybe we're normal. Or maybe I'm kidding myself.

She poured a glass of wine and walked into the living room to admire her handiwork; her spackling was improving so much, she decided to go back and replaster one of the first cracks she'd fixed. The phone rang.

"Mrs. Tabachnik?" said a voice too mellifluous to belong to a telemarketer. "This is Father Sherry at St. Rita's."

Joyce put down her glass and stood up straight to speak to the priest.

He apologized for not calling sooner; he had been away on a family emergency—then asked, "How may I be of assistance?"

Haltingly, using the word *respectfully* at least three times, Joyce explained that she and her family were new to the neigh-borhood, Jewish, and wanted to remove the statue of Mary from their yard.

"Are you the folks who bought the Loquasto house?"

This town is amazing, Joyce thought. "That's us," she said brightly.

"I know that statue." He chuckled. "You're going to have a

heck of a time getting her out of there. Joe poured enough cement to anchor the Washington Monument."

"Wow," said Joyce, watching the rain trickle down Mary's concrete veil and drip prettily onto the ground.

"Why don't I drop by and have a look tomorrow?" he offered. "Six o'clock okay with you?"

As soon as she hung up, Joyce called Frank and told him he had to come up the next day. "No way I'm talking to this priest by myself."

The following evening, Frank arrived a few minutes before six, with a good steak, a bag of salad, and a bottle of red wine. He'd had his hair cut and he was wearing the blue shirt she had given him.

Joyce felt a rush of attraction for her husband and wished they didn't have an appointment with a priest at just that moment. She wished that she felt this way about Frank more often—and closer to bedtime.

She kissed him on the mouth and he held her close for a moment. "I guess you missed me," he said.

"I guess so."

They sat on the front stoop and exchanged news: Harlan had a meeting with some California venture-capital guys, who were gung ho last week but now seemed a bit wary. Joyce complained that her writing was going so slowly that she'd begun reading the help wanted ads. Frank reminded her, kindly, that she always felt discouraged in June, but that by summer's end she was inevitably writing up a storm.

"Yeah, yeah," Joyce admitted as a rusty yellow Pacer pulled up. Watching Father Sherry get out of the hatchback was a little like watching clowns pile out of a toy car at the circus. He was a tall man in a black wet suit; a pair of red suspenders framed a sizable paunch.

Frank and Joyce walked to the sidewalk to meet him.

He shook hands and said, "Pardon my appearance. I have a couple of free hours and couldn't resist. The season is so short, you know."

Barely taking a breath, the priest led them over to the statue. "So here's Our Lady, freshly whitewashed. And you say you've found flowers near her, eh? Probably Mrs. Lupo up the street. Have you met Theresa?"

Father Sherry didn't give Joyce a chance to answer. "She must really be slowing down if she hasn't come over to check you out. She used to be good for a covered dish while she gave you the once-over."

"The Loquastos put the Madonna here, oh, ten years ago as a kind of thanks offering." He crossed his arms over his midsection and shook his head. "One of their kids, Ricky, I think, got caught in the undertow over at Good Harbor and was nearly swept out to sea. The lifeguard got to him in time, thank God, and they wanted to express their gratitude."

He crouched to poke at the pedestal, and Frank hunched down beside him. "Joe was in construction. He had some of his guys come over to do the foundation.

"That was just a few months after I came to St. Rita's. They asked me over to do a blessing. Hoo, boy, did I ever get the hairy eyeball from the neighborhood ladies. I had to eat everything they offered, just to be polite. And I never stopped, as you can see." The priest laughed, standing and patting his stomach.

"Theresa Lupo was there that day, and she told me a long story about her mother, who was sick with breast cancer." Father Sherry's hand was resting on the statue's shoulder. "Theresa was heartsick and just frantic about it. The day after the Loquastos put up their statue, she swore she saw a tear on the Virgin's face. Joe said it was raining, but you couldn't tell Theresa that. She was sure the Virgin was weeping with her.

"So she started bringing flowers. Mary Loquasto was sweet about it; she'd invite her in for coffee. The mother held on for another six months, long enough to see Theresa's youngest's first communion, which Theresa took as a gift from the Virgin of Forest Street. I'll bet she's been bringing flowers ever since.

"And that's the story of your statue."

Joyce suddenly felt like an anthropologist, or an ugly American, or maybe just a tourist.

Frank whistled softly and shook his head. "What should we do?"

Father Sherry rubbed his chin. "I say we wait until the end of the month, till after the Saint Peter's fiesta. It's a madhouse now getting ready, and then there's that whole week. I'll call Joe Loquasto, and I should visit Theresa anyway. She'll like being consulted."

The priest checked his watch, and Joyce and Frank walked him to his car. "I'll be back in touch in July, first thing. I appreciate your sensitivity. And once we get it taken care of, you'll have a great story to tell."

Tossing off their thanks, the priest folded himself back into his car.

Frank went inside to start dinner, but Joyce returned to the statue for a moment. The mild smile suddenly seemed secretive and wise. "Mary, honey," she whispered, "can you do anything for my friend Kathleen?"

"HELLO? THIS IS a message for Kathleen Levine? I got your name and number from Rabbi Hertz? My name is Brigid Gallagher-Steinberg, and Rabbi Hertz wanted me to contact you about the library at the temple?"

Kathleen stared out the window while she listened to the string of questions. Back from treatment, with the day ahead of her, she noticed that her tomato plants needed staking.

It was a nice day. But she didn't feel like walking the beach alone. Joyce was back in the city now, getting Nina ready for camp. Kathleen sat at the kitchen table and glanced at the calendar.

It was almost July, which meant it was almost August.

Danny would have been twenty-six. He could have married by now, Kathleen thought. She folded her arms and put her forehead down. Of her three boys, he had been the most social. He was fascinated with little babies; he tried to swaddle his teddy bear like an infant. She would have been a grandmother. She lowered her cheek to the cool-hard Formica, but there were no tears.

"No!" she thought, sitting upright. She had no idea what Danny would have been like. He was a three-year-old who sucked his fingers and wanted *Goodnight Moon* five times a night. He thought his big brother walked on water. He never met Jack, never got to be a big brother himself. He was barely out of diapers on the day that car knocked him into the tree, headfirst.

The day before the accident, Kathleen had taken Danny to Muchnik's Shoes downtown and bought him new sneakers. Red Keds. He wanted the red ones. Twenty-five years ago. The red sneakers against the white sheet on the stretcher. They could have looked like bloodstains, but they didn't. They looked like roses.

Kathleen shuddered and started looking for her car keys. There was no rule against visiting the cemetery on days other than the anniversary, she thought. She would go by herself. Right now. Why not?

The phone rang.

"Mrs. Levine? This is Brigid Gallagher-Steinberg again? I couldn't remember if I left my phone number or not? So I thought I'd call and leave it on your machine? But there you are."

"Here I am," Kathleen said abruptly.

"I'm sorry if this isn't a good time," Brigid said, her cadence flattened by Kathleen's tone.

"No, it's okay. I was going out. But there's no rush."

Brigid had been deputized to chair the library subcommittee for children's books. "Rabbi Hertz picked me because I asked why there were no books for my little boy at the temple? You've got to be really, really careful what you say around her. My husband is running a committee to see about adding a handicapped-accessible bathroom because he told her about a case he's doing on the Americans with Disabilities Act? He works for the attorney general's office?"

"Yes," said Kathleen, putting the keys into her purse.

"Rabbi Hertz says you're a professional children's librarian? So I wonder if I could bring over the books we already have and also a bunch of catalogs? Oh, and there's a really good children's collection at this temple down in Lexington? They have a full-time librarian. I talked to her, and she was really nice and said we could go down there for a visit?"

"I'm not sure I'm up to that."

"I could drive."

Annoyed that Brigid hadn't taken the hint, Kathleen said, "I'm afraid that the radiation treatments are making me tired."

"Radiation?" Brigid gasped. "I'm so sorry. Rabbi Hertz didn't say anything about any, anything, any treatment. I'm so, so sorry. I don't understand why she didn't. Really, I am so sorry."

Kathleen flushed, ashamed at the way she'd blindsided this poor woman. "Oh, it was probably meant as a gift, her not treating me like an invalid. I don't really want to be treated like I'm sick." Except I do, thought Kathleen. "I'm having radiation for breast cancer. My doctors tell me I'll be fine."

"No chemo?"

"No."

"Oh, that's good. My friend, Nancy? She had radiation and chemo after her surgery? The chemo was awful." There was a long pause.

"I'm not that bad off." Kathleen made herself add, "I'm lucky."

Brigid said she'd understand if Kathleen would prefer not to get involved. "You've got plenty on your plate."

"Actually, I don't. Besides, you're right about the rabbi. I'm not sure I didn't agree to do it. Why don't you drop off the catalogs. But I think I'd rather wait and see about the field trip. I am pretty tired these days." Kathleen wasn't sure she wanted to spend hours in the car with Brigid of the Perpetual Question.

When she got off the phone, Kathleen went out to the deck and tended to the flower boxes. Slipping off her shoes, she walked barefoot over the warm paving stones to rescue her two drooping tomato plants, which is where Brigid found her.

"I knocked on the door and rang the bell?" she said as she rearranged the little boy straddling her hip. "This is Nathan." She brushed thick red hair off his freckled forehead. "Can you say hello to Mrs. Levine?"

"Nathan?" asked Kathleen. "Now there's a name I haven't heard in a long time." Nathan buried his head in his mother's shoulder. "Hello, Nathan. Do you like teeny tiny toads?"

"No!" said Nathan, his voice muffled.

"Oh, too bad. Because there's one right under this leaf. Are you sure you don't want to see him?"

Brigid crouched down and Nathan peeked. "Oooh," he said, catching sight of the thumbnail-sized creature as it hopped away.

Kathleen invited Brigid and Nathan in for cookies and milk, but they were on their way to a play date. Brigid—a slender red-head in denim shorts and a Rockport T-shirt—carried a shopping bag filled with catalogs to the deck. She put Nathan down while she fetched a box from her car.

"Are you two years old?" Kathleen asked.

Nathan nodded warily.

"Don't worry," she whispered. "I won't pinch your cheeks or kiss you. But I hope you'll come back and find the teeny tiny toad with me. He lives in my garden in a teeny tiny house with an itsy-bitsy mouse and a squeaky beaky grouse."

Nathan stuck his thumb in his mouth, but his eyes smiled.

Brigid returned with a cardboard box that held the entire contents of the temple's juvenile collection. "There isn't much here. The rabbi said to recycle anything—or everything. It's up to you."

Brigid lifted her son, kissed him on either cheek, and asked, "Um, Mrs. Levine? I gotta ask. With a name like Kathleen? Are you Catholic?"

"I converted to Judaism before I married my husband. What about you, Brigid?"

"That would kill my mother. But the kids are going to be Jewish? I mean, we're raising them Jewish? Actually, *I'm* raising them Jewish. My husband isn't all that into it? You know?"

"Yes, I do."

Kathleen walked Brigid to her car.

"Will you come back sometime, Nathan?" Kathleen asked.

He looked at her for a moment and nodded.

"So you'll call me when you've gotten a chance to look through this stuff?" Brigid asked.

"Yes."

"Say bye-bye, Nathan." But Nathan shook his head no.

"Bye-bye," said Kathleen.

The house felt empty. She switched on the radio, but that only made the rooms seem even more desolate. The phone rang. "How 'bout a fish sandwich for lunch?" Buddy asked.

"Okay," Kathleen said, thinking of the way Nathan nodded with his thumb in his mouth. Danny had sucked his two middle fingers.

Buddy showed up twenty minutes later with the sandwiches, french fries, and two chocolate milk shakes. Kathleen had dropped eight pounds since the surgery. Buddy had noticed; she saw it in his eyes every time she changed into her nightgown.

Marcy had noticed and asked about her appetite. But Kathleen liked being thinner. It made her feel younger. Besides, food didn't appeal to her much these days.

Buddy coaxed her to finish his shake after she polished off hers. "I guess I was hungry," she said, spooning the last of Buddy's coleslaw onto her plate.

"Good. Now, how about a nap? You were up again last night, weren't you?" he said.

"Maybe I could sleep." Kathleen shrugged. "Would you lie down with me for a moment?"

"Sure."

He lowered the blinds and turned back the bedspread. Kathleen took off her gardening pants and stretched out. Buddy came out of the bathroom in his shorts. He lowered himself to his side, his eyes on her.

"What are you looking at?"

"My beautiful wife."

Kathleen smiled. "Keep the glasses off, m'dear."

"You are beautiful," he whispered. "Even more than when we met." She kissed him and ran her fingers over his kind, rugged face. He was still a good-looking man, but he had aged. His face was craggy, his chin was starting to slacken into jowls, and there were thick white hairs in his nose and ears. She could go for days on end forgetting how much she had changed, but Buddy's face reminded her of the passing of time.

Of course, she never said that to him. There were lots of things she never said to Buddy. Kathleen believed it was the secret of their marital happiness.

She'd known a man, once, to whom she had said everything that popped into her head, but that was years ago. Stan might be dead, for all she knew.

It was good to have Joyce to talk to.

She smiled at her husband, whose eyes were still clear and tender. "I love you, too."

He leaned in to kiss her. A real kiss, mouth to mouth. He drew her toward him. Kathleen was flattered on the occasions Buddy got aroused. He reached around, holding her backside in his big hands, a move that still made her feel like a girl. She pushed into his embrace, feeling his erection.

"One second," she said, and turned to get the lubricant from the drawer.

Kathleen woke up an hour later and found a stem of Sweet William on the pillow beside her. She stared at the red-and-white stripe of the flower and ran a finger around its pinking-shear edge. Does anyone still own pinking shears? she wondered.

She was restless. She hadn't climaxed with Buddy. She reached under the sheet and touched herself. She tried to remember what it was about Stan that had been so tempting, so compelling. She had risked everything for those afternoons, each one thrilling not just for the sex, but also for the talk. Stan was a great talker, and she had never made anyone laugh so much. Now she couldn't even remember what he looked like.

She closed her eyes, and Dr. Singh's face materialized. Kathleen giggled. She wondered whether all his patients fantasized about him.

She thought of his full, cupid-bow lips. She remembered his hands on her. The nut-colored skin. Hands with long, tapered fingers, long, oval nails. Oh, those hands.

JULY

JOYCE spent another whole week behind the wheel of her car, working her way through a long list of errands in advance of Nina's departure for camp. And then there was her daughter's urgent social calendar: she *had* to sleep at Sylvie's house; Rachel's sleepover was *the last one until September;* going to the movies with Jesse was the *only thing* she wanted to do.

"What if I sit on the other side of the theater?" Joyce asked as she drove the girls to the multiplex. "You won't even know I'm there."

"I would, too, know it," Nina snapped.

Joyce opened her mouth to argue, thought better of it, and said nothing.

Nina finally agreed to spend a few hours with Joyce, shopping for camp clothes. They bought sneakers and shorts at the sporting goods store without incident. The underwear purchase went smoothly, but at Old Navy, Joyce said, "Honey, I'm not going to spend forty-nine dollars on a pair of pants that are going to get wrecked at camp."

"I am not going to wreck them," said Nina, her eyes instantly glazed with furious tears. "These are the only ones that fit me." She slammed the dressing-room-cubicle door.

A woman outside another door caught Joyce's eye and shrugged. "They're all like that," she whispered. "They get better."

"Promise?" Joyce whispered back.

The well-dressed stranger nodded as her daughter—tall, chubby, and pouting—walked out of another cubicle carrying a stack of jeans. "Nothing," she said, glumly handing the jeans to her mother in a messy heap.

"Do I look like the maid?" the woman asked in a strangled voice that Joyce recognized. The girl shot her mother the Teenage Death Ray look, grabbed the pants, and shoved them at another sullen teenager wearing a headset, whose miserable job was to fold rejected items.

"Nina," Joyce said softly through the door, "let's just buy those pants and go home."

Nina opened the door and smiled. "Thank you, Mommy."

Joyce and Frank drove two cars to see Nina off. Side by side, they watched as the buses pulled away. "Seven weeks," Frank said. "I don't know whether to cry or cheer."

Joyce nodded.

Frank took her hand. He chewed the inside of his lip. "She'll come back more mature."

Joyce, fighting tears, didn't respond.

"You're a great mom."

"You're not so bad yourself," she said. "Want to grab a cup of coffee?"

"Sorry, Joyce, I'm already late for a meeting that I can't miss." He kissed her on the cheek. "See you later?"

"Are you going to come up to Gloucester?"

"Looks good. I'll call this afternoon."

Joyce watched Frank drive off. She sat in her car and promised herself that she would write every single day that Nina was gone. She would walk the beach with Kathleen every day. She would start Nina's room this afternoon. And she wouldn't wait for Frank to make the first move. She'd ask him what was going on. She'd do it tonight.

Or maybe she wouldn't have to. Maybe he would show up at the house with flowers and they would make love every night for a week. Maybe things would be fine.

FRANK DIDN'T COME up that night. He called at four to say he'd just been informed of an evening teleconference with a new set of potential buyers. He called at eight-thirty the next morning to check in. "I should make up it there tonight." But at four, when Joyce was at the supermarket, he left a sheepish message about a programming bug that might take all night to correct. In the morning he said he probably couldn't come up that evening since they had a 7 A.M. meeting the following day and that it was possible he'd be stuck working through the weekend.

Joyce let that bit of news hang on the line between them.

"Joyce? I'm really sorry, but it's crunch time here."

"I know," she snapped. "What about Sunday? Can't you at least take off Sunday afternoon?"

"I'll try. I'm sorry. Is it nice being up there?"

"It's beautiful," she said icily.

"Are you getting work done?"

"Yes."

"You seeing Kathleen?"

"Yes." Joyce wasn't going to let him off the hook by making her life sound pleasant.

"I'll call tomorrow."

"Fine." Joyce slammed the phone down. Son of a bitch, who needs him anyway? She was enjoying the physical labor of painting. She was sleeping ten hours a night. And her time at the beach with Kathleen was wonderful.

They seemed to have an endless supply of things to talk about. Headlines, bathing suits, books, and story by story, themselves. As soon as she caught sight of Kathleen at Good Harbor, Joyce became aware of the clenched tightness in her jaw and noticed how it eased as they walked together.

"I think I'm relieved Nina is gone," Joyce said as they started across the beach. "In fact, I'm so relieved that I don't even feel guilty."

"It's probably good for you to have a break from each other."

When two women stopped Kathleen to ask about how her treatment was going, Joyce stared out at the horizon. By the time they reached the end of the beach, she marveled at the change in her mood. "I can't believe how much better I feel already. Why is that?"

"I think it's the emptiness," Kathleen said, rolling up her trousers. "Or that straight line between the sea and the sky. Or the size of it all. I don't know, but it does put things in perspective."

As the week progressed, Joyce and Kathleen permitted longer silences into their conversations, confident that the lulls would end in new territory. Like troughs between waves, Joyce thought.

After a few minutes of quiet, Joyce said, "You've told me a lot about your sister, but I don't know anything about the rest of your family—your father, your mother . . ."

"My poor mother," Kathleen said, shaking her head. "Pat, my mother, and I lived with my gran, my father's mother, after he walked out on us. My grandmother decided it was my mother's fault that he was a drunk, which was terribly unfair, but there was no challenging Gran.

"My mom worked for an insurance agency to support us all. Gran stayed home with Pat and me, and she was good to us—as good as she knew how to be. But she made my mother's life miserable. My mother bore it in silence, as far as I know, and I suspect she did blame herself for my father's desertion. I was fifteen when we heard he died.

"My mom and my gran died within a year of each other. Strokes, both of them. Neither one lived to see my boys."

"I'm sorry," said Joyce.

"Yes. And what about your mother, is she still alive?"

"My mother is alive and well on a golf course outside of Prescott."

"Where is that?"

"Arizona. She and my dad got divorced when I was a freshman in college, and she remarried a couple of years later. Bob, the second husband, had four kids, and she raised the two younger ones. Her life revolves around his children and golf. And since I hate golf, our conversations are pretty brief."

"I'm sorry," Kathleen said.

"Yeah, me, too. But it's been like that for twenty-two years, so I don't expect anything else. Boy, was I ever determined to be totally different from her. To have a house full of kids, instead of an only child like I was. And to never ever let that kind of distance come between Nina and me. Of course, I'm learning how little control you actually have over what happens between you and your kids."

Kathleen nodded and linked her arm through Joyce's. "Hang on. Nina still has a lot of growing up to do, and you are not doomed to repeat your mother's mistakes."

"The universal fear of women everywhere," Joyce said. "I suppose Nina has already joined that club."

Kathleen squeezed Joyce's arm closer. As they approached Salt Island, Kathleen asked, "When do you want to go on our little adventure?"

"Whenever you say, fearless leader."

"I'll check the tide and let you know."

KATHLEEN CALLED ON Sunday morning and asked if Joyce was ready to climb Salt Island. "I could pick you up at five, and we'll get to see a sunset over the water."

"Nice of you to arrange that," Joyce said.

By the time they arrived at Good Harbor, a cool breeze was chasing the last of the stragglers off the beach, which meant that Joyce and Kathleen had the sandbar virtually to themselves. On sunny weekend afternoons, it could be as crowded as a city side-walk. Everybody went for the walk, tourists and locals alike; most just strolled out and headed straight back; a few lingered to peer into the tide pools, but only a handful climbed up to the top.

The deserted sandbar was flat, hard-packed, and cool under their feet. "It's like a magic highway," Kathleen said. "It appears and disappears. Brigadoon."

"Mont-Saint-Michel—minus the castle," said Joyce. "And it's pretty close to walking on water."

"Or parting the seas."

"With a hint of danger, don't you think? The outside chance of getting stranded, like Robinson Crusoe."

"Well, within sight of a snack bar," Kathleen said, pointing at the weather-beaten shack onshore.

Their laughter carried over the water.

On the island, only three wiry boys were visible, hunting for wildlife in the tide pools, nets in hand. Their excited cries were insistent and shrill.

"Hey, Carter."

"Hey, look!"

"Hey, over here."

Joyce looked up. From the beach, the climb to the summit of Salt Island looked relatively easy, but here, at the bottom of the fifty-foot rise, the path seemed like nothing but a deep gap between two vertical boulders. A knotted yellow rope lay across one of them. Would she need to haul herself up, arm over arm? She imagined herself dangling from it, hollering for help. Joyce had done such a good job of avoiding heights, she had nearly forgotten how much she hated them.

"We don't have to do this if you don't want to," she said, hoping her hesitation wasn't obvious.

"Don't worry about me. Being out in the air like this gives me energy, and I usually sleep better afterwards. I'm hoping for a full eight hours tonight."

"Okay." Joyce pulled sneakers and a sweatshirt out of her backpack. "I'm game."

She tried not to think about falling and kept her eyes on Kathleen's feet ahead of her. In five breathless minutes, they'd reached the top.

Joyce shaded her eyes and moved slowly, like a searchlight, taking in the panorama of Good Harbor. The tidal river was gone, and the footbridge looked like a Japanese miniature. The salt marsh glittered bottle-green in the late light, while oblivious drivers sped through the deepening sky, heading home for supper.

She turned. The balconies of the red motel were deserted, but next door, a fortunate few sat, in proprietary silence, on the decks of houses perched above the private stretch of the beach. Joyce imagined their vista, focused on Thacher Island and its twin light-houses.

She turned again to scan the broad arc of dark ocean, one hundred eighty degrees of sky-skimmed water, full and empty, blue on blue, cool and far. Joyce felt dizzy—a momentary, champagne kind of dizzy. She looked to landfall at the rocky stretch below Atlantic Avenue where the Bass Rocks wore their customary mantle of gulls and cormorants, prehistoric birds, drying their mangy-looking wings in the breeze.

Joyce strained to memorize the colors, the specific shape of rock, roof, breaker, and beak, bathed in this light.

She faced the mansion on the bluff, a boxy Yankee castle that inspired fantasies of wealth in everyone who walked Good Harbor. Funny how it was not so grand from here, swallowed by the tree-covered hills above and behind. Next time she would bring binoculars.

Kathleen, meanwhile, stood perfectly still, facing straight out to the sea. She soaked up the late sun's warmth. She savored her own breath, in and out, slowing down, after the climb.

Joyce watched a solitary woman walking the beach, a long, beige caftan fluttering at her ankles. Joyce looked over at Kathleen, now facing up, studying the overhead sky.

"What color would you call that?" Kathleen asked. "Cerulean?"

"It's nearly purple, isn't it? So rich, you know? Almost"—Joyce searched for a word—"chocolate."

Kathleen laughed. "Blue chocolate? That doesn't sound very appetizing."

"Oh, no? Blue is the color of heaven, where you have as much chocolate and sex as you want. In fact, I've never understood how anyone could have a favorite color other than blue."

"Then I won't tell you that mine is the color of the sand at Good Harbor."

"I forgive you."

"There is only one place I love as much as this," Kathleen said. "Halibut Point."

"Never been."

"In all these years?" Kathleen reproached her. "You've got to go. It's wonderful. Very different from this. All rocks and crags—no sand. Magnificent. I used to take my boys. One day every summer, just before dawn, no warning at all, I'd roust them out of bed. They'd fall asleep in the car, and I'd bribe them awake with cookies and a thermos of hot chocolate. We'd walk out to the biggest, farthest-out rock we could find, and the minute we saw the sun, we all cock-a-doodle-doo-ed like roosters." Kathleen cupped her mouth and crowed.

The boys on the rocks below looked up.

Kathleen crowed again. Joyce waved at the boys.

"Did Buddy go with you?"

"No. He took the boys fishing without me, so Halibut Point was my little adventure with them. I told Buddy we were going out for a sunrise breakfast, which we did. We went to the diner in Lanesville. Hal always got buttermilk pancakes and Jack had French toast.

"You have to go for the sunrise sometime, Joyce. It's just . . . well"—Kathleen reached out to the view and held it between her hands—"as good as this."

"You talked me into it. But I don't think I'll be able to drag Nina along."

"Hal stopped coming the year he turned fourteen. But Jack went until he graduated from high school. The last year we went, he drove, and when he got there, he opened the door for me." Kathleen smiled at the memory. "Very gallant."

A sleek powerboat skimmed across the horizon, bouncing lightly on the water. The engine's sharp whine sounded a tinny note above the splash of the hull, cutting across the waves.

Joyce lay back on a flat rock, which held the warmth of the sun and the acrid smell of birds. "Should we be getting back?" she asked, her eyes closed.

"There's no rush for the tide, if that's what you mean." Kathleen looked over her shoulder toward the center of the island. "There used to be a kind of pond in the rocks. It must still be there. The boys and I used to visit it."

"Let's go see."

"Are you sure?"

"I'll follow you anywhere," said Joyce.

"You're good for my ego."

Joyce smiled. "About a year ago, I met an interesting woman at a PTO meeting. We really hit it off, chatting in the driveway afterwards. But when I asked her if she wanted to have coffee, she said no, she already had more friends than she had time for. Imagine that."

"It's been a long time since I made a new friend. But I think that's mostly my own fault," Kathleen said. "I'm so private. I don't . . . what's the word? . . . disclose. Especially if something's wrong. It was drilled into me that you don't put your business out where anyone else can see. It makes for a lonely life. My grandmother used to say the Irish are a lonely people. She said it with a kind of pride.

"I sometimes think one of the reasons Pat was attracted to religious life was the closeness we saw among the Sisters who taught us. The Sisters of St. Joseph were such good women—none of that smacked-knuckles business—very kind to us and generous with one another." Kathleen paused. "I haven't thought of them in such a long time."

Joyce watched the sunlight shift in Kathleen's white hair, making her eyes seem much bluer. Suddenly they were brimming. "Kathleen?"

"I'm okay. I just miss her. My sister."

"Of course. But you can talk to me, you know. About anything."

"Yes." Kathleen put her hand on Joyce's shoulder for a moment. "I know that." Waves splashed in the deep grotto beneath them and sent up the smell of cool brine. Kathleen got to her feet. "Are you ready to explore?"

"Lead on."

They made their way across a fairly level plain of rock, clambering around granite boulders strewn by ancient ice. It didn't take long for Kathleen to find the pond, which turned out to be a brackish puddle surrounded by scrubby weeds. Tiny wasps buzzed across its glazed surface.

"Sorry," Kathleen said, wrinkling her nose. "I guess what I really remember is how much Hal and Jack loved finding it."

Joyce crouched down. "I can see why. It's crawling with life, heated by the sun and nourished by bird shit."

Kathleen laughed.

"Boy, are you a cheap date. All it takes is a single four-letter word, and you're on the floor."

"You're a bad influence. I'm swearing a blue streak these days. Well, for me it's a blue streak. Buddy gets a kick out of it, actually."

"Oh, great. So now I'm known in the Levine house as the woman who corrupted Kathleen."

"Buddy calls you Dr. Joyce."

"Ha."

"Well, Doctor, I think we'd better be going."

"Okay, but, Kathleen, I need to pee."

"Well, go ahead."

Joyce hesitated.

"I'll join you." In one fluid motion, Kathleen crouched and pulled her pants and underwear around her knees.

"Wow. For such a ladylike lady, you're very good at that."

"Thank you," Kathleen said with mock dignity. Joyce laughed and managed a reasonably good imitation.

"Didn't you have peeing contests as a kid?" Kathleen asked, watching as it ran down the rocks, drying without a trace. "Patty and I did it in the backyard, summers. My grandmother caught us once. Chased us around the house with a hairbrush, but we were too fast for her."

"I don't think I ever had a peeing contest in my whole life. This is like a milestone!"

"Mazel tov," said Kathleen, starting to laugh. "Today you are a woman."

That set Joyce off, and soon they were on their sides, gasping for breath, hiccuping laughter.

"Oh, oh, oh," said Joyce, pulling her pants up. "It's not even all that funny. Can you imagine what we look like?"

"I'm afraid so." Kathleen wiped her eyes and stood. "I think we'll go back around the other side. It might be a little faster."

She headed down a cascade of rocks that seemed more and more menacing to Joyce as they descended. Kathleen pointed out good footholds and hummed under her breath; Joyce tried to manage her rising panic. I will not wimp out, she thought. Shit, I *can't* wimp out. What would Kathleen do? Carry me?

They were on the sand within fifteen minutes and walked back to shore in water lapping at their ankles. Kathleen took Joyce's hand and raised it like a prizefighter's. "Now you can tell the world you conquered Salt Island."

"Let's have T-shirts made," Joyce said.

"Okay," said Kathleen. "But first, let's go for a drink."

BUDDY WAS WAITING at the door when Kathleen got home. "I'm so sorry," she said. "Joyce and I had a margarita out on Rocky Neck after the beach."

He followed her to the kitchen, where she began to describe the walk to Salt Island. "It was so beautiful, Bud. We found that little pond the boys used to love. I think Joyce was a little nervous climbing down, but I was calm as a clam. Pretty good for an old lady, huh?"

He stared at her for just a moment. "Good?" he said, straining to keep his voice level. "What if you fell? What if she fell? The lifeguards were gone. It's been dark for over an hour. I almost called Jack at work. I was close to calling the cops. Didn't you even think what I might be going through here?"

He was nearly shouting, and Kathleen went cold with shame. Buddy sat down heavily and put his head in his hands.

"I'm sorry," she said quietly. "I should have left a note. I wasn't thinking. It was just . . . I forgot myself."

He didn't move. The clock ticked above their heads.

Kathleen heated a can of soup and they ate without speaking. Soon after, she went to bed with a copy of *Library Digest*. Buddy stayed in the den, the TV on.

Sorry as she was for worrying Buddy, Kathleen tried not to feel too guilty about her day with Joyce. She was too tired to read and turned off the lights. Running her hands over the muscles in her thighs and calves, she thought about taking some aspirin; she'd probably be sore in the morning.

She woke up, hours before dawn, uneasy. In the bathroom mirror she pulled up her nightgown and stared at her breast. The skin was red and raw, the nipple was sore, and there was a dull ache inside her chest. Kathleen stared at her haggard, frightened face. What had she done?

Later that morning, Dr. Singh reassured her that the symptoms had nothing to do with exercise. "Please, Mrs. Levine," he said gently. "Put that out of your mind. Skin problems are a normal side effect. This happens to many patients, and the symptoms resolve once the treatment is over."

He looked at her breast from every angle and laid a finger gently against the scar. "I think it is not so bad that we can't continue."

Marcy clucked her tongue. "You're not using any new lotions or soaps are you?" Kathleen glared. "Of course you're not," Marcy said quickly, handing her samples of two thick, unappealing creams.

The techs were sympathetic. "It's pretty bad," Terry agreed. For the first time, she looked at Kathleen's breast as if it were entirely separate from her.

"Sometimes it comes on fast like this," Rachel said. "But it can clear up fast, too. Try keeping a few damp washcloths in the refrigerator. That feels good."

The clinic-wide chorus of reassurance didn't help. Kathleen took it personally. These symptoms were just nasty reminders so she wouldn't forget—not even for a few hours—that she had cancer. As if she *could* forget.

Lying on the treatment table, her arm above her head, her breast exposed, Kathleen chewed on it. Cancer, cancer, cancer, cancer. It never became a meaningless noise the way almost any other word did when you repeated it endlessly. There was something about the way the letters hung together that was oddly malignant.

There's another terrible word, she thought, *malignant.* The machine moved into place and Terry's voice sounded over the speaker. "You all set, Mrs. Levine?"

"Malignant," she whispered.

"Are you okay?" Terry asked.

"Yes," she said. No, she thought.

When Joyce called later that morning, Kathleen told her what had happened. "No fuckin' fair," Joyce said, and showed up two hours later with a carton of lemonade and a bag full of cotton sports bras with the tags still on.

"I can't believe you went to this much trouble," Kathleen said.

"Hey, this is exactly the least I can do."

It was the first time Joyce had been to Kathleen's house. She admired the built-in bookcases in the living room and stopped to study the chronology of family pictures: from Hal and Jack as smiling infants to Hal and Jack as smiling adults.

When they reached the deck, Joyce marveled at the garden, where Kathleen's daylilies were in full bloom. "What's that one called?" Joyce pointed to a lush stand of deep red flowers.

"I think that one's College Try."

"You're kidding."

"I could go look it up."

"Don't bother. You go sit under the awning, and I'll bring you a drink."

They sipped their lemonade, not saying much. Joyce thought Kathleen looked worn-out. Had her arms been this skinny yesterday?

"Buddy was upset with me," Kathleen said after a long pause.

"Because you were late?"

"Yes. And I know it's stupid, but I feel like I'm being punished for yesterday."

"For not calling?"

"For having a good time."

"Don't do that to yourself."

Kathleen didn't say anything, and for the first time, there was awkwardness to the silence between them.

"Can I get you anything else?" Joyce asked.

"No. I think I'll try to nap."

"Okay. I'll come by tomorrow and pick up the bras that don't work." At the door she gave Kathleen a hug and thanked her for saying what she was really thinking. "Call me if you need anything."

The next day was worse. Kathleen woke up feeling as if she'd been hit by a load of bricks or flattened like the coyote in those Road Runner cartoons. She felt encased in cotton wool. She felt like their old dog, Kirchel, on his last shaky legs before Buddy had taken him to the vet, to have him put to sleep. She came up with one image after another, lying in bed, trying to marshal the energy to stand.

It took all her strength just to get dressed. Reluctantly, she asked Buddy if he'd drive her to the clinic, where she asked to speak to the doctor again. She felt guilty about taking his time two days in a row, but he walked in wearing a sympathetic face. "I will order some blood tests, but I suspect there will be no explanation for your exhaustion there," Dr. Singh said after listening to her heart and lungs. "I do not mean to imply that your fatigue is not genuine. This is a well-documented side effect. But it, too, shall pass, Mrs. Levine."

On the way home, Kathleen closed her eyes and replayed the doctor's accent. "Pahss." What would it be like to be kissed by a man who spoke so beautifully? she wondered, and dozed until Buddy leaned over and whispered that they were home.

She revived a little, straightened up the kitchen, read the newspaper, did the exercises for her arm. But then everything drained out of her and she lay down on the couch.

Kathleen opened her eyes three hours later, feeling stiff, groggy, and sweaty. She must have been dreaming because her heart was pounding. Buddy had left a note on the kitchen table, saying he was sorry he'd been angry with her the other day, and that he'd be home early. Kathleen felt abandoned.

"I hate this," she said out loud, disgusted by the sour smell of her body and the unfamiliar taste of self-pity in her mouth. "I refuse to live like this."

She went to the computer, dialed into the library system, and searched for *Final Exit.* The subtitle, "The Practicalities of Self-Deliverance," struck her as creepily funny, and she laughed out loud at the message line: "Copy lost." That's a good one, she thought. I guess someone used it and forgot to return it. Joyce would get a kick out of that.

But she didn't mention it to Joyce when she called to ask about walking. Kathleen begged off: "I'm so tired, I just want to read and nap all day. I hope you don't mind."

From the chaise on the deck, Kathleen worked through the box of children's books from the temple. She was appalled at the quality of the writing and illustrations from the 1960s, but also ashamed by how little she knew about some of the basic Jewish concepts they contained. She wrote the rabbi a note saying that nothing in the "collection" was worth keeping but added that she really wasn't feeling up to meeting with Brigid.

With that out of the way, she turned on the television and watched old sitcoms. That night, Buddy sat with her while she watched news programs that seemed intent on terrifying their audiences: doctors made terrible mistakes without remorse; supermarkets sold spoiled meat and poison vitamins; the police were vicious.

Kathleen slept badly. When Joyce called the next day, Kathleen put her off again. In the evening, she watched a report about automobile manufacturers cutting corners on safety equipment; about teenage murderers; about how the Internet was a minefield of pornography and hate-mongers. The phone rang.

Buddy put his hand over the receiver and said it was some lady from a breast cancer support network. Would Kathleen like to talk? She shook her head.

"Are you sure, Kath?" Buddy asked.

She stood up and, without a word, walked past the TV and out the back door. Buddy followed and fell in beside her.

"I got a nice-sized striper today," he said as they reached the end of the block and looked out at the water in the moonlight. He talked too quickly, about how one of his suppliers was going out of business, about how much Miguel, his assistant manager, liked the striper Buddy had caught for him and how his mother had fried it in spicy cornmeal. Kathleen knew Buddy was making an effort, but she couldn't rouse herself to ask the questions that would have eased the conversation. She took his arm, and they walked back.

The following morning as the lights went down in the treatment room, Rachel said, "We're half-done, Mrs. Levine." The laser cut the room in half. Kathleen closed her eyes, but the red string of light remained before her.

I'm half-done and July is winding down, she thought. Is the summer going quickly or slowly?

"You all set, Mrs. Levine?" asked Rachel.

"Mrs. Levine is as set as she can be at the moment," Kathleen said.

"Well, that's honest," said Terry. Rachel laughed softly behind her over the intercom. The machine hummed its fifteen-second song, and then it was time to go home.

That afternoon, Kathleen got a call from Jack. Hal phoned during dinner and said he'd be home for a visit soon: "Maybe by the beginning of August, if I can get it together."

Kathleen thought about having her sons at home. Acting as if everything were fine would take a lot of effort.

"When did you call them?" she asked Buddy.

"What do you mean?" he said, turning away.

"Never mind." She switched on the television.

JOYCE TRIED NOT to take Kathleen's daily rejections too much to heart. She called an oncology nurse she'd once interviewed, who reassured her that severe fatigue in cancer patients was normal. So Joyce took to sending silly postcards and tried to be funny and entertaining on the phone, turning her thin scraps of news into low-key shtick: the latest offering to the Madonna of Forest Street was a bunch of sorry-looking orange-dyed carnations; the smelly boy who mowed the lawn for Joyce had hidden some *Playboy*s in their garage. Joyce concluded their conversations with a progress report on her painting. "You've got to come and see my ethereal bathroom," she said, hoping to sound intriguing, but Kathleen didn't rise to the invitation.

"I could come over there," Joyce offered.

"Let's talk in the morning," Kathleen said.

After she finished Nina's room, Joyce painted the hallway and then her office. She worked slowly, meticulously. She spackled and sanded even the tiniest hairline cracks and primed the fresh plaster before painting it. In the bathroom, she sponge-painted a layer of white over the blue, suggesting clouds on sky. She got so skillful with the smaller brushes she didn't even bother taping the windows and barely smudged the glass.

She was on a first-name basis with the hardware store clerk who had the starfish on his wrist. Ralph had a girlfriend, Linda, who brought him a peanut butter cookie every afternoon, but Joyce put on mascara and lipstick whenever she went in for joint compound or a new brush.

Frank called every morning and every evening, with a new addition to his litany of work-related excuses. After a week, she stopped asking him whether he was coming up and he never asked her to drive down. She was mad at him, but also back into a comfortable routine. She got up before eight and walked through the house, running her hands over yesterday's project, studying her brushwork, planning the next task.

Joyce didn't even bother turning on the computer. She wrote postcards to Kathleen and letters to Nina, who sent back a series of breathless notes. She was having an awesome time. The kids were awesome. She needed socks. Could Joyce please send frosting-in-a-can? She'd been chosen cocaptain of a coed soccer team. Could they send extra money for candy at the canteen?

Joyce's days became more and more stripped down. Frank called. She called Kathleen. She wrote to Nina. She painted, and by four in the afternoon she could recite the day's top stories, verbatim, with the announcer on National Public Radio. She bought prepared dinners at the supermarket and ate them while she read the newspapers and drank two glasses of wine. She kept her mind off Frank, the way she kept her tongue off the chipped filling in her right rear molar.

She fell asleep after the eleven-o'clock news and dreamed of painting enormous walls in a palace by the ocean. "I'm like a nun, or something," she thought, looking at herself in the bathroom mirror.

"Me and my BVM."

One afternoon, she managed to get herself to Good Harbor but walked only partway across the beach. It felt too lonely without Kathleen.

After five days alone, she drove home to Belmont, feeling a little like a thief as she unlocked the door to her own house. She left the rooms dim behind drawn blinds as she looked through the mail. Only a few things required her attention. Frank paid the bills and threw away the junk. She stuffed the last of her underwear into a plastic bag. She lay down on Nina's bed and inhaled the lingering scent of strawberry shampoo.

Joyce walked from room to room. Frank kept a clean house without her. There were no dishes in the sink, and the bed was made; only the overflowing hamper testified to his bachelor life. She closed the door behind her without even listening to the messages on the phone machine. Nina's camp had both numbers, and Frank told her about anything that really needed her attention.

On her second trip to Belmont a few days later, Joyce felt less like a thief and more like a ghost. The outside of the refrigerator had been cleared of last season's soccer notices. The inside was empty except for a collection of Chinese take-out containers. She started to write Frank a note: "Hi. I was here," but stopped. What did she want to say?

"Where are you? Don't you think it's strange that we haven't seen each other for two weeks? Should we make a date for a movie—or with a lawyer?"

She crumpled the paper and stuffed it into her pocket. She left the radio off on the drive back to Gloucester and wondered whether they really were heading toward divorce. She wished she could talk this through with Kathleen, but she was too exhausted by her treatment. Joyce needed a walk; this didn't seem like something she could bring up on the phone, especially since they hadn't talked about their husbands yet.

Maybe she should stop over there, Joyce thought as she drove over the bridge, or maybe that would be pushing it. Kathleen was battling cancer, after all; how could Joyce whine about her marriage? Joyce went home.

That night, a loud crash startled her awake with a jolt that had her sitting up in bed before she could even open her eyes. Trembling, she saw the digital clock click 4:24. Goddamned raccoons.

She lay down. The darkness was not quite solid anymore, but it would be hours before she could start painting.

A bird trilled outside, too early for the sun. Maybe it was singing in its sleep, she thought, pressing her palms over her eyes. Maybe birds dream of singing and sing in their dreams.

She stood up, remembering Kathleen's story about Halibut Point at sunrise. She pulled on a sweatshirt, pants, and sneakers, reheated the remains of yesterday's coffee, and headed out to the car.

The quiet was so thick, she could almost smell it. Joyce stopped before opening the door and held her breath. The Madonna's veil gleamed in the streetlight. The perfect mother, she thought, and walked over toward the statue. Not me. I get all pissy because Nina doesn't want to go to the movies with me. She put a finger to Mary's lips. What do you know, anyway, Miss Mary? Boys are easier. Everybody says so.

Joyce reached the main road without seeing a single car. Yawning, sipping her coffee, she drove under the speed limit, until a pickup truck roared up behind, and then passed her. Music blared through the open windows, and she could feel the bass from the truck's radio vibrate in her chest.

"Asshole!" Joyce yelled, her heart pounding. She straightened up and paid closer attention to the road all the way into Rockport center, which seemed completely asleep, except for the sudden smell of frying potatoes.

I'll come back for breakfast, Joyce thought. I'll sit at the counter and chat with the waitress and tell Kathleen about that, too.

Starting up the hill past Rowe Point, Joyce pushed down on the gas pedal, racing past churches turned into private homes, past inns and modest Capes and granite walls, past condos, a ramshackle hotel, houses she'd coveted for years.

Do I even know where I'm going? she wondered, then spotted the small brown State Park sign. She winced as the brakes squeaked and the tires squealed into the silence. But, hey, here she was, pulling up beside the padlocked parking lot. Or maybe I should go home.

Joyce was, she knew, a fundamentally timid person. She talked a brave game, but even as a teenager she had been afraid to take risks. In college, she'd never dropped acid or even once gotten stupid drunk. The idea of hitchhiking through Europe with her roommates had been too scary, the dangers much too vivid.

She talked herself into stepping over the chain at the entrance to the park. What would the headline say? *Middle-Aged Woman Caught Trespassing.*

She walked slowly, squinting at the ground to avoid roots and ruts. A flashlight would have been a good idea, but she could manage. The air under the trees was green and loamy. Little rustling sounds in the bushes startled her. Mice, she supposed.

What if it's overcast and a rotten day for a sunrise?

What if there's a rapist on the beach?

What if she just relaxed and kept walking?

The forest ended abruptly and the sky opened over a low landscape of scrub and sand. The sharp salt breeze hit her face and cleared her head, and now she could hear the ocean.

Gravel scattered as she followed a narrow path through beach roses and poison ivy. A huge mountain of granite slag rose on her left, ten stories of rubble from long-abandoned quarries.

You did it, Joyce congratulated herself, and started out across the black-and-white moonscape of slabs and boulders. She placed one cautious foot at a time, careful of crevasses that cut down to dark, wet pools below. At least it was easier than climbing Salt Island.

And it was just as magnificent as Kathleen had said. Every time Joyce walked a few yards or moved her head, the shape of the world changed altogether. The random architecture of crags and croppings, smoothed by water and time, framed a perfectly flat ocean, barely distinguishable, in this light, from the sky.

It must be unbelievable in a storm, Joyce thought. But this horizon was flat and empty. Not a gull, not a cormorant, not even a lobster pot in view.

It was empty, but not silent. She listened to the endless wet smooch and sigh of the tide breathing beneath her, breaking through to slap against the infinite in-and-out of the shoreline. Seawater smacked and sucked between stone, on stone, breaking stone into sand, eventually. Forever and ever.

The light was stronger now, but still colorless. The day was dawning in the clouds. What kind of painting could you make out of all this gray? she wondered, scanning the coast as far as she could see. It was all gray light, gray water, mottled-gray rock. And me in gray sweatpants and gray sweatshirt and gray funk.

Joyce felt as if she were at the end of the earth. She reached up, arched her back, and stretched, with her hands reaching wide above her head. She sighed, turned, and saw him.

A hundred feet away, on a cliff that hung over the water at a seventy-degree angle. He was barefoot, wearing cutoff jeans and a long-sleeved work shirt. He stood very still, a cigarette in his mouth.

Joyce was so startled it took her a moment to be afraid. Should she walk away? Had he seen her? What was he doing out here? What was she doing out here?

He watched her take notice of him and flicked his cigarette

into the sea. He raised his arm and waved in a big, goofy, side-to-side motion, as if he were hailing an ocean liner.

"Halloo," he called.

Probably not a murderer, she thought, and waved back.

He started toward her. She looked around, hoping to see someone else, but there was no one. In a moment, he was at her side.

"Not a maniac, are yeh?" he said to her, a beautiful smile showing small, crooked teeth.

"Not me. My friend Kathleen recommended the view at sunrise, and I couldn't sleep."

"I've a sister named Kathleen." He was Irish.

"The raccoons woke me up. I couldn't fall asleep again."

"What about your husband?"

"He's in the city during the week."

"Poor fella."

Joyce shrugged. "Do you come here often?" She winced at the cliché.

"First time," he said, smiling again. "It's a grand view. Reminds me of home."

"Ireland?"

"Yeh."

Black hair pulled into a scant ponytail at his neck; he was fair-skinned, smooth at the knuckles and wrists. In his thirties, Joyce thought, but she couldn't tell if he was four years younger than her or ten.

"Any other questions?" he said.

"Aren't you cold?" she asked, horrified again at the suddenly maternal tone of her voice. What was wrong with her?

"You must have a little one at home."

"Well, I have a twelve-year-old daughter. She's at summer camp." So now he knew she was on her own.

"You miss her."

"Yes."

"I miss my little girl, too. But not her mother."

"You're divorced?"

"Never married her."

And now Joyce knew that he was on his own.

A gull appeared. Together, they watched it trace the horizon. The black-and-white scene had turned sepia. Low clouds on the horizon turned out to be a fog bank, which was filtering toward them, shrouding the water, and exhaling mist into their faces.

"A mysterious morning, isn't it?" he said, and shivered. "And I am a bit chilled. Shouldn't have left my shoes in the truck. I could use a cup of coffee."

"Sorry. I didn't bring any." Joyce clapped her hand over her mouth. He must think I'm an idiot.

He laughed. "Would you join me for a cup? There's a lovely diner down the road a bit."

"Sure." Joyce wondered what her hair looked like as they started back.

She paused to negotiate a three-foot gap between two boulders, and he reached out a hand to help her across. He held on for an extra split second after she jumped over. Joyce let him break the hold.

As she got into the car to follow him to the diner in Lanesville, she thought about turning left instead of right. She could tell Kathleen about meeting a handsome Irish stranger at dawn at Halibut Point, flirting a little, and disappearing into the morning. That would be a good story and a good place to end it. The man might be a sicko who lured women to their death.

But Joyce didn't really think he was dangerous. He had a sweet smile, and the way he looked at her was . . . It was like water in the desert. His hand was soft. She wanted to know his name. And it was just a cup of coffee in a public place. It would make an even better story.

The diner was a cheerful-looking hole-in-the-wall she'd passed a thousand times, always meaning to stop. It might have been the same place Kathleen had taken her boys.

He smiled at her as she opened the door. His name was Patrick. They ordered eggs and toast and drank cup after cup of coffee as he smoked and talked. He'd been in the States for six months, working for the cousin of a friend who ran a messenger service. He drove nights and sent earnings home to his two-year-old daughter, Clare. He sent the money orders to his mother, though. Not to Elizabeth, the girlfriend. He spit out her name like a curse.

Patrick had grown up outside of Dublin, dropped out of high school but got a night school diploma. He wanted to go to university to study geography. "Geography?" Joyce asked.

"Yeh. And poetry." He reeled off a list of his favorite modern Irish poets, with names that sounded like a sonnet of beautiful nonsense syllables: Padriac, Ciaran, Donagh, Nuala. She watched as the words dropped from his mismatched lips—the lower more generous than the top.

He offered her a Marlboro and she took it. She hadn't smoked since college, but it was an excuse to touch his hand as he lit her cigarette. Her arm warmed from the contact. His eyes were almost indigo blue.

Patrick threw a crumpled $20 onto the counter as they left. Outside, Joyce stood against the cab of his panel truck, letting the cool damp of the metal seep through to her back. Patrick leaned over her, propped on a hand he placed beside her cheek. Five foot ten, she guessed. His breath smelled of tobacco.

"Why did you drop out of school?" Joyce asked.

"That's a story." Softly, almost whispering, he told about how he'd gone, one Saturday morning, to fix a window in his math teacher's room. She was waiting for him, a woman in her first year on the job. Young, black hair, brown eyes. "A tall girl. Tall as me.

Pretty." They thought they were alone in the building, but they got caught in the cloakroom and he never went back.

Joyce stared at his mouth. He leaned down and kissed her gently.

"Can I see you again?"

Joyce nodded.

"Meet me for lunch here, tomorrow?"

She nodded again and he took her phone number.

He walked her to her car and kissed her hand. Joyce realized that she wouldn't be telling Kathleen about her morning at Halibut Point, after all.

KATHLEEN PUT ON her seat belt and sat, distracted, her fingers on the unturned key. Buddy came over to the driver's side. "You all right?"

"I'm fine." She started the car and pulled out of the driveway. Kathleen drove down the block slowly and waited for the traffic to break. Why are there so many cars today? Why are they all going so fast? Why won't anyone let me in? She gripped the wheel.

Finally there was a gap in the traffic and she eased out into the road. A trucker blasted his horn and set her heart racing. Riding the brake, Kathleen edged into the rotary, merged right toward the bridge, and realized she was panting. Climbing over the river, she noticed a long line of passing cars. She looked down at the speedometer. I'm not really going twenty miles an hour, am I? As another car passed, she turned to see the driver mouthing curses at her.

She fixed her eyes on the bumper of the car ahead of her and tried to keep up. Oh, my God, she thought. Oh, my God.

Once she got off the bridge, Kathleen pulled over to the side of the road, crawled over to the passenger's seat, opened the door, and vomited onto the sandy shoulder.

What on earth had she eaten last night? Or was this some form of radiation sickness?

She counted to one hundred and felt her pulse slow down a bit.

It wasn't food poisoning or radiation sickness, she thought. It was all in her head. And if she didn't pull herself together, they would drag her to a psychiatrist.

She found a breath mint, brushed her hair, and started the car again, forcing her right foot down until the speedometer registered forty-five, which was as fast as she could bear to go. "I can do this," she said, glancing at her panicked eyes in the rearview mirror. "I have to do this."

Kathleen arrived at the office ten minutes late, but no one commented or seemed to notice her agitation. I must be a better actress than I thought. Or maybe they just weren't interested.

Actually, the whole office was a bit out of kilter. Dr. Singh was at a conference in Boston. His replacement, a heavyset woman with a Russian accent, came in to check on the settings and barely looked at Kathleen. Rachel had called in sick and Terry was on vacation. The substitutes called her "honey" and took too long getting her positioned.

On her back, arm raised, breast bare, she tried not to think about driving home. She closed her eyes against the red laser line, but it remained on the backs of her eyelids, vibrating and fading, a crimson tightrope.

After her treatment, Kathleen drank a cup of tepid tea in the too bright hospital cafeteria and then walked around the small gift shop for as long as she could. At least there won't be much traffic now, she thought. She could drive like a little old lady and they could all pass her. I can do it, she told herself. I've done it a million times.

She had done it with children screaming in the backseat. She had done it with brushfires smoking in the woods on both sides of the road. She'd driven this stretch of road after the unveiling of Danny's headstone, Buddy sobbing beside her.

I can do it, she thought. But as she approached the bridge, she started to shake. "What *is* this?" she wailed, and pulled off the road again.

"Okay, okay," she said in the tone she used with the kindergartners. "You don't have to take the bridge. You can go around."

But that would add so many more miles to the trip. Which was worse? She stared at her knuckles and realized her hands ached from grasping the steering wheel so tightly. All she wanted was to be home.

"Let's go home," she said to herself firmly in the rearview mirror. She turned off the highway and took the longer route, forcing herself to breathe slowly: in two-three-four, out two-three-four.

That evening, she asked Buddy if he would mind driving her tomorrow. "It would be nice to have the company."

"Only if you let me take you to breakfast after."

With Buddy at the wheel the next morning Kathleen wasn't quite as terrified, but the trip over the bridge still made her pulse speed up and her hands clammy. She kept her eyes on the guardrail and counted. Buddy didn't notice.

No one seemed to notice. One of Marcy's daughters had chicken pox, so she was out of the office. When Joyce called, Kathleen said she was feeling a little unsteady on her feet, but even Joyce didn't seem concerned. She'd thought Joyce might guess that something was wrong.

Kathleen sat under the awning on the deck and tried to read but couldn't concentrate. She ended up in the cool of the den, dozing in front of the television. She didn't answer the phone unless she heard Buddy on the answering machine. She listened to a message from Rabbi Hertz, and one from that young woman, Brigid.

She stayed out of the car. Buddy ran the errands and did the grocery shopping. He came home after work to find her asleep on the couch. He sat on the chair beside her, leaned his head on his hand, and worried. Hal and Jack had called him at the store to find out what was wrong with their mother: she sounded weird when they spoke to her on the phone. Buddy told them that Kathleen was just tired. That's what she kept telling him.

She woke up and saw the look on Buddy's face and said it again. "I'll be okay. It's the radiation. They all say I'll be fine." Then she made up another story about walking at Good Harbor with Joyce.

JOYCE FELT ELECTRIFIED and breathless. She woke before six and walked to the end of Rocky Neck in the wispy stillness. Back home, she turned on the computer, wrote a poem about the sunrise, and deleted it. When Frank called, she was sitting on the kitchen floor, staring at the purple swatch she'd painted.

"I'm trying that eggplant color," she told him, coughing to clear her throat.

"Are you okay?"

"I think it's just the fumes getting to me. But I think I'm almost ready to get serious about the book now that the painting is nearly done."

"Great."

Joyce said nothing.

"Well, then, I won't keep you."

"You're not," said Joyce, instantly annoyed at him for ending the conversation so abruptly. "Things okay at work?"

"Yeah, crazy." She could imagine him shrugging.

"Well, I have to get going. I should call Kathleen."

"You're a good friend," said Frank. "Talk to you later."

As soon as she hung up, Joyce got into the shower. Washing away my lies, she thought. Not that I've lied to anyone. Yet.

In the car, she switched the radio from NPR to a heavy metal rock station and turned up the volume. It was noise but it drowned out her misgivings and it seemed to sharpen her senses.

Patrick kissed her absently when she sat down at the counter for lunch. He wasn't nearly as talkative as he'd been the day before. He hadn't shaved either. "I had a long night," he explained. "Double shift. I didn't get off till just now." He smoked one cigarette after another and only smiled as Joyce tried to make conversation, which wasn't easy. She couldn't very well talk about her family, so she told him the story of the statue in her yard, from Ricky's near-fatal accident to Theresa's recent devotions.

After the waitress delivered their sandwiches, they chewed in silence, and Joyce began to think that this would be their last meeting. But Patrick asked her if she had time for a quick walk at Plum Cove before he went home and crashed. They walked silently past chatting mothers and playing children on the small, rocky beach.

Patrick leaned against Joyce on the way back to the cars, brushing his hand against hers. "I've been so lonesome here," he said. "You're a good egg to put up with me, Joycey."

She squeezed his hand and lifted her mouth to be kissed. He obliged. He got into her car and took her face between his hands, kissing her. For ten minutes, he kissed her, then moved his lips to her ear and said, "Tomorrow, Joycey, would you come visit me in my poor little room?"

"Yes."

"Noon again?"

"Yes."

He wrote down the address.

Joyce turned up the volume on her radio even louder and kept it there, turning it down only for her daily phone call to Kathleen, who said no again. When Frank called, she let the machine pick up. "Looks like a great beach day," he said. "I hope you're having a good one."

It was a long one, which she filled with ceilings, her least favorite job.

In the morning, she took a bath instead of a shower. She filed her nails and finally left the house early, arriving in Rockport an hour before she was supposed to be there, which turned out to be a good thing since she couldn't find Patrick's apartment. She located the sub shop he mentioned, but there was no door at the address he'd given her. Finally, she walked around to the parking lot behind the storefront, where he was waiting, on the wooden stoop, smoking.

Joyce followed him up a flight of stairs that opened into a dim kitchen with empty spaces where there should have been a refrigerator and a stove. They walked past a line of hollow-core doors, each of them padlocked from the outside. "Who lives here?" she asked.

"Workingmen," Patrick said, leading the way. "Mostly Irish. Working two jobs, a lot of them. Sending money back home."

Patrick's room was at the end of the hall. The two windows, hung with old floral bedsheets, overlooked the street. Five oversize wrestling posters were taped to the walls. "Not mine," he said, pointing to the lurid masks and rippling muscles. "The kid before me had 'em up, and they cover the cracks." He lit another cigarette.

Jeans and work shirts were folded neatly and stored in blue milk crates that also held a half dozen books, a carton of Marlboros, an ashtray, and a gooseneck lamp. The king-size mattress took up most of the floor space, a worn, green acrylic blanket tucked into hospital corners. It looked, oddly, like a monk's cell. Or an odd monk's cell.

He took her hand and kissed the inside of her wrist. She could barely breathe.

When he closed the door, Joyce panicked. Was she out of her mind? No one knew where she was.

"Are you all right?" he asked, stepping back and holding an

open palm out to her, as though she were a wary dog. He let her make the first move.

She paused, then put her mouth to his. They kissed, standing. He was in no rush. They held each other, and he ran his arms up and down her back. He held her head and tangled his hands in her hair. His attentions—deliberate, almost chaste—made Joyce feel light-headed.

She had to sit, to lie down. But he held her standing, kissing, running his hands down to the small of her back, her midriff, her ears, her ass, everywhere but her breasts and her crotch.

She moaned. Patrick pulled back a little and smiled at her, as though he had won some kind of victory. "You can go now if you like."

Joyce pulled away, feeling as if she'd been slapped. "What do you mean?"

"Well, it's hardly a palace where I live, is it now?"

"What difference would that make?"

"I don't know." He shrugged. "Americans are, can be . . ."

Joyce imagined a string of women coming here, turning up their noses at the squalor. Though it wasn't really squalid. It was shabby, but clean enough.

She put her hands on his hips and pushed herself up against him. He laughed. "All right then."

He drew her to the mattress and they necked like a couple of high school kids until Joyce thought she would pass out. Patrick got up and excused himself to go to the bathroom.

He's getting a condom, thought Joyce, who took off her shoes.

The lock clicked shut behind him when he returned. Patrick lay down and started kissing her. He unbuttoned her jeans and slipped his hand under her T-shirt, kissing her. He stripped her slowly. With his tongue and with his fingers, he caressed her slowly, head to foot.

He held her head between his hands and whispered in Celtic—sibilant, purring nonsense warming the inside of her willing ear. He ran the silky insides of his forearms on her thighs in a way that nearly brought her to orgasm, then paused for long, aching moments, before taking her the rest of the way with his hand.

He put her toes in his mouth, and she nearly laughed at the intensity of that pleasure. He reached up her thighs, and up inside her. Fingers and tongue, turning her inside out. He was practiced, and generous. He took his time and seemed to know just when to apply a little more pressure. He cooed as she climaxed, "Ooh, Joycey."

Joyce grinned at herself in the mirror on the way home. Her skin glowed. Her lips glowed. She looked young. Was it really the most intense, satisfying orgasm she'd ever had, or was it just new?

She painted three closets that afternoon. She finally lied outright to Frank when he asked about her day. "Antique shopping," she said. She slept for twelve hours and woke up at eight-thirty, to Frank's phone call.

Then Patrick called, as he said he would, at ten. "Give me a couple of hours to sleep. I'm done in."

He was waiting outside for her and kissed the back of her hand as he took the sack of coffee and muffins from her. She sat on the folding chair in his room, watching him eat.

He ate in big bites and drained the cup. Joyce watched him wipe his mouth with the napkin. "You're the cure for loneliness," Patrick said, putting the cup back into the bag.

He leaned against the wall, stretching his legs on the bed, and pulled a book from his shelf, a big, dog-eared collection of contemporary Irish poems. "Come sit by me, Joycey." He patted the space beside him. "Let me read you something." He read three poems full of longing for a lover and for a green piece of land, which turned out to be the same thing.

When he finished, he kissed her on the cheek and jumped up. "Back in a sec."

He took off her clothes, standing up this time. Nuzzling her breasts, stroking her thighs, kneeling before her, he steadied her with his hands when she swayed. There was a moment when Joyce grew fearful that he would stop, or that he would do something cruel. But that never happened.

Three days running, Joyce left his room high as a kite, but more and more perplexed. As she drove back to Gloucester, she fretted over the way he never took off his clothes, never let her touch him below the waist. He even stopped her from running her hands under the shirt he never removed, holding her wrists, gently but emphatically, until she stopped trying.

Joyce longed to give him what he gave her, but he refused. He shifted his weight when she tried to lean against him. When she reached down for him, he shook his head no.

"Why?" she asked, panting, wanting him inside her.

"Your pleasure is my pleasure," he said, removing his face from between her hands, kissing a path down between her breasts, down to her toes and up to her clitoris, where he stayed until she stopped him.

And he stopped only when she stopped him, when she was drenched, weak, sore with pleasure. When she said, "Enough." Or when it got to be two-thirty.

The lobster shift, he called it, three in the afternoon until eleven at night, though often there was overtime until early in the morning. His regular route took him all over the North Shore, though he'd been as far as Maine and New York City.

He told her that sometimes, too wound up to sleep after a long night, he would find a spot and watch the sun rise over the ocean. Like the morning they had met at Halibut Point. "I won't go back there without you now," Patrick said as they lay on top of the threadbare sheets. "It'll be our own piece of sky. On the edge of the morning, the off-chance meeting of lonely hearts."

Joyce shivered.

"You enjoy hearing me go on a bit, don't ya?" he whispered, lips to her ear.

As she drove home, she plotted ways to pry off his shirt. She practiced asking him why he wouldn't get naked with her. Was he impotent? Did he have AIDS? Was he a priest? Was there a camera in the room? Was he a psychopath setting her up for a brutal murder?

She'd think of something before their next time together. He was going on a three-day run, all the way down through Connecticut, he said. He'd call at ten, the morning he returned. Joyce didn't know how she'd wait that long. She'd probably finish the bedroom and start on the kitchen.

As the supermarket came into view, Joyce decided she couldn't wait another minute for a cold drink and pulled up to the soda machine out in front.

Rummaging through her wallet for change she heard her name.

"Joyce!"

It was Buddy Levine. "I am so glad to see you," he said. "I've been meaning to call and thank you. Kathleen's been so blue at home lately, if you two weren't spending so much time together, I'd be a lot more worried about her."

THE NEXT DAY, Joyce showed up at Kathleen's front door at noon. "I am taking you to lunch. No excuses."

Kathleen offered none. "You look good," she said. "Is the writing going better?"

"No. But I did find a great little store in Rockport." Joyce twirled around to show off a new sundress. "Put on some shoes, and we're out of here."

They went to Traveler's, a newly renovated restaurant on Main Street where the fish sandwiches were served on sourdough rolls. Sitting under a ficus tree by the front window, Joyce studied Kathleen's face as she read the menu. The hollows in her cheeks were too pronounced, and she seemed tense and vague. Joyce had seen Kathleen gripping the door handle in the car all the way into town.

"How about a glass of wine?" Joyce asked.

"I'm fine, you know," said Kathleen quickly. "I'm just ready for this treatment to be over. It's knocked me out."

"Is it just fatigue, really?"

"I think so. Buddy is nagging me to go talk to someone. But I've got you, don't I?"

"Yes, you do." Joyce studied the menu. What could she say? "I'm sorry I've been too busy not-quite-screwing my boyfriend to pick up on the hints you probably dropped on the phone every day"? Or maybe, "Good thing I ran into Buddy, who spilled the beans about your lying to him."

There was a rap at the window. Kathleen waved at a young state trooper in full regalia: black shiny boots, peaked cap, holstered gun. "Jimmy Parley," she said to Joyce. "An old student." She motioned for him to come inside.

"Look at you," she said, shaking his big hand.

"Hey, Mrs. Levine. You know my little girl is going to kindergarten next year?"

"Impossible. Alyssa, isn't it?"

"Yes!"

"Hard to believe. Forgive me, Jimmy, this is my friend Joyce Tabachnik. She bought the Loquasto house over on Forest. Near where your cousin Bob lives."

The trooper shook Joyce's hand, then asked Kathleen, "How are you, uh, feeling these days?"

"I'm going to be fine," Kathleen said firmly.

"Good. Well, that's what I heard. Good. Well, I've got to go, but say hi to Mr. Levine and tell Hal he better call the next time he's up."

"Tell Cynthia I said hello, too.

"I remember him in kindergarten," Kathleen said. "Such a shy little guy. He fell sound asleep once during story time. He graduated a year after Hal. Now look at him. And a father."

Their food came, and Kathleen relaxed a little. She told Joyce her neighbor had brought over three more marijuana cigarettes. "For my appetite," Kathleen said. "I guess Louisa thinks I need fattening up."

"I'd have to agree with her there," said Joyce. "But who is this Louisa person? A drug dealer?"

Kathleen laughed. "You should see Louisa; the epitome of the genteel New England lady. She must be nearly eighty. But when her husband had stomach cancer a few years ago, the marijuana helped him get through the chemo." Louisa Moore Bendix's life was a great story, from her grandmother the prohibitionist to her great-grandchildren who lived in Kuwait. Joyce listened gratefully, realizing how little she had to talk about.

Nina loved camp, but her notes were unremarkable. And what can you say about painting? Frank was still missing in action, and this wasn't the best time to begin a conversation about her marriage. Most of all, Joyce didn't want to talk about the only thing on her mind. I've been so obsessed with Patrick, I didn't even notice that Kathleen was in trouble.

Kathleen started to fold her napkin.

"Oh, no," said Joyce, "we're having dessert."

"Tell me again how blue tastes of chocolate," Kathleen teased, as Joyce coaxed her into finishing the brownie sundae, taking every bite as a personal victory. Kathleen's watch was loose on her wrist.

As they got into the car, Joyce said, "Let's go for a walk. Doctor's orders."

Kathleen tucked her hands under her thighs to avoid gripping the handle again and said with a heavy sigh, "I don't know."

Joyce pretended not to hear and turned toward her house. "We can stop and pick up a couple of hats. And I want to show you inside."

"Maybe I'll just wait in the car."

"Please come in for a minute? No one's seen it yet."

"What do you mean? Surely Frank's seen it."

Joyce shook her head.

"He hasn't been up at all?"

"No."

"But it's been weeks, hasn't it?"

"A few, I guess. He's busy at work."

Kathleen wondered whether she should ask about Frank again.

"Mind your business" had been the motto of her childhood. But now that seemed like a failing in a friend.

Joyce's face betrayed nothing as she swung the car into her driveway and got out. "Ta-da," she sang out as they walked into the house.

The living room, empty except for a beanbag chair and an off-white rug, was honey-colored—almost golden—in the full light.

"Wonderful," Kathleen said.

"Come see." Joyce gestured for her to follow down the hall. Her office, a translucent pink, was bare except for a calendar over an uncluttered desk.

"How pretty," Kathleen said in the bathroom.

"Don't look at this," said Joyce, closing the door on the paint cans and ladder in the master bedroom.

Nina's room looked the most lived-in, with posters on the walls and a low platform bed made up with purple sheets, which looked cool against the pale blue walls. She misses her daughter, Kathleen thought.

The kitchen floor was lined with newspaper. Joyce had finished the cabinets and walls in a rich tan. Random swatches of dark purple bloomed in several spots below the chair rail. "I still haven't quite decided whether I can live with this color," she said, handing Kathleen a long-sleeved shirt and one of Nina's baseball caps.

"It's lovely. The colors are so perfect. Where did you get the idea to paint that one wall darker in the living room?"

"I hired a decorator to tell me what to do," Joyce said a little sheepishly.

"But why hasn't Frank seen it?" Kathleen asked softly. "He hasn't even been up on weekends?"

"He's too busy." Joyce waved her hand as if she were shooing a bug. "I don't even care anymore."

"You don't care?"

"Let's go to the beach."

Kathleen was quiet as they drove over the hill, concerned and confused about the way Joyce had answered—or hadn't answered—her questions about Frank.

"I'm going to drop you off and park," Joyce said.

Kathleen crossed the bridge and sat down to wait. It was a sun-worshiper's day, hot and almost cloudless, with a cooling offshore breeze. Kathleen shuddered with pleasure as the warmth soaked through her clothes. She buried her hands in the sand, wiggling her fingers down through the soft, sun-baked layer, pushing into the cool, packed surface beneath.

"I feel like a vampire released from the curse of doom," Kathleen said, wiping her hands as Joyce sat down. "I've been avoiding the sun. I wonder if that's making things even worse."

"Things?"

"The treatments, I guess. And August. It's almost August. August is . . ." Kathleen stopped. Why tell her? she thought.

Joyce tried to find Kathleen's eyes under the brim of the hat.

"August is hard for me."

Kathleen glanced up to see Joyce looking at her, waiting, nodding. Oh, why not. "August is hard for me. Because my son died in August."

Joyce's mouth opened and closed. After a moment she asked, "You had three?"

"Danny. The middle one," Kathleen said quietly. "He died on August fourteenth."

"Danny."

"He was three years old. Hal was four. Nearly five." Kathleen straightened her shoulders and looked right at Joyce, who reached over and put her hand on top of Kathleen's.

"They were playing in the front yard on their bicycles. Danny was on Hal's old tricycle. Hal had a new two-wheeler with training wheels. The phone rang." Kathleen stopped.

"I went inside to get it." It had been so long since she had told this story, the words seemed small and far away in her mouth.

"The driver was an old man. Too old to be driving. He lost control of the car. He wasn't even speeding, really. I think he was going thirty miles an hour, if that.

"But he drove up onto the lawn and into the driveway and . . . He didn't even know what he'd done. When he got out of the car, he . . . Well, he shouldn't have been driving. I couldn't blame him. I blamed his daughter. He probably had Alzheimer's, though I don't know if we called it that then.

"That was on August eighth," Kathleen said with a catch in her throat. "At first, we thought he had a chance. Pat came that night. Did I tell you that she was a nurse? She slept with us in the hospital. She talked to every doctor, every specialist. The nurses were wonderful. He had the best care because of Pat.

"But there was too much damage. To his brain.

"We let him go on the fourteenth." Kathleen paused and her shoulders drooped. She pulled her hand gently from under Joyce's and wrapped her arms around her knees.

"Oh, God," Joyce whispered.

"I was pregnant with Jack then. I didn't know it yet. I knew in September, but not in August."

Kathleen looked out toward the horizon. "Every year, from the middle of July there's some part of me that's waiting. I'm never fully aware of it, and after all these years, it still sneaks up on me. First, I wait for it to be August, then for it to be the eighth, then for the fourteenth. At some point I look at the calendar and I remember. Oh. I'm waiting for Danny to die."

Joyce hadn't taken her eyes off Kathleen's face, which had relaxed a little after the tension of telling. She stood up, held her hand out to Joyce, and said, "Let's walk."

It was a noisy day at Good Harbor. The surf chuffed into shore, where crowds of children squealed and teased and laughed. Three little girls, up to their thighs in the water, held hands and leapt up shrieking whenever a wave slapped up onto their convex bellies. A young mother dunked her giggling baby's feet into the waves. A group of three women chatted, their arms crossed over their stomachs while their boys roughhoused in the surf.

Joyce winced at all the mother-and-child tableaux, which now seemed like a series of coldhearted insults to Kathleen's loss. "There are so few men here during the week," Joyce said.

"There are more women even on weekends," said Kathleen, pleased that Joyce, too, had noticed. "Why do you think that is?"

"More moms are home with kids? More moms take care of kids than dads?"

"Yes," said Kathleen. "But you see lots of women without kids, too, walking and talking. You and I aren't the only ones here without children to entertain. Why, do you suppose?"

"Women are smarter than men?"

"I'm not sure about that." Kathleen shook her head. "Though we do seem to take advantage of the opportunity to talk. And this is such a perfect setting."

The tide put an end to the beach just past the red motel. They turned and started back.

"Kathleen, I'm sorry if you don't want to talk about it anymore, but I have to ask you something. The story about Danny, and August, and all. Don't you think that your symptoms, your fatigue, has something to do with him? How many years is it?"

Kathleen felt her throat tighten. It was twenty-five years, but she wouldn't say that. Not even to Joyce. That would make it all a simple equation: Poor Kathleen; of course she's suffering. After all, it's twenty-five years. She wasn't having any "Poor Kathleen."

"It's a lot of years."

Joyce heard the hesitation in Kathleen's answer and they

walked most of the way back in silence. Below the mansion, children with nets squatted near the edge of the tidal river. One small girl wearing a yellow swimsuit sat on the wet sand with a red bucket between her legs.

Kathleen walked toward her. "What have you got there?"

"Fishies," she said seriously.

Kathleen looked inside and nodded.

She must be about three, Joyce thought.

Kathleen leaned in and said, "You can catch little crabs around here, too."

"Do they bite you?" asked the girl.

"Oh, no."

It would have killed me to lose Nina at the age of three, Joyce thought. I would have walked into the ocean.

Kathleen said good-bye to the little girl, returned to Joyce, and answered her unspoken question. "Hal kept me alive. Cooking his meals, taking him to the playground. When I realized I was pregnant, I didn't want a new baby. I only wanted Danny back. But then Jack was born, and he was the happiest, most joyful little guy. And I fell in love with him."

Joyce nodded. "There is nothing I can say, is there?"

"No. There is nothing to say. But it's good that you know."

"Thank you for telling me."

Kathleen dozed off almost as soon as they got into the car. Joyce pulled into Kathleen's driveway slowly and kept the engine going.

Joyce watched her friend sleep and remembered Kathleen's questions about Frank. She hadn't known how to answer her. She didn't have anything to say about Frank. She didn't think about her husband from his morning phone call to his evening phone call. She went for hours without even wondering what Nina was up to. She thought only of Patrick. Patrick's fingers, Patrick's lips.

She had dreams about him, dreams set in a boat on the ocean. The owl and the pussycat.

What *could* she say about Frank? She could have shared a couple of half-truths. It's always nonstop when you work on a start-up. He was probably even enjoying it, staying up all night, drinking beer, eating pizza. But the other times, he'd had Nina to come home to, and Joyce, too. She wasn't home anymore.

Kathleen moaned softly in her sleep.

Frank and I have had long dry spells before, Joyce reminded herself again, picking at her cuticles. Of course, I wasn't having an affair before. And I am having an affair, even if we haven't technically consummated. For a while, Joyce had talked herself into believing that stopping short of penetration made a difference. But that was bullshit. It would be easier if Frank were having an affair. That would let her off the hook.

Kathleen startled and sat up. "Why didn't you wake me up?"

"You were only out for a few minutes. And you needed the sleep. So here's the deal, Miss Kathleen. From now on, we will walk on Good Harbor beach every afternoon, but I think later would be better, when the sun isn't so strong. I'll call tomorrow morning to set it up. This is not an invitation, by the way. It's a prescription from Dr. Joyce."

Kathleen leaned over and gave her a long hug. The smell of lavender lingered on Joyce's cheek as she drove away.

Thank God for Kathleen. I don't have to be just an adulterous fraud anymore, Joyce thought. I can be a friend—a good enough friend to be trusted with what happened to Danny. God, poor Kathleen.

I wonder if she'd still be my friend if she knew about Patrick.

Oh, well. Nina will be home in a few more weeks, and Frank will show up eventually, and everything will change, but not yet.

Not just yet.

AUGUST

K ATHLEEN lifted her head from the pillow: 5:50 P.M. Buddy would be home from work soon. She closed her eyes again and stretched. She and Joyce had done the length of the beach twice that day, resulting in a wonderful, long nap. Maybe their walks would help ease the panic that had spilled over from the car into the rest of her life.

She wasn't driving at all anymore. Buddy took her to and from the clinic in the morning, and Joyce picked her up for a walk at three-thirty, plenty of contact to diffuse suspicions about her mental health. But Kathleen had developed several other odd, secret habits that were less obvious.

She was avoiding the mirror altogether, but at least her hair had grown so long she could pull it up into a ponytail without looking. She used a washcloth in the shower so she wouldn't have to touch her own skin. She stayed out of the kitchen as much as possible and ate only when Buddy was around. She avoided the front door. Kathleen knew that she was acting peculiar, but she told herself she'd be back to normal as soon as the radiation was over. She was counting on it.

A car door slammed. Kathleen rolled to her side and tasted sea salt on her lips. She wondered what Buddy had brought home for supper.

"Mom?"

Kathleen was up in an instant. "Hal?"

He was hugging her before she could get to her feet.

"Surprised?"

"Completely."

"You are way too thin, Mom."

"Aren't you the charmer?"

"Isn't the doctor concerned?"

"No," she said. "I'm fine."

Hal frowned.

"Let me get a look at you," she said.

"I'm going bald."

"Impossible!"

"See for yourself." He tipped his head forward.

"Oh, dear. That makes me feel ancient. I have a balding son."

Kathleen was perpetually surprised at how her genes and Buddy's had yielded two such distinct replicas: Jack was a McCormack—a compactly built Irishman—while Hal was a Levine, cut out of the same large, sandy cloth as Irv and Buddy. "Too bad you didn't inherit the Levine hair, though even bald, you are one handsome man."

"Not that you're in the least bit prejudiced," Hal said.

They walked into the kitchen just as Buddy arrived, carrying two bags of groceries.

"Surprise!" he said, beaming.

"You knew? You sneak."

"I got tuna steaks to grill." He deposited a six-pack of beer on the counter.

They settled on the deck while Buddy started the fire and Hal tried to get Kathleen to talk about her treatment.

"I don't know what to tell you," she said with a dismissive wave of her hand. "I'm in and out so fast. The girls, the techs, are nice kids. The best thing is that it's almost over."

"No side effects?"

"Not really."

Buddy frowned at her.

"What? Oh, my fatigue? Yes, I'm tired, but that will pass."

Kathleen could tell that Hal didn't quite buy her version of the summer, and she walked into the kitchen to fetch place mats and napkins.

When she returned to the deck, Hal was telling Buddy about work.

"It's fine," said Hal. "I'm making great money, but . . ."

"Great money is great," said Buddy.

"But what?" asked Kathleen.

"It's just a job." Hal shrugged. "I'm not interested in what I do all day, and when I go home, I have nothing to talk about."

"So you're thinking about making a change?" Buddy asked.

"Change is in the air in my house." Hal proceeded with news about his many roommates: Tom, the cycling nut, had bought an insanely expensive bike and entered a big race; Ruthie, the nursing student, had decided to specialize in pediatric oncology; Leona was burned-out from teaching city kids and was looking for a job in the suburbs.

"And what about Josh?" Kathleen asked. Josh had been Hal's roommate at Michigan and had moved to California with him.

"I was saving this for last. Josh is getting married."

"Married?" Buddy asked.

"Yup."

"To whom?" Kathleen asked.

"Sarah Bley."

"Do we know her?"

"You met her last time you were out. She's the big blonde from Los Angeles."

"The one who was visiting Ruthie?" Buddy asked.

"Yeah. That's when they met."

Buddy raised his eyebrows at Kathleen, and she realized Buddy had also guessed that Josh and Hal were lovers.

After dinner, Hal pulled a thin bottle from the refrigerator. "My newest discovery. Dessert wine." He poured the gold-colored liquor and Kathleen wet her lips. "It's sweet!" she said. "I love it."

"I knew you would. And I brought you a few books I think you'll like."

"I'm sure I will," she said, beaming. Hal may look like Buddy, she thought, but he took after her in temperament and interests.

As Buddy started on the dishes, Hal suggested a walk, and he and Kathleen set out down the block.

Kathleen told Hal about Joyce, and how much she wanted them to meet. "She's been so great through all this."

It was the first time she had volunteered any information about her illness or treatment to Hal. "Your father has been wonderful, too," she added quickly.

"I know. But some things are easier to talk to friends about."

"I suppose," she said, wishing it weren't quite so true, wishing she could ask Hal about his life in a way that wouldn't seem like prying. Instead she said, "I'm glad you're here."

"Me, too."

They stopped at the spot overlooking the water, between the Craddocks' and the Longs' houses. Kathleen realized it was the same spot where she had stood early in the morning before her first appointment with Dr. Truman. That felt like years ago, but it had been only fifteen weeks.

Hal watched his mother's face as she counted the weeks. "Mom, I think you're depressed."

Kathleen patted his arm.

"I mean clinically. I think you should see someone."

"Oh, Hal, it's not that bad."

"No, really. It's important. It's all connected to what's going on with you physically. I go."

"You go where?"

"To see a therapist. It's been very good for me."

Kathleen stared.

"Mom? You knew about the therapy, didn't you?"

"Why would I know?"

"Well, I assumed Dad told you."

"He didn't say anything to me." She didn't know anything about her son anymore. Or about her husband.

"It's helped me work out a lot of issues, not only about work, but about, you know, the family and"—he paused, choosing his words—"how, uh, losing someone sets you apart, especially as a child."

Kathleen said nothing.

"Mom?"

She was stunned, not so much by Hal's revelation, but by the sudden rush of shame it called up in her. What had he told his therapist? Why was her grandmother's disapproving voice so loud inside her head? And how could she begin to talk to him about Danny now? They had never had a real conversation about what had happened. Hal was still hurting. And she was still unable to comfort him.

"Mom?"

"Hal, I need to go back. I'm tired. And no more medical advice from you. Please."

Hal lowered his head—just the way Buddy did when he was angry—and turned back, starting at a pace that was a little too fast for her. He relented after a few steps, and she took his arm, squeezing it gratefully.

"Nice walk?" Buddy asked as they walked into the kitchen. Hal made a beeline for the bathroom.

"Lovely," said Kathleen.

When Hal returned, he and Buddy squabbled over who would drive Kathleen to the clinic in the morning, but she settled it quickly; it was her time with Buddy. The last thing she wanted was for Hal to discuss her weight or state of mind with Marcy. Hal insisted on taking his mother to lunch afterward. "My pleasure," Kathleen agreed.

In the car the next morning, Buddy seemed to choose his words carefully. "Well, what do you know about Josh, huh? Hal's going to be best man. He says we're going to be invited."

Kathleen struggled hard against the rising terror she felt as the car climbed the bridge. She sighed, trying to disguise her labored breathing. Thank heaven Buddy always kept his eyes on the road.

Once they reached the mainland, Buddy asked again. "So what do you think about Josh's news?"

"I thought he might be gay," Kathleen said softly. "And you did, too, didn't you?"

Now it was Buddy's turn to be silent. He signaled and pulled into the passing lane before answering. "Yes."

"We never talked about it," Kathleen said, sounding a little angrier than she intended. And now we don't have to, she thought.

"It was okay with me," said Buddy.

"What?"

"It took me a long time to get used to the idea, but I would have told him that it was all right. That he was my son. That I loved him. Hell, I love Josh, too." Buddy let out a hoarse laugh. "I love Josh even more now!"

Kathleen tried to smile.

"You thought I'd be some kind of Neanderthal about it, didn't you?" he said, eyes straight ahead.

"I didn't know how you'd react."

"You should know. For crying out loud, Kathleen! After all this time, you should know."

"I'm sorry, Buddy." She squeezed her eyes closed, shutting out the kaleidoscope of passing cars and rushing trees, trying to hold on through the panic.

He glanced over. "It's okay, Kath. You just take it easy. It's only four more days and we're done, right?"

She nodded and stared at the door handle. Four more days. She counted them out as they drove the rest of the way: today, tomorrow, Monday, and Tuesday.

On the way home, she changed the mantra: tomorrow and Monday and Tuesday. And then it would be August 8.

LIKE KATHLEEN. Joyce had fallen asleep after their walk in the heat. She'd collapsed on Nina's bed and woke at sunset, disoriented, hungry, and crazy to see Patrick. He was gone on another three-day run, to northern Maine this time. And then it would be the weekend, so there was no chance of seeing him for five days.

He never called on Saturday or Sunday. On the morning they'd met, Joyce had made it sound as if Frank spent weekends in Gloucester, and she'd never got around to correcting the story. After all, there was the possibility that Frank might actually appear some weekend.

And what would that be like? she wondered as she walked through the house, cranking the windows all the way open. Would one look at his familiar face make her comprehend the terrible error of her wanton ways? She knew that Patrick was just a fling, or at least, she knew it in her head. Her body was a different story. Joyce was unsure about her heart; she was in lust, in longing, in heat, even. In love? Maybe a little. Oh, definitely a little. But probably not enough to do anything drastic—Patrick had certainly not given any indication of wanting anything more from her than their afternoons. "My lifeline," he called her. "The cure for loneliness."

"I suppose I could say the same for him," Joyce murmured, then opened the refrigerator and groaned. "I can't face a bowl of cereal," she announced to the empty kitchen.

The air, heavy and still, absorbed the sound of her voice like a sponge. She grabbed car keys and considered the options as she started the car: she could go to the supermarket and take out a healthy meal or get a slice of pizza down the street.

She drove past the pizzeria and the Star Market and found herself on the road to Rockport. The scene of my crime, she thought. She would buy an ice cream cone and sit out on Bear Skin Neck. On a night like this, the tourist strip on the little peninsula by the harbor would be great for people-watching. Besides, she needed a few more postcards for Nina.

But as she pulled into town, Joyce decided she'd rather have a tuna sandwich. As she passed the sub shop looking for a parking spot, she saw that the lights were on upstairs, in Patrick's room. A shadow moved behind the shade. Her mouth went dry. It took her five minutes to find parking, a dozen blocks away. She counted them, hands in her pockets, head down, walking as fast as she could.

From a bench across the street, Joyce sat and watched Patrick pace. His gait, his profile, his hold on the cigarette. He was on the telephone.

But there was no phone in his apartment. He couldn't afford a cell phone. He called her from the pay phone downstairs.

He was lying to her.

And she was lying to everyone in her life.

Maybe the job had fallen through. Maybe he was just talking to his business partner. Maybe he was talking to his mother, in Ireland. Maybe he was sweet-talking another woman.

But where did the phone come from? And why hadn't he called her?

Don't ask him, Joyce, she drilled herself. Don't ever ask.

He lit another cigarette, his back to the window.

She stared until her eyes ached. Leave, she told herself. Leave now. Finally, she took her own advice and drove home.

The streetlight on the corner had burned out, and she'd forgotten to turn on the porch light. The Madonna was deep in shadow, but Joyce saw something moving behind it. That's way too big to be a raccoon, she thought.

"Mrs. Lupo?" Joyce said softly.

There was no answer.

"Mrs. Lupo, it's okay."

A tiny, white-haired woman hurried out of the yard up the street.

"Theresa?" Joyce called, and then stopped. What could she say to Theresa Lupo? The adulteress and the acolyte. Sounds like a romance novel, she thought, or an X-rated movie.

The phone rang as she walked into the house. Sure it was Frank, she listened as the machine picked up. There was a long pause and a hang-up. Frank would never do that.

Maybe it was Patrick. Maybe he wanted her to come to him.

"Shit," she screamed. The sound in the empty house shocked her.

The phone rang again and she lunged at it.

"Joyce!" Kathleen said. "I hope it's not too late to call. Would you mind including an extra person on the beach tomorrow? I'd like you to meet my son Hal."

KATHLEEN TRIED HARD to appear calm. She tucked her hands under her thighs, breathed slowly, and kept her eyes on Hal's face as he drove her to lunch. Thank goodness the trip was short, she thought, getting out of the car, and thank goodness he hadn't noticed anything.

"Look at this place," Hal said as they walked into Traveler's. "Hanging plants? I'll bet they serve raspberry iced tea. You sure this is still Gloucester?"

"Don't be such a snob."

"I just don't want it to get glitzy."

"Don't worry. There was a good little French restaurant down the street that folded after a few months. But all the bars are doing fine."

As they sat down, she heard a voice behind them: "Mrs. Levine?"

Kathleen turned to see the rabbi getting up from another table.

"Hello, Rabbi Hertz. Let me introduce my son Hal. He surprised me by showing up from San Francisco last night."

Hal stood up to shake her hand. "How long have you been the rabbi?"

"I started in the fall."

"How do you like it here?"

"It's a great community. People have been very welcoming."

"Really?" Hal asked. "It used to be kind of a tough place for newcomers."

"Well, so far so good," she said, smiling.

Hal smiled back. "Do you do a Torah study session on Saturday morning? I've been going lately. Not services so much, but the study sessions before."

"You have?" said Kathleen.

"It was Josh's doing. Josh and Sarah," Hal said to his mother, then explained to the rabbi, "That's my roommate and his fiancée. Sarah isn't Jewish, but the two of them took an Introduction to Judaism class together. I went with them once because they were raving about one of the rabbis who taught there. Now I go to her shul, sometimes."

Michelle Hertz, it turned out, knew the California rabbi, who had been two years ahead of her in school. "Did Debra ever cut her hair?" she asked.

"No."

"Wow. We used to call her 'Cousin It,' and that was years ago."

"Behind her back, I hope," Hal said.

They laughed as Kathleen looked on. There was a pause in the conversation.

"San Francisco is almost as beautiful as Gloucester," Michelle said finally.

"Yeah," Hal agreed. "I've been there for nearly six years. At first, I thought I'd stay, but the fact that I never got rid of my winter clothes was probably a sign. It's a drag being so far away from your family, and since my mom's, um, well, I'm thinking about coming back East."

"You are?" Kathleen said.

"I was going to talk to you about it over lunch."

"I'd better let you two catch up," Michelle said. "And we do have a Torah discussion group on Saturday morning. Nine o'clock. I'd love it if you could come. Both of you."

Kathleen watched Hal's eyes follow Michelle out the door. When he turned back to her, she waited for him to say something and finally asked, "Are you really moving home?"

"I've been thinking about it for a while, actually. The Bay Area is way too expensive. Josh and Sarah will probably move to L.A. Besides, I thought you'd want me near you," he teased.

"Nothing would make me happier."

Hal squeezed her hand. "Can I get a good fish sandwich here?"

During lunch he entertained her with details of Josh and Sarah's wedding plans. Then he asked how she'd met Joyce. Kathleen recalled the scene, and Hal smiled. "At temple, eh? Aren't we all becoming *frimme yidden*."

"Translation, please?"

"It's Yiddish for 'religious Jews.'"

"Do you go to temple every week?"

"Almost. I like the Torah study. I like knowing that at least once a week I'll have a conversation that's about something important."

"Like about God?"

"Sometimes God. Not always. Sometimes ethics, sometimes politics, sometimes family dynamics. It depends who shows up that Saturday—and on the *parashah,* the portion for the week, you know."

"I know what a *parashah* is," Kathleen said. "I was there for your bar mitzvah, if you remember."

"Yes, you were." Hal kissed her hand. "And I appreciate it." After they ordered he said, "When we're done here, I'll drive you over to Good Harbor, but I wonder if you'd mind my just saying hello to Joyce and then maybe she could drive you home? I have something I need to do."

"Sounds like you're not going to tell me why, right?"

"You'll know everything soon enough," he said, hinting at big news. "Just not today."

When they arrived at the beach, Hal and Kathleen leaned on the hood of the car and shared the view until Joyce arrived.

"Here he is," Kathleen said triumphantly.

Kathleen watched as Hal and Joyce exchanged hellos and sized each other up. Then Hal kissed his mother on the cheek, made a formal little bow to Joyce, and left.

"Wow," Joyce said. "He's a hunk."

"Isn't he, though?" Kathleen threaded her arm through Joyce's. The sand burned the soles of their bare feet, so they rushed toward the water's edge.

"I have so much to tell you," Kathleen said, and described Hal's arrival, what seemed like a flirtation with the rabbi before her very eyes, his announcement about moving East. She let it spill right out . . . like a pile of blessings, she thought, and stopped in mid-sentence.

Suddenly she was aware of the heat rising from the sand, the heaviness in the air, the sweat trickling down from under her hatband, the thumping in her chest. The panic from the car had followed her, even here.

"I think I need to go back."

"Sure," Joyce said, alarmed at the change in Kathleen's voice and posture. "It's way too hot out here."

"WILL YOU MISS US?" Rachel asked as Kathleen got up from the table.

"You're going to have to let me know about the baby," Kathleen said.

"You're already on the mailing list," Rachel said, patting her belly, which now pushed against the buttons of her blue smock.

Buddy reached over for Kathleen's hand as they crossed the bridge on their way home. "Last Friday," he said.

"What?"

"This is our last Friday. Next week you can start sleeping in."

"I suppose you're right," she said, thinking only that next week she wouldn't have to ride over the damn bridge twice a day.

At the house, Hal relayed phone messages from Brigid, who was mailing something to Kathleen, and from Michelle, who had told him about the temple library project.

"I'm planning to go to services tonight, Mom. Want to come?"

Kathleen said she was too tired. "Next week. I'll be done with radiation then."

Hal looked disappointed but didn't insist.

Joyce called a little later and announced that it was too hot for an afternoon walk, but that she was coming over for a visit. She arrived at two with a paper bag from which she produced a dozen limes, a bottle of tequila, and margarita mix. "Take me to your blender," she said.

As they sat in the den with the blinds drawn against the heat, Hal regaled them with San Francisco stories. Slightly tipsy, Kathleen put her feet up on the couch and listened as her friend and her son engaged in a spirited conversation about movies she'd never seen and pop music she'd never heard. She beamed at the sight of Joyce being charmed by her charming son, and at Hal, impressed by her wisecracking friend.

But when Hal asked Joyce about her work, Kathleen heard Joyce's voice go up a tone and saw her smile turn tight and artificial. I don't ask enough about what's going on with Joyce, Kathleen thought. Joyce was taking good care of her, but she wasn't returning the kindness.

Kathleen dozed off. Waking up in the darkened room, she realized that she was only a little embarrassed; if she had fallen asleep like that in front of anyone but Joyce, she'd be mortified for life.

It was past six. Joyce was long gone and Hal had set the dining room table with the Sabbath candlesticks and wine cup.

Standing by the table, Kathleen realized she was deeply touched by Hal's new interest in his Jewishness. Not that she could say why. Religion had never been central to her life, not in an obvious way. And yet she was moved at the sight of Hal carrying a challah and wearing a crocheted blue yarmulke. He'd bought the challah at the supermarket, along with a roast chicken and salad. "My brother would shudder," Hal said, pointing at the ready-made feast.

"Your grandparents would be tickled," Kathleen said.

As she lit the candles, she remembered how she'd done the same thing two months before, when she'd found out that the cancer wasn't going to kill her. She stared at the flames.

"Mom?"

"I'm okay," she said, wondering whether he would disapprove of her Hebrew pronunciation, now that he'd gotten so religious. But he smiled as she recited the prayer, then hugged her tight. "Shabbat shalom," he said, hugging Buddy next.

He said it again on his way out the door later.

"You, too," Kathleen said.

Kathleen was out on the deck, wrapped in a cotton blanket, when Hal got home. It was one in the morning. He stood at the sink and wolfed down a sandwich. He didn't see her, but Kathleen had a clear view of his face. She watched him rinse his hands and smile. She would have given anything to know what he was thinking.

Hal turned off the light, and Kathleen leaned back in the chaise lounge to look up at the sky and make wishes. After a little while, she got into bed, pressing her arm against her breast. The scar and the skin around it were numb.

In the morning, she found Buddy and Hal in the kitchen, drinking coffee and reading the paper. Hal was already dressed, wearing the blue yarmulke again.

"I thought I'd go to Torah study," he said as Kathleen kissed the top of his head.

Buddy raised his eyebrows. "I hope you're not becoming a religious fanatic."

Hal frowned a little and shrugged.

After he left, Kathleen told Buddy about Hal's meeting with the rabbi in the restaurant and his late return last night. Buddy pumped her for more details but Kathleen had nothing more to add.

"I sure hope they're not just talking about theology," Buddy said.

"That might be a good place to start."

"As long as it doesn't end there."

Kathleen put a finger up to her lips. "Shhhh."

"Oh, I won't say anything," Buddy groused. "But I sure am going to cross my fingers."

Kathleen crossed hers, too.

JOYCE WAS CONVINCED Patrick had seen her spying on him that night through the window. She had no proof, of course, and she knew it was irrational. But as she faced the weekend, she grew more and more certain that he wouldn't call next week, that she'd never see him again.

Frank called three or four times a day on weekends, to apologize mostly. And weekends were hard, because that's when Joyce missed Nina most.

She didn't want to go too far from the phone, just in case Patrick did call (not that he would), but now she couldn't stand to be inside the house either. All the rooms were painted, and every surface reproached her. The hallway trim had been finished in the afterglow of her first meeting with Patrick. The kitchen windows were completed after her first day of panting and grunting in Patrick's bed. She finished the bedroom—hers and Frank's—while plotting ways to peel off Patrick's shirt.

Joyce called Kathleen a few times, but hung up before the machine clicked into gear. She couldn't read, couldn't even watch TV.

She stared out the window at the yard and winced at the mess. The kid they'd hired to mow the lawn had stopped showing up two weeks ago, and he'd never touched the borders and flowerbeds. The space around the untrimmed bushes had turned into a knee-high jungle.

Joyce knocked on her next-door neighbors' door and borrowed Ben and Eric's lawn mower and rake. She pulled Frank's hand tools out of the garage and trimmed the bushes. Then she got down on her knees and started pulling weeds.

Gardening had always been Frank's exclusive domain, to the point that it was a family joke. "Mom was attacked by a dandelion when she was a baby," Frank had told Nina. "She's been afraid of plants ever since." Frank—who had grown up in apartment buildings—had acquired a shelf full of gardening books since they'd moved to Belmont, and a headful of facts about temperature zones, soil pH, and growing seasons. When they'd closed on the Gloucester house, he'd splurged on a fancy new set of shears that came with a suede holster. Frank probably misses this garden more than he misses me, Joyce thought.

She was surprised at how much she enjoyed yardwork. After paint fumes, the dirt and roots smelled sweet. She caught a tang of mint and chive in one of the overgrown flowerbeds. Did Mary Loquasto grow herbs, or was it someone from long ago? A fisherman's wife's kitchen garden? Magnolia's great-granddaughter, perhaps?

It was the first time she'd thought of Magnolia for weeks, and she let her mind wander in the direction that Kathleen had suggested that time at Good Harbor. What if Magnolia did end up here, in Gloucester? She'd have to kill Jordan in order to provide her heroine with new romantic tension. Poor Jordan. She smiled as she considered whether to finish him off by scurvy, storm, or pirate attack.

On Sunday, she filled two more bags with weeds, dead leaves, and bits of paper. Ben and Eric stopped to admire her progress and offered her some orange lilies from their yard. "They're totally overgrown and we need to divide them," Eric said. "You'd be doing us a favor."

Joyce accepted, knowing how Kathleen would get a kick out of her joining the daylily club. She thought a lot about Kathleen as she worked outside: her health, her fears, her sons, her confidences. God bless Kathleen, Joyce thought. It's strange how effortless friendship seems, especially compared to family. Just showing up qualifies you for a medal. I really need to find something to celebrate the end of her treatment. Maybe I can find a "Duck and Cover" poster somewhere.

For some reason, as she worked outdoors, Joyce didn't think about Patrick at all.

By Sunday afternoon, only one big cleanup project remained. Joyce squared her shoulders and headed for the bed surrounding the statue of Mary. She felt sheepish about leaving this for last. "You are a superstitious nitwit," she lectured herself as she grabbed the trowel and an empty bag and headed for the "grotto." Did she think the Madonna was going to come to life and paint a big red *A* on her chest? Did she believe Mary even cared about her sorry Jewish sins?

Father Sherry had called and left a few apologetic messages. His mother was ill and had taken several turns for the worse. Someone from the rectory had called yesterday to say the priest was still in Detroit.

Oh, well, at least no one has left any wreaths lately, thought Joyce, as she got down on her knees and reached for the tall grass that had grown past the statue's knees. A moment later she was back on her heels. "Oh my God," she whispered.

The overgrowth was a blind, hiding a heap of trinkets and coins. Joyce picked them up, one by one: six religious medallions (four Marys and two St. Christophers), a tarnished silver thimble, a collection of tricolor ribbons from St. Peter's festival. She found a miniature china teacup and saucer, and a pile of nickels and dimes.

The soil under the coins had been turned over. With one turn of the shovel, Joyce unearthed a diamond engagement ring and a pair of pearl earrings. Oh, no, she thought. That poor woman is really crazy.

She wrapped the "offerings" in a kitchen towel and called Kathleen, who agreed to meet for a walk. "I feel a little like I robbed a grave or something," Joyce said as they set out under a dramatic, cloud-filled sky. "But I couldn't just leave it all there, could I?"

"You did the right thing," Kathleen said. "It sounds like Theresa is now way past reverence for the Virgin. She's got to be eighty. She lives just around the corner from you, with her daughter, Lena. Maybe you should call Lena."

"I'll do that."

They walked on quietly for a few moments. A steady wind pushed the high cumulus clouds, blocking the sun and then revealing it. Huge shadows fell on the sand, so that Joyce and Kathleen walked through disappearing walls of warmth and light.

"Joyce, what's going on with you?"

"What do you mean?"

"You seemed sort of edgy when Hal asked about your writing."

"Oh, that." Joyce brushed the question away with her hand.

Kathleen waited for an answer.

"I haven't written anything all summer. Sometimes I think I'll never write anything again."

"You're just becalmed."

"That's a nice word," Joyce said wistfully.

"You'll catch a breeze. You won't stay becalmed. Or maybe you could think of it as lying fallow."

"That's a less attractive image."

"Not really. You've only just started digging around in your garden, but after a year you'll get to see how flowers thrive in places that have been uncultivated. Those will be the most beautiful parts."

"Actually, I had a thought about Magnolia while I was rooting around out there. I imagined one of her descendants living up here, planting a kitchen garden."

"So Magnolia becomes a mother, does she?"

"I suppose she does, eventually."

"Then you can plumb your own mother-daughter issues."

"Oh, great," Joyce said, shaking her head. "Part of me can't wait for Nina to come home and another part of me is dreading the fray. Sometimes, I fantasize that she comes back as ten-year-old Nina who wants to play Monopoly with me. Sometimes, I imagine that she'll be totally mature and my best friend. But then reality strikes and I remember that we're only just starting the whole adolescent thing."

"You know," Kathleen said, "I sometimes wonder if people who see us walking on the beach think we're mother and daughter. I don't think of you as my daughter, not at all, though you're young enough to be."

"I sure don't think of you as my mom. Mothers and daughters, huh? It's never easy."

"Mothers and sons are complicated, too. Hal seems angry with me these days."

"Why?"

"I'm not entirely sure. I used to think we were close, but now I'm wondering whether the reason he moved to California was to get away from me. I suspected that he was gay," she said, turning toward Joyce. "Did I ever tell you that? For years, I assumed that's why he lived in San Francisco with Josh. But I was wrong. And now I feel like I don't know him at all, and that it's my fault.

"I knew him so well when he was a little boy, and even in high school . . . I thought I did." Kathleen stopped. "How did I get all of this so wrong? Was I just not paying attention?"

"I have no wisdom or comfort to offer here," Joyce said. "I feel like a total washout in the intergenerational family communication department."

"I'm hoping to get another chance with Hal, now that he'll be closer to home. And I suppose motherhood is a work in progress. Oh, dear. That sounds like a sampler, doesn't it?"

"I'd put it up in my kitchen." Joyce laughed and put her arm around Kathleen's shoulder.

"Failure, success. It's moment by moment." Kathleen looked at the sky. "This is a beautiful moment. I feel like we're walking right through the clouds in these shadows."

Joyce turned to admire Kathleen's profile. "My turn to ask you something," she said softly. "What will you do on August eighth?"

"Oh." Kathleen took a quick breath at the turn in the conversation. "Nothing, really. We go to the cemetery and light the anniversary candle on the fourteenth."

"Do you think that Hal's anger has something to do with Danny?"

Kathleen stopped and turned to Joyce.

"I'm sorry," Joyce said. "It was just a thought."

"But you're right," Kathleen said, a little breathless. "That's it. And of course, he has every right to be."

"What? Oh, for heaven's sake, Kathleen. What are you blaming yourself for?"

"I wasn't there."

"What do you mean?"

"I was in the house when it happened, when the car . . . The phone rang, and I went in the house to get it. That's when it happened.

"People used to say to me, 'How horrible to see your child struck by a car.' And I never corrected them. But Hal knew that I didn't see it at all. Only Hal saw it."

"And you think he's angry at you because of that?"

"Oh, I don't know," Kathleen said, suddenly unsure of that theory. "I really don't."

"Couldn't you ask him?"

"I could. I mean, it's possible to ask. I just don't know if I have the nerve. We never talk about Danny."

"Never? In all these years?"

"It was too painful. Too painful to bring it up."

"For whom?"

"For Buddy. He couldn't even bear to hear Danny's name, so I didn't . . ."

"And with Hal?"

Kathleen shook her head.

Joyce took Kathleen's arm and they walked quietly back to the footbridge. Turning for a last look at the beach, Kathleen said, "Look at that," pointing at the sky. "I'm not sure I've ever seen such perfect clouds."

Joyce turned to Kathleen. "You're healthy, Kathleen, aren't you?" she half-asked, half-challenged. "You don't have cancer anymore, right?"

"I suppose so. I mean, there's no medical evidence that there's any left, and the radiation is supposed to make sure of that. But, it's still with me. When I go to sleep at night and when I get up in the morning. I try to tell myself how lucky I am, that it was only DCIS, that it didn't spread. But it's always there."

"Oh, Kathleen," Joyce said, her voice full of frustration and good wishes. "I want to be able to make it all better for you.

"I love you, you know."

"I love you, too," said Kathleen. "And that helps."

IT WAS THEIR LAST trip home from the radiation clinic. Kathleen was finished. She should have been smiling and sharing a sigh of relief with Buddy. But instead, Kathleen wept quietly into her hands, unable to explain why.

Rachel and Terry had bantered with Kathleen as she moved into position. Over the intercom, Kathleen heard them count to three and suddenly break into song: "Is Miz Levine all set?" to the tune of "I Could Have Danced All Night." Kathleen laughed so hard, Rachel had to come out and make sure she hadn't moved off the mark.

Afterward, they escorted Kathleen to the staff coffee room for cake and a card signed by everyone. The girls kissed her. Marcy hugged her and didn't say anything about support groups, which Kathleen took as a parting gift. Dr. Singh dropped by and ended the celebration with a kind of benediction: "Whenever this time comes to mind, may you recall the kindness of these faces."

As they neared home, Buddy said, "I wish I could say something, Kath. I wish I could do something."

She blew her nose. "There's nothing you can do. I'm just, well, it's just an emotional day."

"What's this?" Buddy exclaimed as they pulled in behind a Ryder van parked in their driveway.

"What's going on?" Kathleen asked.

"Beats me."

Jack opened the front door as they got out of the car.

"What's with the truck?" Buddy called.

"Hello to you, too," Jack said, reaching out to hug Kathleen. "Congratulations on being done, Mom."

"Thanks, hon. But what's in the truck?"

"I should have called, I guess, but I didn't want you to worry. Where's Hal?"

Hal, Buddy explained, had taken his mother's car to Boston to run some secret errand. "Do you know what he's up to?" Kathleen asked.

"No clue." Jack had already turned the kitchen upside down, a griddle set out and pancake batter ready to go.

"And the truck?" Buddy asked again.

The truck, Jack explained, was full of his stuff because Lois had gotten the lead in a touring production of *The Music Man*, and the sublet in the apartment was up.

"Oh, Jack, I'm so sorry," said Kathleen.

"It's not that big a deal." He shrugged.

"Separating with Lois isn't that big a deal?"

"Separating? We were roommates. Friends."

"You were?" said Buddy.

"You were?" Joyce said.

"You didn't think we were, oh." Jack shook his head. "No, no. We're good friends. She still wants to meet you guys.

"But jeez, parents, aren't you curious about why I'm *here* with all of my stuff in a truck?"

"No guessing games, Jack," Buddy said. "Not today."

"Okay, okay. Do you remember Ed Frisch? He was on the wrestling team with me in high school? Big guy with kinky, blond hair? Anyway, he's a developer in Boston now, and he's opening a new seafood restaurant in the new waterfront hotel downtown? And"—Jack paused for effect—"you are looking at its new executive chef."

"Wow," said Buddy, who hugged Jack and started pumping him for details. "When do you open? Do you get to design the whole menu?"

But Kathleen only smiled and nodded. She was still on the verge of tears and ashamed that she couldn't muster any enthusiasm for her son's news. She fled to the bedroom and, when Buddy checked on her a few minutes later, pretended to be asleep.

Life was crowding in on her. Jack was home. Hal was home. She had finished treatment. So many prayers answered. And here it was, August 8, again. Tomorrow.

Every year, Buddy asked whether she wanted him to stay home. Every year she told him to go to work, assuring him that she would be all right and that they'd be together on the fourteenth. He always stayed home on the fourteenth.

She listened as Buddy and Jack banged in and out of the house, carrying boxes into the basement and garage. In the bathroom, Kathleen locked the door, unbuttoned her blouse, and forced herself to look in the mirror.

The scar wasn't quite so red, the skin no longer chapped, but the breast didn't seem to belong to her anymore. She stared at it. Her babies had nursed there. Buddy had fallen asleep there. Now, it looked like a war zone. "Armistice Day," she whispered, buttoned her blouse, and readied a smile.

She walked into the kitchen but found Jack on the deck, ordering Buddy to wash down the weathered picnic table.

"Where did these come from?" Kathleen asked, fingering a set of peach-striped linens.

"Souvenirs from the big city." Jack grinned. "I'm making you a fabulous dinner tonight."

"So what else is new?" Kathleen smiled.

As the day's heat faded into a cool seaside evening, Jack set out an old brass storm lantern he had brought with him, lit it, and pulled out a chair for Kathleen.

"Should we put that on the menu?" he asked about the grilled-eggplant appetizer, the marinated swordfish, the garlic mashed potatoes, the roasted asparagus.

"Why wouldn't you?" said Kathleen. "It's all delicious, Jack. You'll be a big success, no doubt about it."

"Can you get bread like this in Boston?" Buddy asked, twisting off another piece of the crusty baguette Jack had brought from Manhattan.

That launched them into a discussion of suppliers. Buddy asked if Jack would be part owner of the restaurant. "If you need a lawyer, David Koch has always been a stand-up guy for me."

Kathleen watched the two of them talk business, approving of the way they listened to each other, seriously and generously.

"Earth to Mom," Jack said gently, and put his hand on hers.

"Dessert?" he repeated.

"You had to ask?"

As Jack served warm peach upside-down cake, the phone rang. "It's Hal," Buddy announced, and handed the phone to Jack. "He wants to talk to you."

Jack returned ten minutes later and announced that Hal probably wouldn't be back until Friday.

"What's Mom supposed to do without a car until then?" Buddy sputtered. "What the heck is he doing down there?"

Jack shook his head and shrugged, but couldn't help smiling.

"Oh, so you know?"

"Maybe I do, and maybe I don't. I'm going to take the train into the city tomorrow and hook up with him. And if it's okay, I'm going to use Mom's car to check out some local produce vendors and a baker or two. Hal and I will probably drive back together, by Friday at the latest."

"It's okay about the car," said Kathleen. "So we'll all be together for Friday-night dinner?"

"Do you know that your brother is going Hasidic on us?" Buddy said.

"That's overstating it a little," Kathleen objected.

"I'll get a kosher chicken," Jack said. "They really do taste the best."

Kathleen smiled. "Hal will approve. But if you two moguls will excuse me, I think I'm going to lie down."

Jack walked her down the hall and gave her a long hug. "You're going to be fine, Mom."

"It's great to have you home, hon."

She lay down on top of the bedspread and looked at the ceiling. What had she been doing twenty-five years ago, right this minute?

WITH THE WEEKEND behind her, Joyce started waiting for the phone to ring. Frank called. A telemarketer called. The mail arrived. She walked with Kathleen. Frank called again. She wrote to Nina. The day passed.

After dark, Joyce drove to Rockport and passed Patrick's apartment. The windows were dark. She went around the block two more times, but no one was home.

The next day, Kathleen called to say Jack had arrived: her house was in an uproar and she wouldn't be able to walk. Joyce thought about killing some time at the mall, but in the end she painted the stairwell to the basement. At night, she drove to Rockport, past dark windows, again.

Joyce woke up early the next morning and lay in bed thinking about Kathleen. It was the eighth. Maybe she should go over there.

At seven-thirty the phone rang, and Joyce dove for it.

"I didn't wake you up, did I?" Frank asked.

"No," Joyce said, catching her breath.

"Look. I'm coming up tonight. I should be there by six."

"Oh, really?" Joyce said, trying to sound as if it were no big deal.

"We have to talk," he said flatly.

Joyce felt her stomach drop. How had he found out? She got up and started sweeping the kitchen, even before putting on coffee. She washed all the floors in the house. She called Kathleen, who sounded a little breathless but claimed that Buddy was on his way home. Joyce went to the supermarket and bought too much food, and flowers for the table. She headed outside to clip stray blades of grass at the edge of the driveway. Anything to keep herself occupied.

Joyce was in the shower when Frank arrived, earlier than announced. She found him running his hands over the kitchen walls. "Very professional," he marveled, pointing at a silky stretch that used to be badly cracked.

"And you even cleaned up the yard. Those lilies you planted will be pretty next summer."

He looked pasty and exhausted. The stray gray hairs at his temples had multiplied. Joyce kissed his cheek lightly and said, "I'm making pasta." He smiled but avoided meeting her eyes and reached into the refrigerator for a beer. The kitchen clock ticked overhead. Joyce thought she would scream if he didn't say something.

"Frank, what's going on? What do we have to talk about? I've been going nuts since you called."

"Oh. Sorry I made it sound so dire. Let's sit." He lowered himself into a chair.

Joyce ran down the list of possible bombshells. He knows. He's dumping me. He's dying of cancer. *He's* having an affair.

"First of all, I want to apologize," Frank said, peeling the label off the beer bottle with his thumb. He was nearly whispering. "I've been very distant. I've kind of abandoned you this summer."

"No," Joyce started, but he gestured for her to stop.

"Just let me get this out. Things are bad at work. Really bad. It turns out that Harlan has a serious drinking problem and Tran wants to move back to San Jose to be near his family. All the potential investors opted out, and I think the company's going to fold within a week. Maybe two." He put down his beer.

"I ignored the warning signs, and for a while I thought maybe we could squeak by until the financing came through. I'm sorry, Joyce, but I've been working without pay for a few weeks now, hoping it might help. I think we may end up in a real financial bind."

"It's okay," Joyce said softly. "The way you walked in here, I thought you were going to tell me you had a week to live. Or that you were dumping me for a cute programmer chick."

"No," he said, shaking his head, keeping his eyes on the beer bottle. "The other thing is, I don't want to keep doing this."

Joyce felt her face flush. He does know, she thought. He wants a divorce. "Keep doing what?" she asked, trying to sound calm.

"Working in high tech." He started to talk more forcefully, as though he'd rehearsed this part. "I realized that what I enjoyed the most about my last couple of jobs was teaching people how to do stuff, how to write code, how to program. And the thing I like doing best in the rest of my life is coaching soccer—being around kids.

"I hope you won't be too upset about this, but I've been looking in the help wanteds, and I applied for a job at a junior college outside of Worcester. I'd teach a few programming classes and act as assistant dean in the new technology department they're starting.

"I had one interview last week, and today they called back for a second one. The pay isn't so good, Joyce, but I'm . . ." He finally stopped and looked her in the eye. "I can't go on like this."

Joyce was so relieved she was afraid she might laugh. She put her hand on his. "You take the job when they offer it. That'll take care of health insurance, right? I'll make more money this year. We could even sell this place if we have to."

"I hope it won't come to that." Frank looked so pathetically grateful that Joyce had to turn away. She got up, emptied a box of spaghetti in the boiling water, and stirred, keeping her back to Frank. He wants me to forgive him?

I'm risking my whole life—Nina's life, Frank's life—for a roll in the hay with a man I barely know? What do I know about Patrick after all? That I love the way he smells? That I love the way he doesn't stop kissing me until I'm on the moon?

Is it really just about sex? God, I am such an asshole. Besides, it's over. He hasn't called in a week.

They ate dinner without saying much. "I'll wash the dishes," Joyce said and watched through the kitchen window as Frank walked around the yard.

Maybe I'll go down to Belmont for a few days, Joyce thought. I should call Mario. I should get back to work.

What am I waiting here for anyway? Patrick isn't calling. And the next time he does, I'll tell him it's over. That's what I'm going to do. If he ever calls me again.

KATHLEEN PUT ON the old pants she wore for gardening and said good-bye. Buddy offered to come back after he dropped Jack at the train. She told him no. "Joyce is coming by," she said, and waved them off.

Kathleen hung up after Joyce's phone call and sat at the kitchen table as the coffee cup cooled between her hands.

Finally, she stood up and walked into the den. She pulled out the one album with all the photographs of Danny and leafed through it, as she did every year, page after page, remembering the way he waddled, the way the little toe on his right foot turned in, his giggle, his passion for mashed peas.

Kathleen remembered the smell of his hair when it was wet. The way he twisted his hands, like a Balinese dancer, whenever he was excited or tired.

She began to weep and closed the book, taking her tears down to the basement, to the laundry room, where she lay down on the cold cement floor, letting herself fall all the way down to the bottom of her grief.

She cried, loud and hard, until she had no tears left, until her back ached and her bones were chilled. Then she went upstairs and took the coldest shower she could bear. Wrapped in a towel, she sat on the edge of the tub, her limbs heavy, her head throbbing.

An involuntary shudder took her to her feet.

She went back to the den, to the desk, to the check register, to see that Buddy had performed his annual ritual, too: $100 to the Sisters of Saint Joseph Retirement Fund, for Pat; $100 to the Jewish National Fund, for Mae and Irv; $500 to the Daniel Levine Memorial Fund, so that no one should ever have to buy a coffin for his own little child. She found a few more tears.

Buddy came home at four, with daisies. They walked around the block, holding hands. After a dinner made from Jack's copious leftovers, they sat on the deck and talked about their sons: Was Jack just sparing their feelings with that story about him and Lois? Would Jack make a good enough living to afford a decent apartment in Boston, now that rents were so high?

They tried to guess what Hal was up to. Was he looking for a job? Were they way off-track about his interest in the rabbi; they'd been plenty wrong before. Maybe he had a girlfriend in the city.

"I hope he finds something to keep him nearby," Kathleen said. "I don't suppose he'd actually live up around *here.*"

"Why not?" Buddy said. "It's a great place to live."

They fell silent and Kathleen felt Danny's memory settle over her again. She closed her eyes and remembered the day Buddy had taken him for his first haircut. She thought the barber had cut it too short, and they had quarreled.

Buddy took her hand in the gathering darkness and cleared his throat.

"Are you catching cold?"

"No," he said, blowing his nose. "I'm okay. And you?"

"I'm okay, too."

ON FRIDAY MORNING, Hal and Jack returned with a carful of groceries. As Jack ferried bags into the house, Hal presented Kathleen with a small brown package: "This is from both of us."

She unwrapped a signed, first edition of Sendak's *In the Night Kitchen*. "Hally, it's wonderful. But what's the occasion?"

"Occasion? Let's see. How about the end of your treatment? How about, oh, I don't know, the beginning of my course as a paramedic at Northeastern? How about me checking out the MCATs schedule? Is that enough to celebrate?"

"Oh, my," she whispered, holding the book to her chest. "I'm so glad. I can't believe you're both going to be close to home again."

"Leave it to Jack to steal my thunder and do it the same month."

"Oh, Hal."

He put his arm around her. "Just kidding. And I'm sorry I was gone so much this week."

"That's all right, hon. I really don't expect you to spend every day with me."

But Hal exploded. "What are you talking about? Of course I should have been home." Kathleen stared. Hal, still angry but embarrassed, walked out of the room as Jack walked in with the last of the bags.

"Hal and I went to Brookline," Jack said, "which isn't Brooklyn by a long shot, but I got a nice kosher chicken. And three challahs so we can have a taste test. Save your appetite."

That evening, Hal sang the long blessing over the wine, as Jack stood in the kitchen door, waiting to serve the meal. During dinner, Hal explained the details of his "master plan." He would get certified as a paramedic and work as an EMT. Meanwhile, he'd take refresher courses in chemistry and physics to prepare for the MCATs. "I figure I'll apply to U. Mass. in Worcester, BU, Tufts, and maybe Harvard, just for the heck of it."

Jack raised a glass. "To my brother the doctor. But why didn't you try the marinated calamari I put out before dinner?"

"I don't eat shellfish anymore."

"You're kidding," Jack said. "Why not?"

"I don't eat pork, either."

Buddy whistled. "You really are going religious on us."

"I just don't eat shellfish or pork. No big deal. Okay?"

"Okay," said Kathleen. "To each his own, right?"

"What's that supposed to mean?" Jack asked.

"It means we love you guys whatever you eat or don't eat," Kathleen said, raising her glass in Jack's direction. "And here's to the success of the Bay State Seafood Café and its brilliant, handsome new chef."

"Here, here," said Hal.

"I suppose you can eat fish when you come," Jack said grudgingly.

"I love fish. And all the desserts," Hal offered.

"The dessert chef makes those, not me." Jack was still put out.

"For goodness' sake," Kathleen said, getting up from the table.

"Sorry," Jack said, starting to clear the table.

"Sorry, Mom," Hal said, adding, "Are you and Dad coming to services? Jack is."

"I've got to see this lady rabbi he's raving about," Jack said, waggling his eyebrows, à la Groucho.

"Not tonight," Kathleen said. "Next week. We'll all go then. You know"—she paused—"for the anniversary."

"I only go if she goes," Buddy said.

Hal's smile evaporated. Kathleen remembered how, as a little boy, he would put his pinkies into the corners of his mouth and pull them down into a deep frown when she said no to his request for a later bedtime or a second bowl of ice cream.

"I'm sorry, Hally. I'm just worn-out. Don't be mad. Please?"

He shrugged.

"Say hi to Michelle for me," she called as they walked out the door.

KATHLEEN WAS DOING laundry when the doorbell rang. She ran upstairs and, slightly out of breath, opened the door on Jimmy Parley. He was out of uniform, in a sports shirt and pressed jeans. Shifting his weight from one leg to the other, he apologized for interrupting. His face seemed flushed.

"What's wrong, Jimmy? Is Buddy okay?"

"Yes. He's fine. It's nothing to do with your family. It's your friend, Mrs. Tabachnik."

"Oh my God. Has Joyce been in an accident?"

"No," Jimmy said. "Look, there's no good way to say this. Can I come in for a sec?"

Kathleen opened the screen door and Jimmy stepped into the foyer. He stood close to her and talked in a hushed rush, as though someone might walk in on them.

"There's going to be a drug bust in Rockport within the hour. There's a man we've been keeping under surveillance, and . . ." Jimmy took a breath. "Mrs. Tabachnik has been, uh, seeing him. I know she doesn't have anything to do with his, uh, activities. But she could get caught in the middle of something.

"I shouldn't even be here. I just found out, and, well, I'm just saying that you might want to go stop her. It might be too late to find her at home. You'll have to go Rockport before she's inside that apartment.

"If she goes, when she goes, she gets there at noon. So if you just happen to be around there a few minutes before then, you'll catch her."

He handed her a folded scrap of paper. Kathleen opened it and read an address.

"It's behind that sub shop on Broad. The door's in the back, off the parking lot. If she isn't there by twelve-fifteen, you just leave, okay?"

Kathleen nodded.

"Like I said, I just found out it was today, and I had to decide. So I hope I did right by coming to you, Mrs. Levine."

"You did right, Jimmy." Kathleen thanked him, closed the door, and started looking for her car keys. It had been a while since she'd used them or even seen them. They weren't in her purse. Or on the table in the foyer. Or in the junk drawer in the kitchen.

Oh, Lord.

She went to the closet and rummaged through the pockets of her raincoat, her jacket.

Oh, no.

She ran up to the bedroom and looked in her other purse, in her sweatshirt pockets.

"Please, please, please," she muttered.

Feeling through the drawer in Buddy's nightstand, she thought she heard something jingle. She dumped the contents onto the bed. Lots of change but no keys.

Then, remembering the spares, she ran to the back of the garage.

What would she have done if Hal had taken the car today? she thought, pulling out of the driveway. What would she have done if Jack had been home and wanted to know where she was going without brushing her hair or putting on shoes?

She raced out of her driveway and down the street, leaning forward, honking to get the car ahead of her to hurry up and pull out onto the highway.

Take it easy, she told herself. This is no time to get a ticket. She didn't even have her license. No money, no watch even. The clock on the dashboard hadn't worked for years.

She had time, didn't she? Jimmy had come to the door—when was it, eleven-fifteen? Or was it later than that? How long had she wasted looking for the keys?

Her hands were sticky on the wheel, and she could feel her heart pounding, but not the way it did when she was on the bridge. She just had to get there before Joyce . . . What was Joyce doing at noon with a drug dealer?

"As if I didn't know," she muttered, grateful to find a parking spot only a few doors up from the sub shop. She retrieved a pair of Buddy's thongs from the trunk and peered through the realty storefront window, looking for a clock. It was 11:48. She walked around to the back, clutching at the key in her pocket.

The parking lot was empty except for a rusty panel truck up on blocks. An open Dumpster buzzed with wasps. The midday sun raised welts of heat from the cracked macadam.

Kathleen caught sight of herself in the truck window. She was wearing her gardening pants, traces of dried mud on the knees. She hadn't showered that morning or even pulled her hair back off her face. The thongs were far too big for her feet. She looked like a bag lady.

Hurry up, Joyce, she thought. We've got to get out of here. Hurry up.

A few long minutes later, Joyce appeared around the side of the building, her eyes focused on the two coffee cups she was carrying. She was smiling. Then she saw Kathleen.

"Come on," Kathleen said softly, taking the cups from her. "We have to go."

Joyce's face was a mess of confusion and fear and mortification. "What?"

"Not now." Kathleen guided her by the elbow out of the parking lot and back toward her car. She opened the passenger door for Joyce, who slid in meekly.

"I'm going to take you home," Kathleen said as she pulled into the street.

"No," Joyce groaned, looking down at her lap.

"What about coming to my house?"

"No."

"All right. We'll go to the beach."

Joyce stared out the window. Kathleen stole glances at her and tried to think of ways to spare her feelings.

They didn't speak the rest of the way. At Good Harbor, Joyce followed Kathleen to a spot near the tidal stream, as far from other people as they could get. A few children clambered nearby with nets and buckets. The sky was overcast but bright.

Joyce sat with her head bowed while Kathleen told her about Jimmy's visit.

"Drugs," said Joyce. "Boy, that explains a lot of things. What an idiot I am. What a total jerk."

"Don't."

"Why not? I've been having a weird, kinky affair with a drug dealer, an addict, too, come to think of it. I've been sneaking around in the broad daylight, risking my life, my family. Nina! For God's sake, I can't even look at you. You must think I'm the scum of the earth. And I probably am."

"No, Joyce. I'm not judging you. Believe me."

"Why not? You have no idea how sleazy this whole thing was. I want to say it's like I was a different person in that room, but that would be a lie. It was me, all right. Joyce Miller Tabachnik, moron. Bored suburban housewife. Empty-nest cliché. Oh, God, this is so awful."

Kathleen put her hand on Joyce's.

"Don't touch me," she snapped.

"Oh, stop it." The anger in Kathleen's voice startled Joyce. "What? Do you think you're the only woman who ever made a mistake?"

"I suppose the divorce courts are full of women like me."

"Are you and Frank getting a divorce?"

"Maybe we should."

"I didn't," said Kathleen evenly.

"You didn't what?"

"I didn't get a divorce after my, after I . . ." Kathleen took a breath and continued, "I had an affair."

"You?" Joyce looked Kathleen in the face for the first time.

"His name was Stan, and he was artist-in-residence in the Cape Ann schools. It was two years after Danny was born." Kathleen paused between phrases, listening to herself say things she'd never said out loud. "He was from Hingham. He had a wife and kids. Three kids. He rented a room in Salem while he worked on the North Shore. I spent seven afternoons with him. I counted. Seven afternoons. Five in February, two in March.

"He was wonderful in the classroom. He had those children making the most beautiful, heartbreaking little paintings you can imagine. His own art wasn't as good, I'm afraid. But, Lord, he could talk like an angel."

"And you never told Buddy?"

"I never told anyone."

"You don't mean to say that I'm the first person, ever?"

"I never had a good reason to tell anyone until now. I don't see why you should ruin your marriage and hurt your daughter just because you need to confess. You told me. You don't have to tell anyone else."

"I'm not sure that will work for me."

"Well, you don't have to do anything today, do you?" Kathleen said firmly. "Or tomorrow, for that matter. Wait awhile. Let things settle down."

"Were you in love with him?"

"With Stan? I'm not sure." Kathleen looked down at her hands in the sand. "He was exciting to be with. He made me feel smart. And at that moment in my life, I was sort of lost. Buddy was having a tough time in the store, but he wasn't talking to me about it. I was exhausted, taking care of Hal and Danny, who still wasn't sleeping through the night.

"And then my mother-in-law decided that I should get out of the house a few afternoons a week, so she watched the boys. I'm sure Mae thought of it as a gift, but I was completely at loose ends. I didn't know what to do with myself. I volunteered at the school library just to have somewhere to go, and that's where I met Stan.

"He turned my head. What an old-fashioned thing to say, but that was it. I was flattered. I was . . . infatuated.

"He was totally different from Buddy," Kathleen said, glancing up to meet Joyce's unswerving, sympathetic gaze. "Buddy was never much of a reader, and also"—Kathleen cleared her throat—"well, Buddy was the only man I'd ever been with before.

"But I think I always knew that I wouldn't leave Buddy. From the very start, even. I didn't trust Stan the way I trusted Buddy. Stan was cheating on his wife, wasn't he?"

Joyce shook her head sadly.

"I ended it. I couldn't stand the sneaking around."

"And you never told Buddy?"

"I almost told him a thousand times. For weeks afterward, months, but it didn't make sense to me. Why hurt him like that? I made an awful mistake, but then I put a stop to it. It was over."

"You never told your sister?"

"Heavens, no" Kathleen shook her head. "Her good opinion meant too much to me. And besides, how could she possibly understand? She was a nun."

"How does it feel now? To have told someone."

"Not as bad as I thought it would. Besides, it worked, didn't it? You're not going to tell Frank right away, are you?"

"I don't have to do anything today. Isn't that what you said?"

"Or tomorrow."

"But I can tell you, right?" Joyce said. "I met him at Halibut Point, at dawn."

"Oh, dear. Just like I told you."

"Now that I think about it, he was probably there signaling to a drug boat or something.

"We never actually, uh, did it, you know, consummated. He wouldn't or maybe he couldn't. Maybe because of the drugs. I mean, he never took off his pants. It drove me crazy, but now I'm grateful. I guess I was lucky."

Joyce pulled up her knees and wrapped her arms around them, making herself as small as she could. "I was going to end it today. I know that sounds like a lie. I should have done it over the phone, but when he called, I just wanted to say good-bye in person. Or maybe I was kidding myself. I would have probably jumped in bed with him again. I don't know.

"I've been such a rotten wife. Frank came up, finally. It's been weeks and weeks since he was here, you know? He came to tell me that he's totally miserable at work. He's hated his job for years, and I hardly noticed. Why didn't he tell me? And then he apologizes for losing his job." Joyce groaned. "Meanwhile, I'm cheating on him. Poor Frank."

Kathleen sighed. "I think he left you in the lurch this summer. And now it also sounds like he needs your support, a lot."

"I know," Joyce said. They sat quietly. "But, Kathleen?"

"Yes, dear?"

"I need a bathroom. And there are way too many people around here for us to have another peeing contest."

Kathleen stood up and reached her hand out to Joyce. "Let's go to your house."

THE PHONE WAS ringing as they walked through the door. Joyce pointed to the answering machine and put her finger to her lips. What if it was Patrick? What if the police hadn't raided the place? What if they had arrested him, and he wanted her to bail him out?

"Joyce?" Frank sounded frantic. "Where the hell are you?"

She picked up the phone and Kathleen turned away to give her some privacy, but turned back when she heard Joyce say, "Oh, God. Is she okay? . . .

"No. I just walked in the door. I didn't . . . When? When did it happen? . . .

"Yes. I'll be there as soon as I can. . . . Yes," said Joyce. "Hanover. The medical center. Is she really going to be okay? . . . Yes. . . . Yes, I'm sorry. I'll find you. I'm leaving now."

"What happened?" Kathleen asked, trying to sound calm.

"Nina fell out of a tree."

"What?"

"She was climbing a tree near her cabin this morning. She broke her collarbone. Frank's been calling for hours. She lost consciousness for a minute, which means there was a concussion, so they took her to Dartmouth-Hitchcock for observation. Frank says there's a map in the car.

"Oh, shit," Joyce shouted. "My car is in Rockport."

"Don't be silly, I'm driving. Go use the bathroom, loan me a pair of sandals, and we'll leave."

As Kathleen eased the car into the first traffic rotary, she said, "Now tell me exactly what Frank said."

Joyce ran through the few details she knew. "The break was on her left side, and she regained consciousness quickly, which is good. But I have no idea what she was doing up in a tree. Was she there on a dare? Was it an accident? Was she trying to, I don't know, hurt herself?"

"That's way too big an assumption," Kathleen interrupted. "Kids do lots of stupid things for no reason at all."

"I guess. But Nina doesn't. Or she hasn't."

"Well, doing stupid things is part of adolescence, I'm afraid."

They were past the second rotary and starting over the bridge. Kathleen gripped the wheel, anticipating panic. But there was nothing.

Exactly what had scared her so much about doing this? It was a twenty-degree rise up to the crest of the bridge, if that. And the whole span took two minutes, at most. Where was her terror?

"Kathleen?" Joyce's voice was trembling. "Would you keep talking? It's probably irrational, but I'm so afraid of what I'm going to find at the hospital, I'll go nuts if I don't have something else to think about. Or maybe it's that I'm afraid to face Frank after what just happened. Could you keep talking to me? Would you mind?"

Starting with the first thing that came into her head, Kathleen described in elaborate detail a meal Jack had cooked the other night, including a mouthwatering pasta dish made with cabbage, of all things. The smell had gotten her remembering her grandmother's house, which seemed saturated with the smell of cabbage, which made her think about how much Pat hated cabbage. When Pat announced that she was going to take vows, she said, "I asked them if I could have an exemption written into the vow of obedience if they ever put cabbage on my plate."

"I felt like I was losing her when she went into the convent," Kathleen said. "It felt like a repudiation of us, of our relationship. Like she was choosing those Sisters over me. I'm glad I never told her that, because it wasn't so. We stayed close, even though we lived in different cities.

"We worked at it, you know, with letters, and phone calls. She came here every summer for her two-week vacation. Pat was devoted to Buddy and the boys. But I'm afraid I always compared other friendships to hers, which was unfair. But that's how it is. Your family makes you who you are. And then she died."

"How long ago was that?" Joyce asked.

"Fourteen years. I felt so helpless during her illness, especially at the end. All the nursing Sisters bustled around, bringing her medications, changing the bed, bathing her. I just sat there and held her hand, weeping. She sent me away the night she died. She told me to go rest. And then she slipped away, so I wouldn't have to watch. She was taking care of me, even at the end."

Kathleen took a deep breath. "At her funeral I felt so strange, so out of place. The Sisters and the priest kept talking about how she was in a better place. They were all smiles—big, heartfelt smiles. But I was sobbing. I could barely stand up, much less smile back at them. I felt there was something terribly wrong with me, but Buddy told me that I was just being Jewish, and there's just no pie in the sky like that for us."

Kathleen shook her head. "After she died, I figured I'd get breast cancer, too. Every mammogram, I thought, this time it'll be my turn. That first biopsy, I thought for sure, this is it. But it wasn't. And this time, well, I got off easy."

"Wait a minute."

"I know," Kathleen corrected herself. "It sucks. But it's true that I'm not going to die from this—at least, it's not likely. I'm going to be around for a while. I'm grateful. I am lucky. I know it."

Joyce nodded and leaned back into the headrest. Her eyes were fixed on Kathleen as she talked on and on, telling stories about Pat. Her boldness as a girl. How she liked Buddy right off the bat. How she'd stood by Kathleen's side, under the bridal canopy at their wedding, which had been a small affair at her in-laws' house.

After they crossed the border into New Hampshire, Kathleen stopped for gas and coffee. Back on the road, she started talking about her sons. Hal's shyness, his childhood terror of bugs, his science honors in high school. Jack's outgoing nature, his fearlessness in the water, his trophies for swimming, for wrestling, and track. The way the boys used to fight over their toys, and the way they looked, side by side, walking out to the car the other night, on their way to temple.

And then, Kathleen found herself telling stories about Danny. He loved trucks. He was pigeon-toed. He fought sleep, even when he was exhausted. When he got his first tooth, he bit Hal's finger so hard he broke the skin.

There were hundreds of people at Danny's funeral. People Kathleen had never seen before: customers from the store, acquaintances of Mae and Irv's. Louisa Bendix had stayed home to look after Hal. "The coffin was tiny. Obscene. It was small enough that just one man from the funeral home could carry it."

Joyce hugged her knees to her chest and listened intently. They passed Manchester and the road emptied, so that it seemed they were alone in the world.

Kathleen felt a little like she was in a confessional. As a child she hated the dark wooden booths in church. They always scared her, and after she saw her first Dracula movie, they reminded her of coffins. The car was an intimate space, too, a good place for telling secrets, but it held no threat. Maybe it was the changing light, or Joyce's rapt attention.

"It's twenty-five years this month," Kathleen said, her eyes fixed on the road ahead. "Remember you asked me how long ago it was that Danny died? I didn't want to tell you because, well, I didn't want you making allowances for me." She lowered her voice to a mock-reverent whisper. "Poor Kathleen. It's twenty-five years since her little boy died. Poor woman."

Joyce started to speak, but Kathleen cut her off. "I couldn't stand that because, I . . ." She stopped, and Joyce waited.

"Remember I told you the phone rang, and I went into the house? Well, it was Stan on the phone."

Joyce sat up straight in her seat.

"I ran inside just to see who it was. Just for a second, you know. I thought it might be Pat, who was due to visit that month. But it was him.

"I hadn't seen him or even spoken to him for five months. He called and said his wife was kicking him out of the house. He said he loved me and wanted to marry me. He wanted to come to the house. He was sobbing.

"I told Hal, 'Watch your brother.' I said, 'I'll be just a second.' But it wasn't just a second. And then I heard Hal scream. Not Danny. Hal.

"It was . . . That was . . ." The car filled up with the noise of the engine, the tires on the road, the air rushing over the windows.

"What a horrible sound. I can't begin to tell you. Like a siren. Louder than you'd ever think a child could scream. Screaming and screaming.

"And you know what I did? What 'poor Kathleen' did? I hung up the phone. I didn't drop it when I heard Hal. I didn't leave it dangling. I took the time to hang up the damn receiver.

"I don't think I said anything to Stan. I don't remember really.

But I do remember replacing the phone on the hook before I went to see why my son was screaming. I never forgave myself that moment. I never will."

"Why not?"

Joyce had been so quiet, Kathleen almost jumped at the sound of her voice.

"Why wouldn't you forgive yourself for that half second? It was a reflex. It was nothing. You couldn't have stopped the car. Even if the phone had never rung."

"Kathleen," Joyce said firmly, "it wasn't your fault. Hanging up the phone doesn't make you a bad person. Or a bad mother. You didn't kill Danny. The old man behind the wheel of that car killed Danny, by accident. It was an accident. It wasn't your fault."

"I should have been there," Kathleen whispered.

"You were there."

The physical sensation of that morning returned to Kathleen. With her hands on the wheel of a car hurtling across New Hampshire, Kathleen felt herself back at the scene outside her house. Hal screaming. A lawn mower droning in the distance. The blood on the ambulance driver's white shirt. The heat.

"It was blazing hot. My neighbors called the police. The ambulance came. Two ambulances. I got into one of them with Danny. Hal was still screaming. I got into the ambulance with Danny and tried not to scream myself.

"Buddy was at the hospital when we got there. Pat came that night. The days in the hospital were . . . I don't remember them as days; it was a long blur of waiting and crying. But Danny couldn't . . . He didn't get better. And then we had to let him go."

Joyce wiped her eyes and put her hand lightly on Kathleen's shoulder.

"We donated his corneas and his organs."

"It wasn't your fault."

"It wasn't? I told my five-year-old son to watch my three-year-old while I was on the phone with my lover." Kathleen spit out the words.

"It wasn't your fault. And it isn't your fault that you're going to survive breast cancer and Pat died from it."

"No?" Kathleen said sharply, then relented. "I suppose not."

They drove in silence as the mountains grew greener in the afternoon light. Kathleen asked, "Do you know what absolution means?"

"I think so." Joyce blew her nose. "Does Hal feel guilty?"

"Why would Hal feel guilty? He was five years old. There was nothing he could have done."

"There was nothing you could have done, either. That didn't stop you from making it into your fault."

Kathleen shook her head. "We tried to protect Hal from Danny's death. These days, the child psychologists tell you that's the wrong thing to do. But back then, I didn't want to frighten him all over again or make him relive it. Besides, I was too guilty.

"Oh, dear," Kathleen said, her eyes filling with tears, "I think Hal must feel guilty." She remembered what he had said the other day, about not being home with her.

"I was wondering when you'd finally spring a leak," Joyce said, handing her a tissue.

They drove on for a few minutes. Kathleen pointed to a road sign for Dartmouth-Hitchcock Medical Center.

"Oh, God," Joyce said, almost moaning, thinking the worst. Permanent nerve damage? Suicide attempt? Brain injury?

"It's going to be okay," Kathleen said as they pulled up to the emergency room entrance. "Go ahead. I'll park the car and be right in."

JOYCE SPENT FIVE frantic minutes trying to locate Nina. The woman at the front desk couldn't locate her name in the computer, then sent Joyce to the wrong room. When she finally opened the right door, she found Frank and Nina sitting on the bed, calmly watching TV. Nina's arm was in a sling, her hair pulled into a neat bun. For a moment, she looked composed and grown-up, but the moment she caught sight of Joyce, she dissolved into tears. "Mommy."

"Oh, sweetie," Joyce said, sitting down on the bed. "It's okay. I'm here. I'm sorry it took me so long. It's okay."

"I'm sorry, Mom," Nina said, snuffling.

"Just as long as you're okay." Joyce looked over Nina's head and raised her eyebrows in a question mark. Frank nodded slowly, but without smiling, signaling that he'd give Joyce the full story later.

"No cast?" she asked.

"Not for the collarbone," he said.

Nina clung to Joyce with her good arm, nestling against her chest like a baby. When a nurse came in to check her vital signs, Joyce signaled for Frank to move out into the hallway.

Frank hugged her close. "I'm so glad you're here. She really wanted her mother."

"I'm sorry, Frank," Joyce whispered. "I got here as fast as I could." She pulled back, tucked her hands into her armpits, and asked, "So what exactly did the doctors say?"

"She wasn't groggy after she came to, and they don't think the concussion will have any lasting effects. Since I couldn't find a motel room close by, they're going to let her stay here the night. We can stay with her. We have to wake her up every hour or so."

"Mommy?" Nina called in an urgent voice. Joyce and Frank rushed back; Nina was pointing to the TV screen. *The Simpsons* was about to begin, a rerun of one of the show's many Halloween specials. "Halloween in August?" Joyce asked.

"Why not?" Nina said with a flash of impatience.

Joyce and Frank sat on either side of the bed and the three of them watched as aliens devoured Bart. Frank reached for Joyce's hand behind the pillow, and she held on tight.

Downstairs, Kathleen found a bathroom. Using Joyce's hairbrush and some paper towels, she cleaned herself up as best she could before searching for Nina's room. Waiting for the elevator, someone grabbed her elbow from behind.

"There you are," Buddy said.

"What are you doing here?" Kathleen yelped.

"Nice welcome," he said as they got on the elevator together.

"Buddy, how did you get here?"

"I flew," he joked, but Kathleen wasn't smiling.

"I had a delivery near home around two, so I stopped by. The car was gone, but when I went inside, your purse was sitting on the table, and drawers were open all over the place, so I got worried. But when I went to pick up the phone, I saw there was a message; it was Frank Tabachnik looking for Joyce because their daughter was hurt in an accident. Their number isn't listed, so before I called the cops, I ran over to their house. The back door was wide open, and the phone machine was flashing away, so I listened to the messages and figured out you must have headed up here with Joyce.

"I got in the car and flew. Honest, Kath, you wouldn't believe how fast I drove."

Kathleen shook her head. "I can't believe you're here." She opened the door to Nina's room and announced, "The cavalry has arrived."

When Joyce and Frank started settling in for the night with Nina, Buddy caught Kathleen's eye and glanced at his watch. She nodded and said, "Give me a minute."

Kathleen took Joyce into the hall and asked for her car keys. "I'll drive with Buddy and get your car back to your house." Handing over her own key, Kathleen added, "Bring mine whenever you get back."

"There is no way I can thank you," Joyce said as they hugged good-bye.

"Thanks returned, dear one."

Buddy pulled onto the highway and Kathleen closed her eyes. She woke to see the sign welcoming them to Massachusetts.

"I guess you were pretty done in," Buddy said, patting her knee.

"Buddy," she said, sitting up and rubbing her stiff neck, "I have to ask you for a favor, no questions asked."

"You want me to stop at the next rest stop?"

"It's serious, Buddy. I need you to do something for me without asking me why, ever."

He glanced at Kathleen, her eyes fixed on his face. "Of course."

"We have to drive to Rockport. You'll drop me off and then meet me back at the Tabachniks' house."

"Sure," he said evenly.

"Okay." Kathleen nodded. "Thanks."

A piano concerto filled the car as they headed up the home stretch, passing the barely visible gates of the cemetery. "I'm going to ask Hal to come with us. And Jack, too," Kathleen said softly.

"Good," Buddy said.

"It's twenty-five years."

Buddy was quiet for a moment. "We never talk about him, do we, Kath?"

"You didn't want to talk about him. You told me it hurt too much."

"I said that?"

"Of course you did. You said that hearing his name felt like a knife in your heart."

"When did I say that?"

"A month after he died. It was a Friday night, at temple. You said his name was like a knife in your heart."

Buddy frowned. "It must have been a bad day. Or maybe it was all the people coming up to me and asking how I was doing. But, Kath, I didn't mean forever. I didn't mean I never wanted to talk about him ever again."

Kathleen was quiet.

"Did you think I meant forever?"

"I guess I did."

"All this time?" He shook his head. "I thought it was you who couldn't stand to . . ."

Kathleen turned off the music. All those years of unspoken grief and unheard condolence. "Maybe it was me who couldn't bear to talk about him, and I just laid not talking about it on you. I'm sorry, Buddy. I'm so sorry."

"No need. No need."

Kathleen put her fingertips to Buddy's cheek. "I was talking about him to Joyce on the drive up. I told her about the trucks. Remember how much he loved trucks?"

"Trucks and coffee ice cream."

"Coffee ice cream! I didn't tell her about that. That was your father's doing. Danny Levine was the only little boy in America who preferred coffee ice cream to chocolate, or vanilla or strawberry.

"We should talk to Hal about Danny, too," Kathleen said softly.

"I do. Or I have."

"What does he say?" Kathleen was crying.

"He used to feel terribly guilty, I think. Like he should have been able to protect Dan. But"—Buddy took a breath—"he says he worked through that in therapy. He worries about you, though. He thinks you're still—oh, what did he call it?—unresolved. But he can't understand what it means to lose a child. A baby. You don't ever get resolved. You just get, I don't know what, you just get older, and life goes on."

"When did he tell you that?"

"He came by the store the other day. We had lunch."

Kathleen looked at Buddy's profile in the passing lights. "And Jack?"

"I haven't talked to Jack about Danny," Buddy said. "He never asked me. Did he ask you?"

"No," Kathleen whispered, wondering how she'd taught him not to ask. "Never."

Kathleen put her left hand over Buddy's right on the wheel. He held her fingers between his as they made their way over the bridge, past the turn to their house, up the road to Rockport.

Buddy dropped Kathleen in front of the sub shop. The only sound was the hum of the streetlights, vibrating in the fog. "I'll see you there," he said, and pulled away. Kathleen followed Joyce's directions to the tan Corolla, pocketed the parking ticket, and got in.

In the ten minutes it took to drive back to Gloucester, Kathleen felt her senses sharpen. It had rained earlier, so the road gleamed in the headlights. She opened the window and inhaled mulch, brine, tree sap, honeysuckle, grass, brine again, all of it sharpened by the darkness, heightened by the moisture in the air. Kathleen shivered with pleasure.

My husband is a better man than I knew, she thought. My sons have come home. I'm going back to school in September. I have a true friend. The cancer is gone.

Thank you for Buddy. Thank you for Hal and Jack. Thank you for Pat, and for Mae and Irv. For my gran, for my poor mother. Thank you for my health. And for Joyce.

Thank you for books and work and for kindergarten children and for my garden. For my life in this garden. For these trees. For this perfumed night. For this wind on my face.

Thank you for Danny. I haven't counted him as a blessing for twenty-five years, have I? God forgive me, I must have wished he'd never been born.

Thank you for Danny. For letting me love him. For his love. For all my sons. Thank you.

"Amen," she said, pulling into Joyce's driveway, past Buddy's truck, idling at the curb. "Amen and amen."

SEPTEMBER

T HE TABACHNIKS' yard looked like a combination interfaith garden party and construction site. The priest, wearing a clerical collar, short-sleeved shirt, and dark pants, and the
rabbi, in a navy suit and yarmulke, shook hands as a flatbed trailer
truck hauling a backhoe pulled up.

"Steve!" Father Sherry called out. "Why the big rig?"

"Sorry, Father," Steve said, "but I've got to move this thing
today, and it's on my way."

"Sheesh," said the priest.

Father Sherry had enlisted the contractor to cut the statue free
and deliver it to the Lupos, who were glad to give it a home. When
the priest had named the date—Sunday around three—Joyce had
asked whether she should ask some of the neighbors for a little
block party. "That would be lovely," Father Sherry said, and
offered to invite the Loquastos. Joyce was a little nervous at the
thought of them seeing how much she'd changed their home, but
she told Father Sherry to go ahead.

The lawn was cluttered with assorted plastic chairs, most of
them owned by the Levines, who had arrived early to help set up.
Buddy and Hal were arranging lawn furniture with Ben and Eric,
from next door. Jack, in the kitchen with Ed, was assembling
strawberry shortcake.

Kathleen followed Joyce to the front steps and whispered, "Did
you get the clippings?"

Joyce nodded. The police blotter from the Rockport paper had announced the arrest of seven men on drug charges. A story in the *Gloucester Daily Times* about drug running on Cape Ann noted the participation of "Russian and Irish nationals."

"Well, look who's here!" Father Sherry boomed as the Loquastos pulled up to the curb. He opened the car door for Mary, who clutched at a black patent-leather handbag, and escorted her into the yard for introductions. Joe, wiry and thin, trailed behind. He lit a cigarette and peered at the house as if it were an attraction at Disney World. Joyce invited Mary inside for a look, but she smiled shyly and said, "Maybe later."

Both Loquastos perked up when Lou and Marge Bono walked across the street. The priest made the introductions. "All our kids grew up together," Lou explained to Frank, who was offering drinks. "You should have seen the neighborhood back then," he said, accepting a Diet Coke. "The children, all running in and out of each other's house. We got the city to put up that sign Children at Play. It's still there, isn't it, Marge?"

Frank called Nina over for introductions. Nina, who'd been painting her toenails on the front step with her friend Sylvie, stood up reluctantly.

"Oh, that's a hard age," Mary Loquasto said when Frank started to apologize for Nina's bad manners.

All conversation stopped with the arrival of the Lupos. Theresa, four feet ten inches at most, wore a black crepe dress with a crocheted white collar and a new pair of Nikes. She headed straight toward the statue and patted its cheek, as though it were a favorite niece.

Lena, a few inches taller and quite a bit wider than her mother, was in black leggings and a pink tunic. Her manicured nails splayed over her hips as she apologized to Joyce, again. "Burying all that stuff in your yard like that?" She rolled her eyes. "I'm so sorry."

"Why do you say *you're* sorry? It was not your fault," Theresa exploded. "Not my fault, too. Don't make no *apologia* for me. It was from the doctors, from the medicine. No old-heimer's. *La miseria.*"

"Okay, Ma," said Lena. "Everyone knows you're all there, Ma."

Taking Rabbi Hertz's arm, Father Sherry quietly explained that Theresa had been prescribed two medications that shouldn't be taken together. "No old-heimer's," Theresa repeated, guessing that the priest was talking about her.

Lena's teenage son, Mike, walked over to the statue, where Steve had already dug a trench around the concrete base. "Hey, Joe," Steve called out. "This thing could have lasted until the next ice age." Joe Loquasto acknowledged the compliment with a wave.

The guests gathered around the Madonna. Safety goggles in place, Steve started the drill, which set up a painfully loud, high-pitched squeal. Five minutes later, Mike and Frank helped him lift the Madonna onto a hand truck. Lena and Theresa wrapped the statue in woolen blankets and tied it with bungee cords for the short trip to their house.

As they covered the face with a towel, Joyce realized she was sad to see "her" Mary leave. Early that morning, before Frank or Nina had been awake, she'd gone outside to say good-bye. "I'm sorry if there's any indignity to all this," she had whispered. "I won't let anyone look up your skirt. But I think you'll be happier with the Lupos." She had slipped her palm under the Virgin's outstretched hand, but the mild face seemed turned away.

Father Sherry raised his paper cup and, in a jovial but decidedly formal voice, began, "Ladies and gentlemen?

"I would like to take a moment to thank our hosts, the Tabachniks, for turning this moment of transition into a celebration, indeed, an affirmation of our community.

"You know, we Catholics are enamored with the idea of incarnation. We speak of the incarnation of God's love in the person of our Lord, Jesus Christ. This sublime metaphor—the creation of an all-powerful metaphor-maker—is extended in our tradition to include the saints, and especially the Blessed Mother.

"Nevertheless, the idea that God's love is incarnate in the world is not limited to Catholics, I think. For all of us here"—the priest nodded toward the rabbi—"Jews and Christians alike, God's love indeed does take shape in the world. In the glory of sky and sea. In the beauty of forest and garden. And most of all, in the faces of the people who surround us with understanding and compassion, with friendship, respect, and with love."

Father Sherry raised his glass above his head to murmurs of "Amen," "Salud," and "L'chayim."

He beamed, turned to Michelle, and said, "Rabbi?"

"I was tempted to tell one of those jokes that starts 'A rabbi, a minister, and a priest were in a rowboat.' But maybe I won't," she said. The Loquastos looked relieved.

"We Jews like to say blessings," the rabbi continued in a more sermonic tone. "There are Jewish blessings for almost everything that happens in the course of a day. There is a blessing for waking up, a blessing before and after eating, a blessing for seeing planets in the sky. There is even a blessing to say if you should hear bad news.

"If we happen to forget which special blessing we're supposed to use, or on a uniquely happy occasion such as this, there is an all-purpose blessing of thanks. It is called the Shehecheyanu, and it praises God for the gifts of the moment. So at this precious moment of fellowship and good feeling, I am moved to say:

"*Baruch Ata Adonai, eloheynu melech ha-olam:* Holy One of Blessing, Your presence fills creation.

"*Shehecheyanu:* You have kept us alive to reach this glorious afternoon among our neighbors.

"*V'keyamanu:* You have sustained us with bonds of friendship.

"*V'higianu lazman hazeh:* And you have enabled us to reach this precious moment in this sun-drenched place of beauty."

At that moment Jack emerged from the kitchen with an enormous tray, and the rabbi quickly added, "And this amazing strawberry shortcake."

Nina and Sylvie squealed in high-pitched unison at the sight of the desserts. Everyone laughed.

"Amen," said Father Sherry, reaching for the first plate.

As people helped themselves and found seats, Kathleen and Joyce walked into the kitchen.

"How's it going?" Kathleen asked in a low voice.

"It's going," Joyce said with a slight shrug. She turned on the faucet and started rinsing whipped cream from the beaters. "Frank started his new job last Monday. We're being nice to each other. The money situation makes things kind of tense, but at least that's out on the table. Taking care of Nina pulled us together— we're both so grateful she's okay."

"Nina looks good."

"She's on the stationary bike for hours at a stretch, trying to keep her legs in shape while the bone heals."

"Did you find out what she was doing in that tree?"

"It was a dare from one of the boys," Joyce said. "I thought she was smarter than that, but she's not only a jock, but a show-off. She feels pretty stupid about doing it. She did tell me that."

"And what about you?"

"I'm writing about bus safety. And you'll be glad to hear that I've finished sixty pages of *Magnolia's Haven*."

"Joyce! That's great!"

"Jordan had to go so Magnolia could have a new love interest."

"Poor man. How did he die?"

"A shipwreck off Rafe's Chasm, but back then it was called Rafe's Crack."

"You'd better go with the old name, or the local history buffs will hang you out to dry."

"The other big news is that I started therapy," Joyce said. "I'm still trying to understand why I did what I did."

Kathleen frowned. "You made a mistake."

"Yes, but I still need to work it out. She says that Frank's absence was a big part of——"

Jack poked his head through the door. "We need more ice."

"Be right there," Joyce said.

"We need a walk at Good Harbor," Kathleen said.

Joyce nodded. But with Nina starting school and deadlines piling up, it would be at least a week before she could come back to Gloucester. "Give me the headlines."

"Oh, dear," Kathleen said. "There is so much to tell. We all went to the cemetery on the anniversary of Danny's death. Jack and Hal brought pebbles from Good Harbor to leave at the grave, and Hal said the kaddish. Afterward we went out for coffee ice cream. I forgot to tell you that Danny loved coffee ice cream.

"Hal remembered the funniest things about him. Like the way he used to kiss the dog's ears." Kathleen paused for a moment. "Jack asked about a hundred questions about Danny. It was a good day—sad but good.

"And what else; Jack is moving into Ed's apartment until he finds a place, and we're invited to dinner there next week. Hal is going to read from the Torah on Yom Kippur. I've got an appointment to talk to an oncologist about tamoxifen."

"That is a lot. And by the way, you look wonderful. This haircut——"

Nina and Sylvie walked in looking for the ice. Michelle followed, in search of napkins.

Kathleen and Joyce smiled at each other. That would have to do for now. They could catch up on the phone, and they would walk on the beach next week. Rain or shine, they promised.

They would meet on the footbridge and exchange a hug. They'd take off their shoes and walk from one end of Good Harbor to the other, then take another turn, back and forth.

They would talk about their husbands and their children, their work and their bodies. Next week and the week after. Wet feet and dry feet, barefoot and shod, in heat and fog, and then bundled up against the cold.

With Kathleen's dog racing ahead. With Buddy and Frank walking a few paces behind. With Joyce's old friends, visiting from out of town. With red and yellow plastic buckets for the grandchildren, eventually. Together, at Good Harbor, they would see how it all turned out.

ACKNOWLEDGMENTS

Thanks to Janet Rustow, MSW, at the Faulkner Breast Centre for her thorough and generous consultation on the emotional and medical course of breast cancer treatment. I also learned a great deal about radiology treatment for breast cancer from Dr. Tania I. Lingos, Sarah Susi, and Karen Donnelan at the South Suburban Oncology Center; and from Karen Thompson. For careful readings and insightful comments, thanks to William Camann, MD, Judi Hirshfield-Bartek, RN, MS, Beth Israel Deaconess BreastCare Center and to Judith Paley, MD, of femailhealthnews.com.

The members of my writing group (past and present) were indispensable: Janice Brand, Ellen Grabiner, Marcy Herschmann, Amy Hoffman, Renee Loth, and Marla Zarrow. Louisa Williams was an expert and thoughtful editor at a crucial juncture.

I am indebted to Amanda Urban at ICM for hooking me up with my wonderful editors, Sarah McGrath and Nan Graham, at Scribner.

Thanks to all of these experts, cheerleaders, hand-holders, family members, and friends (you know who you are and which is which): Susan Beattie, Emilia Diamant, Helene Diamant, Judith Himber, Judy Jordan, Karen Kushner, Stephen McCauley, Valerie Monroe, Regina Mooney, Edward Myers, Marlee Nelson, Rabbi Barbara Penzner, Jane Redmont, Rabbi Liza Stern, Sebastian Stuart, Diane Weinstein, Tom Wolf, Bob Wyatt, and Ande Zellman.

Thanks again and always to my husband for his unconditional love.

The Red Tent
Anita Diamant

'My name means nothing to you. My memory is dust. This is not your fault or mine. The chain connecting mother to daughter was broken and the word passed to the keeping of men, who had no way of knowing. That is why I became a footnote, my story a brief detour between the well-known history of my father Jacob, and the celebrated chronicle of Joseph, my brother.'

Lost to the history by the chronicles of men, here at last is the dazzling story of Dinah, Jacob's only daughter in the Book of Genesis.

Moving panoramically from Mesopotamia to Canaan to Egypt, *The Red Tent* is robustly narrated by Dinah, from her upbringing by the four wives of Jacob, to her growth into one of the most influential women of her time.

In seeking to preserve not only her own remarkable experiences but those of a long-ago era of womanhood left largely undocumented by the original male scribes and later Biblical scholars, Dinah breaks a male silence that has lasted for centuries, revealing the ancient origins of many contemporary religious practices and sexual politics. The result is a beautiful, thought-provoking novel.

Reading group notes are available on our website at www.allenandunwin.com

ISBN 1 86448 679 1